Death Has
A Thousand Doors

DEATH HAS A THOUSAND DOORS

A Novel of Suspense

by Will Cooper

THE BOBBS-MERRILL COMPANY, INC.
Indianapolis • *New York*

Designed by Ingrid Beckman

Manufactured in the United States of America

First printing

Library of Congress Cataloging in Publication Data

Cooper, Will.
    Death has a thousand doors.

    I. Title.
PZ4.C7794De   [PS3553.0627]   813'.5'4   75-30778
ISBN 0-672-52196-2

Death Has
A Thousand Doors

Chapter . 1

WATCHING THE OLD BUCK DIE must have made up the Senator's mind for him. It was a long shot but a clean kill, one of the few on this hunt. We had watched him scamper out of the brush at the bottom of the ravine and start up the steep slope when he heard the riders beating through. I fired from a sitting position when he was about a third of the way up, about six hundred yards from our stand on the opposite slope. The heavy bullet took him in the middle of the back just behind the shoulders, and he collapsed in a heap, as if all the ligaments had been cut simultaneously. I opened the bolt of the Weatherby and waited for Juan Silva to appear out of the brush at the bottom of the barranca. When he pushed his pony out to where I could see him, I waved him toward the fallen deer and turned to the others in the party.

"Well, gentlemen, that's about it for this year. Everybody has a buck, and there are soft beds and hard whiskey back at the house. Let's go see what's for dinner."

Con, the camp cook, started down the slope with two packhorses, and Pony Blue, the wrangler, took an unloaded animal and started across to help Juan with my deer. The

Senator ambled up as I was tightening the cinch on my saddle. He had joined the hunt late and hadn't seemed to enjoy it as much as he had in past years.

"You got anything real important to do for the next couple of weeks, John T.?" he asked.

"Nothing that won't keep, Senator. What's on your mind?"

"There's a little favor you might do me if you have a mind to. I'll tell you something about it when we get back to the ranch." He slapped my pony lightly on the rump and went to get his own horse. I finished cinching up and then looked around to see if everybody was ready.

It was a small group this year. I had decided to limit invitations after a big party had gotten out of hand a couple of years earlier and slaughtered a bunch of my deer. A couple of hunters from this year's list hadn't been able to make it, so there were only Braden Carlsbad, the senior United States Senator from this state; Sam Price; Hector de la Cruz; and Bill Arledge. Sam was already mounted and Bill was standing by his horse. Hector was stowing a sketch pad in a special saddlebag he had had made to carry his artist's materials, and the Senator was climbing on the big-butted quarter horse he always rode hunting on my place. I stepped into my saddle and booted my horse down the slope, and one by one they fell in behind me. It was a five-hour ride to the main house, and they were all beat, so they just settled down to business and rode. We got home at about three-thirty, and they all went to their rooms to clean up. I did the same.

When I stepped out of the shower, there was a tall scotch and soda and a plate of sandwiches on the dressing table, put there by Juana Sanchez, my housekeeper. There would be the same in each guest's room, with variations tailored to individual tastes in drinks. I sipped my drink and ate half a sandwich while I dressed in slacks, moccasins, and a knitted golf shirt; then I went out to see if all the boys had made it back all right.

Juan Silva was cutting up the deer carcass at the long table by the freezer plant, and Pony Blue was pegging out the hide to dry on the wall. I could see the packhorses rolling in the corral, so Con was probably stowing his gear in the cookshack. I walked over to the freezer plant which I had installed the year after I started the annual hunts as a sort of fresh-air lobby for my private earth preserve. Fish and game were brought in here, dressed and frozen and packed in dry ice, and delivered by fastest transport to wherever the guests specified. Heads, hides, and trophy fish were sent to a taxidermist in the city, processed and mounted, then delivered in the same way. It added up to a nice way to hunt and a carefree, relaxed time for my guests.

"Pony, that's the best head in the bunch. See that it gets mixed up with Bill Arledge's kill so he'll have a decent trophy for that new house he's been telling me about. It has a couple more points and weighs about five pounds more, but he won't know the difference. Send the meat down to the village as usual—the Senator's, too. He doesn't like buck venison any more than I do." I prefer a young doe, shot clean and dressed where she fell, when I eat venison at all. Mostly I prefer prime aged Angus beef broiled on an electric grill. I don't like a lot of carbon and oil and grit and ashes on my meat.

"Boss, what's my chances of gettin' into town tonight?" asked Pony Blue. "I'd shore like to see a light from somethin' besides Juan's cigarette." He drove the last nail into the hide and stepped back to admire his work, moving stiffly but daintily on his high bootheels. A cowboy, he wouldn't be anything else, and wouldn't do anything else but ride after one of the stupidest animals on earth. And he hadn't seen a cow on this ranch for half a dozen years, except for the completely wild scrubs that still lived back in the brush. I suspected him of hunting them down and busting them a few with his rope just for fun and to keep in practice in case I ever came to my senses and started running cattle again. Pony doesn't think of the hundred or so black Angus and Jersey milk cows we keep for the table as cattle—they're just beefy pets.

"Pony, ain't you spent enough money on that barroom heifer? She don't even remember your name from one payday to the next." Juan Silva laughed with the sly half-educated, half-Apache humor which made him style himself "Long Juan Silva" and play straight-faced outlandish pranks on man, beast, and landscape. He is half Chiricahua and half whatever has come along in the last four centuries, and inside him are all the worst and best qualities to be had from that mixed heritage. He likes to hunt, fish, drink and fight and make love, and hates cold weather and work in any form. He belongs to my ranch as he can belong nowhere else in the world.

"You can go to town when the meat's frozen and packed, Pony," I said. "Get a week's pay from Juana and take the one-ton pickup. She'll give you a supply order to fill in town. Fill the order, load the truck, and park it in Carson's shed before you get drunk. Then you can take your time about getting back."

I didn't need to tell Juan Silva when he could go to town. He goes three or four times a year, according to some schedule of his own, and he has never asked. He just goes and returns without a word. I would hear about his visit and get a bill for breakage from other people later.

When I returned to the house, my guests were all sitting around the patio with drinks in their hands, reliving the week-long hunt. Bill Arledge was talking about the shot I had made across the barranca, and Hector was working on the sketch of Bill he had started on the mountain. Bill's likeness will appear someday in one of Hector's huge historical oils, wearing rusty armor or greasy buckskin or city broadcloth, caught up in some bloody moment out of the past of this blood-soaked state. Hector painted in a perfectionistic portrait style that disappeared centuries ago when the late-come Renaissance finally died in Spain. He painted scathing portraits that combined the deep awareness of Velázquez with the mystic vision of El Greco and the bloody-mindedness of Goya. People he portrayed rarely wanted to buy what he saw in them, so he put them into his giant panoramic scenes as members of the crowd. Hector is a distant cousin and lives on a neighboring ranch. I had known him all my life, and kept looking for my face in one of his history lessons, but it hadn't appeared yet.

Dinner after one of my hunts is always an elaborate sit-down affair, but in casual clothes. It's an easy transition from the rough living in my private wilderness back to civilization, and seems to hit exactly the right note with most of my guests. Tonight's feast began with a light soup and broiled trout from the headwaters of the valley creek, followed by wild duck and grouse, then a steak the size of a barn door. The vegetables were perfectly cooked in a way that seems impossible outside of Chinatown in San Francisco. Juana Sanchez, during the only three years of her life spent outside this valley, had cooked in a Chinese restaurant and had learned their special skill with vegetables and fish. Two wines sufficed for the entire meal—a Chilean Riesling and a Mouton Rothschild. After the meal one of the maids brought cigars and cigarettes, and Juana served a bottle from the last two dozen of my good port. I switched to brandy when the port was served.

After dinner Sam Price and Bill Arledge, both exhausted from the eight-day scramble over my mountain, went to their rooms. Hector said he wanted to walk his dinner down, so I was left alone with Senator Carlsbad. I took him into my private study, where Juana had already set up a drink tray and more cigars. I closed the windows against the sudden October chill and offered the Senator my attention.

"You said something about a favor I can do for you, Senator."

"Yes, John. Something like the thing you did for Sam Price a couple of years back. That is, if you're still interested in that sort of work," said the Senator, sitting back in the deep leather chair. He looked at me with the total concentration you rarely see outside a high-stakes poker game. I took my time about answering. Yes, I had done a job of work for Sam Price two years ago. Some cute characters had roped Sam's son and had blackmailed him for some sixteen percent of the shares in Sam's growing young electronics company. They were trying various ways to acquire more stock and enough proxies for a takeover when Sam asked me to lend a hand. It got a little hairy toward the end, but I took the characters off his back. Sam paid me a nice fee, and there was enough loose cash lying around in the operation to finance the ranch for a while.

"I take it Sam told you about his trouble and what I did to help him. Did he tell you what my terms are?" It was my turn to watch the Senator, but I guess he had a good enough pair of openers, because he didn't hesitate to call.

"Yes, he did, but I'd like to hear them from you."

"After I hear what the problem is, Senator."

"Latham Cameron. That's my problem." I didn't say anything, but waited for him to continue.

"The grand jury true-billed him and returned an indictment for first-degree murder. He goes to trial in three weeks unless something exceptional happens before then. I want you to make something exceptional happen." I still waited for him to continue.

"You did read about the case?" asked the Senator. "You do know what I'm talking about?"

"I read the newspaper story, Senator. I didn't go any further."

"You've known Latham for a long time, John T. Do you believe he did what they're accusing him of?"

"It doesn't sound much like him, for a fact," I answered.

"Didn't you think of doing anything about it on your own?" asked the Senator.

"It was some of Latham's friends, friends he brought along without an invitation, who slaughtered my deer two years ago. Which was why Latham wasn't invited last year or this. No, I didn't think about doing anything on my own. I assume he has lawyers who know what to do." I turned my back on Carlsbad then and went to the sideboard for a drink. Glass in hand, I turned and said:

"What was it you had in mind, Senator?"

"Latham Cameron is innocent of that murder, John T. Anybody who knows him, or anything about him, should be convinced of that. That means somebody else did it and planted enough evidence to damn near convict Latham before the trial. I want you to find that man and bring him in with enough evidence to get him convicted."

"*You* want that, Senator? Why you? And why me? Latham Cameron is the junior Senator from this state, and he belongs to the opposition party. You and he have never been great friends, to my knowledge, and you're bitter political enemies if the newspapers have any truth in them. So why should *you* hire *me* to get him out of this scrape? And why should you think of hiring anybody to do a police job that the minority party should be able to get done without either of us?"

"All right, John T. I'll take your questions one at a time, and in order. First, my own interest, which is easy. Latham Cameron is a United States Senator, as I am. He is also innocent of the murder of Malena Vasquez, dancer, or of anybody else. Therefore Latham Cameron, United States

Senator, is falsely accused of murder and is probably being framed. I don't want people to get in the habit of framing United States senators. It would be very bad for this state, and for the nation, if a senator were to be executed for the murder of a cheap little night-club singer. It would be bad for him and his party, sure. As a matter of practical politics, it would also harm me and my party. Lord knows we've had enough political scandal in the last few years to last a lifetime." He turned his cigar in his hand, looked at it as if he had never seen it before, then took a long puff and continued.

"You ask why I am personally interested. That was a naive question. I helped to choose Latham Cameron as the opposition candidate, and I helped to choose the wooden Indian we ran against him. I contributed substantially to his campaign fund, and I voted for him in the election. Sounds like a conspiracy, doesn't it? Not at all. This nation has two major parties, John T. Every four years, one or the other elects a President. The Presidency might go from one party to the other every eight years or so, but the Senate goes on forever. The way things work, if this state is to be adequately represented in the Senate, there has to be somebody there who can talk to the President, no matter which party he belongs to. If you'll take a careful look, you'll see that the House is organized the same way. Call it a way of keeping the lines of communication open. Sure, my party has had majority control in this state for half a century, but we do a much better job by keeping the opposition healthy and reasonably happy." He stopped then, took a sip of his drink, and looked again at his cigar as if it were a strange object in his hand.

"The police, now—that's a horse of a different color," he continued after a moment. "Their case against Latham, as you'll see in a few minutes, is damned strong. When they presented it to the District Attorney, he had to prosecute.

On the evidence, the grand jury had to indict him. Now the police have no choice but to close the file and discontinue the investigation, and if the case goes to court the way it is, Latham doesn't have a chance in hell.''

"So the DA is satisfied with the case as it is, and the police have gone about their business. Now what about Latham's party?"

"I'm sure they're doing what they can, John T., but that may not be good enough and it might be far too late. In any case, I'm not satisfied to leave it to them. I want Latham cleared before the trial, for my own reasons, which I've told you about, and that brings us back to you."

"Senator, you probably know very well that I've done little jobs for several people, Sam Price included, and that my rates are the same every time. I take a ten-thousand-dollar advance retainer, with fifteen more on completion of the job. I also take the top half of any loose cash that I find lying around in the case, with the other half going, at my discretion, to any otherwise uncompensated victims of the situation. My rates are high, and you could probably find a lot of people who would work cheaper—but they're willing to live cheaper. As you know, a place like this costs money to maintain.'' And doesn't contribute a dime to my income, which is one of the reasons I like it.

"I'm not quarreling with your prices, boy. You do good work, what I know of it, and this situation is going to call for some good work. Also, it could get sort of rough, which you can also handle if what I hear is true. Last but not least, John T., you belong to the club.'' And that's the big rock in the road, right there. I do belong to the club and always have, and that's where duty raises its ugly head.

Every country on earth, democracy or whatever, is really run by a very small class of people. In a sense, this small group carries the country on its shoulders. Membership changes from time to time, but the men who run nations are all cut from the same piece of goods. I personally have no interest in running the nation, the state, or the county, but my people for a hundred and fifty years have been involved. You can't own a hunk of real estate like this valley and stay completely out of establishment politics. So I can't cop out, either. I can go my own way most of the time, but when the establishment points the finger directly at me and says: You're it, John Thomas McLaren, then I have to stand up. But I also have a right to charge like hell for it.

"I'll take your check for ten thousand and all the information you can give me, Senator," I said, with a mental shrug to fit the armor on my shoulders. The Senator reached into his inside coat pocket and handed me a cashier's check—the amount was ten round ones—issued in the name of an out-of-state bank and countersigned by someone I had never heard of. He carried the title of controller of a corporation that Dow-Jones doesn't list.

"Excuse me for a minute and I'll get you some information," he said, and left the room. He was back immediately with an old brown leather briefcase that bulged and strained the zipper which was almost pulled loose in a couple of places. He laid the case on the table and lit another cigar.

"There is a copy of the brief as presented to the grand jury. There's also a copy of every police report we could lay our hands on, with photographs, coroner's report, and so on. As far as we know, that's the whole case as presented to the DA. We added background sketches of everybody we know to be involved, including Latham and his staff. You can take it from there." He leaned back and relaxed then, as if he had put the whole load down and was ready to rest while I got on with the work. But I knew better. Men like him never relax for more than a few minutes at a stretch, and then only when they have completed whatever step they're taking at the time. Before the end of that cigar, Braden Carlsbad would be chewing on another problem, but I would probably never know anything about it. Then I watched it happen. His heavy old shoulders gradually tightened, and he leaned a little forward in the chair as he retreated far behind the shrewd old eyes that had weighed me so carefully. He sat that way for a moment, then abruptly got up and said good night, pleasantly but with only a minute fraction of his attention on the politeness due a host. I no longer existed as an immediate problem. But I had a problem of my own, so I answered his good night and unzipped the ratty old briefcase.

It had come as no surprise to me that the Senator had a cashier's check for the right amount in his pocket when he walked into my study. He knew damn well that I had three good reasons to accept whatever chore he decided to lay on me. One, my aforementioned membership in the club—not strong enough in itself, perhaps, but a good reinforcement. Second, this valley—it eats money. I own 280 sections— almost 180,000 acres—of the last true wilderness left in the United States. It's a mountain valley, eight miles wide by thirty-five miles long, completely surrounded by the bare rock of a mountain escarpment on one side and the bare rock and sand of a desert plateau on the other. It has been McLaren land for more than a century and a half, passed from eldest son to eldest son without a break. In my grandfather's time and for the few brief years of my father's life it produced an unending succession of prime beef. In my time it produces nothing but bear, deer, elk, lion, and trout, and debts for me. The taxes alone would keep a moderately rich man on the hump.

The reasons for my non-use of the land are far from simple. I studied agriculture and animal husbandry in college, with every intention of continuing the tradition when my grandfather should die and leave it to me. I went into the Army after college, and the old man died while I was away fighting my country's penny wars. I told our business manager to dispose of the herd, keeping some seed bulls and a starter herd of heifers to await my return. But I came home in a basket, with no strength and little interest in cattle ranching. So I sat in the sun on the long gallery of the ranchhouse, or drank quietly in the patio until I was strong enough to ride. I found the valley rapidly reverting to the wilderness my mountain-man ancestor had seen when he rode into the valley on some vague errand of his own in 1810. I rode and walked and hunted the land for another year, until I was as strong and healthy as I had ever been, but I no longer had the slightest interest in ranching or farming. So I sold most of the bulls, butchered the heifers, and watched the wild land creep closer to the long gallery.

The idea of a private wilderness had a growing fascination for me, and I watched the deer herds, the lions, the occasional grizzly, and now a secret pack of timber wolves compete for life as they had done before Columbus conned Isabel out of her jewels. But I couldn't let it go to any other man, so taxes must be paid. I wanted to pay them myself, and refused any offer of assistance from the county, the state, and the Department of the Interior. I could have tax-free status at any time, simply by having the place declared a game preserve or some such thing. It's something my business manager suggests from time to time, but there's one thing I know: if the tax man doesn't come around, the bureaucrat will—and if they aren't bulls in a china shop, nobody is. So I always need money. I stumbled on this way of earning it soon after I got my health back.

Hence the Senator's call for my services and his confidence that I would be available. He also knew the third reason that made me willing to go to work for him. Money —even crude amounts such as I had been spending—isn't enough to protect a chunk of real estate as important as my valley. It takes some powerful friends who are willing to help keep the political wolves at a distance. So I keep my fences up, and I use the valley and its deer herds, trout pools, and wild peace to keep them mended. Of course the Senator had brought a check. All the options were his. So I dug into the stack of material in his briefcase.

After a couple of hours of reading, I could see why the DA had no choice but to prosecute, and why any self-respecting jury wouldn't have to leave the box to return a verdict of guilty. Senator Latham Cameron was boxed in tight, with everything in the book against him and all the doors nailed shut. The gist of the police case went as follows:

On Friday, August 10 of this year, the Senator met with his administrative assistant in his Washington office. They completed their discussion at 10:30 A.M., and the assistant, Sara Connelly, drove him to the airport, where he boarded a plane for home. He intended spending the weekend with some important people in the state capital and at his ranch. His plane was met at 2 P.M. by Sam Anderson, his home office administrative assistant; and by the county chairman of his party. A police escort, one car with a sergeant and a patrolman, preceded Cameron's limousine into the city to the Conquistador Hotel, where the Senator maintained a suite the year round. His intentions were to spend the night in the hotel, meet with several people, and to proceed to his ranch by helicopter the next morning. At 3:30 P.M. Sam Anderson ordered a snack for the Senator and Orman Bridges, the county chairman. While they were waiting for the snack, Cameron made several calls through the hotel switchboard, to confirm appointments made for the weekend.

At 10:45 P.M. Cameron's last visitor left the suite. Sam Anderson called room service for another snack and personally set up a drink tray for the Senator, opening a fresh bottle of Chivas Grand Salute and filling the ice bucket from the icemaker in the suite. Anderson then left for home before the food arrived.

At 11:10 P.M. Ramon Chavez, the room-service waiter, served sandwiches, soup, and a salad to Cameron, who was still fully dressed in a double-breasted light gray suit, black shoes, and a dark red tie. At 11:45 P.M. Chavez reported seeing Cameron, wearing the same gray suit and black shoes but with a light topcoat over the suit, leave the hotel by the back entrance, passing the service door to the kitchen. Chavez then went to the suite and cleared away the remains of the meal. The Senator was not in his room, according to Chavez.

At 1:20 A.M. there was a slight disturbance in the apartment of Malena Vasquez, a flamenco dancer employed at the Club Cielo Azul. A dancer, then. Senator Carlsbad had called her a dancer once, then a singer. The disturbance was slight, and not repeated, so it wasn't reported by neighbors until the following night, after the Vasquez woman had been found dead.

At 8:30 P.M. on the following evening, Raul Ortega, assistant manager of the Cielo Azul, telephoned Malena Vasquez's apartment, as it was his habit to do each evening. The dancer was scheduled to do her first show at 9 P.M., and she was sometimes late. There was no answer, so he assumed she was on her way to the club. When she didn't appear for the 9 o'clock performance, he called again, with no result. At 10 o'clock he became concerned and asked George Laird, the manager, if he should go to the apartment to see if anything was wrong. Laird told him to go ahead. On arriving at the apartment he pressed the buzzer, and when there was no answer, he tried the door. The door was not locked, and Ortega entered the room. He found Vasquez lying on the carpet in the middle of the living room, dead in a pool of blood from several wounds on her head. He used the apartment telephone to call the police and Laird.

The police call was answered by a patrol car dispatched from Central and by Detective Sergeant Vittorio Sanchez, who was off duty but answered the call because he was cruising nearby with his car radio turned on. The duty homicide squad, under Detective Sergeant Charles Pugh, arrived a few minutes later. Sanchez and Pugh searched the apartment together. They found no evidence of forced entry, and no evidence of struggle except for the wounds on the woman's head, which appeared to have been made with a poker from the fireplace. They noted evidence that the victim was a user of drugs, with evidence of a recent heavy hit. The medical examiner confirmed the cause of death and the weapon, and that the woman was indeed an addict, with strong traces of heroin in her bloodstream.

Subsequent police investigation revealed that the apartment lease was in the name of one Lawrence Calhoun, and that rent was paid quarterly by checks written on an out-of-state bank. Investigations at that bank revealed that Calhoun also had a safety-deposit box, which was opened on presentation of a police warrant. The box was found to contain more than twenty thousand dollars in cash and certain papers which implicated Senator Latham Cameron, suggesting that Cameron was "Calhoun." Photographs of Cameron shown to bank personnel were identified as "looking a lot like him," with the addition of a moustache and glasses. A police artist retouched the photograph with moustache and glasses, and witnesses positively identified Cameron as the man who had opened the account, rented the deposit box, and subsequently made several widely spaced visits to the bank.

Cameron, when questioned, stated that he had eaten the meal served by the waiter, Chavez, and had then put on pajamas and a robe in preparation for bed. He had read for a few minutes, became drowsy, and remembered nothing more until he was awakened by the hotel switchboard at 7:30 A.M. on Saturday. The chambermaid testified that Cameron's bed had been turned down, and that it looked as if someone had lain for a time on top of the covers but that the bed had not been slept in.

Police conversations with neighbors and friends of Malena Vasquez and Club Cielo Azul employees revealed that she had been seen several times with a man answering the description of "Cameron-Calhoun," and identified the retouched photograph as being that of the man in question. The Vasquez woman had never introduced the man to friends or neighbors, nor had he ever spoken to any of them.

A search of Cameron's hotel suite revealed nothing except a book of advertising matches from the bank where "Calhoun" kept his account. The checkbook and bank statements covering a period of two years for the "Calhoun" account were found among Cameron's papers at his ranch. Police also found records of several other accounts and deposit boxes in widely scattered banks, with cash totaling $57,000 distributed among them. Papers in the deposit boxes implicated the Senator in several questionable real estate and insurance transactions involving a savings and loan company in which he had an interest. These transactions are all currently under investigation.

So long, Latham, it's been good to know you. A frame? Possible, but from where I sat, not bloody likely. For instance, if it was a frame, somebody had spent around $75,000 at a very conservative estimate, and more probably over $100,000, just to make sure it fit. Then they had blown some very heavy gaffs if the companies listed in the "questionable" transactions were in fact involved in paying off a senator.

On the other hand, if it was a frame, and somebody was willing not only to set up a kill two years in advance but also to spend $100,000 or so in the process just to make sure he got his man, I was getting ready to tangle with a bear. At 5 A.M. I rousted the Senator out of his bed and hauled him back into the study. I gave him a cup of coffee and about three minutes of hell, at the end of which he yawned and looked at me sleepily.

"Sure, John, it's a pure bitch. And you will need a lot of help, which I'm prepared to give you. Here, call this number and you'll have all the heavy back-up you need, plus a staff that's used to handling one crisis after another. That's Sara Connelly's number, and she has the Senator's complete staff on standby, ready to help you from here to Washington. Now you better get some sleep—it's going to be a long two weeks." With that the old bastard pulled his robe around him and ambled back to his room. So did I.

Chapter . 2

I SLEPT HEAVILY until Juana Sanchez woke me up with a glass of orange juice and a pot of coffee on a tray.

"Good morning, Señor McLaren," she said as she put the coffee on my breakfast table by the big window. I scrubbed a fist into my gritty eyes and drank the juice while still in bed.

"Good morning, Juana Sanchez. *Qué tal?*" She didn't answer but poured a cup of coffee and laced it with heavy cream—the kind that rises to the top of rich milk and is skimmed off with a big spoon. A dozen or so Jersey milk cows on the place gave me about a gallon of it each day. I took a sip of coffee when she brought it to me, and then got out of bed and pulled on a heavy robe. It was chilly in the room, but the sun through the big east window would warm it soon enough. I sat down at the table and motioned to the other chair.

"Sit down, Juana, and join me for a cup." She poured a second cup of coffee, about half cream, and sat down.

"Are the others up yet?"

"The Senator is still asleep, señor. Mr. Price called for a helicopter to pick them up, and he and the others are at the helicopter pad seeing to their gear.'' I looked out the window then and could see my guests in a group on the concrete slab which now covered one of the old corrals. Con and Pony Blue were lugging stuff down to them.

"Let the Senator sleep, Juana. He'll be staying on for a day or so. I'll go down and see the others off when the bird gets here. Now, do you have a supply list ready for Pony to take to town? If you don't, make one up. Give Pony a week's pay. That should last him about two days in town, so you can expect your supplies then.''

"Yes, señor. Is there anything you want me to order?''

"Can't think of anything, but I'm going to town myself and I can get it if I do. Any problems around the place?''

"No, señor. Nothing I can't handle. One of the maids is pregnant, and she doesn't want to get married and doesn't want an abortion. So you will have another mouth to feed.''

"Who's the father—or does she know?''

"Quién lo sabe? Maybe it was a masked Indian this time. She didn't tell me.'' She smiled a little, maybe with nostalgia. Juana Sanchez, still a handsome woman in her fifties, had raised a little hell in her time.

"Well, I'll be in town for at least a week, maybe two. Can you handle things okay?''

"No tengas miedo, joven. I can handle it.'' She smiled at her own familiarity and took her coffee cup with her as she left. Well, she was entitled to some familiarity. She had known me since my first yell and had taken care of me since I was ten, when my father and mother died. She had kept this house for more than thirty years, first for my grandfather and now for me. She also runs the village that the home ranch has become. It was a town once, with more than a hundred working hands and their dependents, and often as many guests in the big house. I guess there must be forty-five or fifty—now fifty and a half—living on the place, all part Apache. We have always had Apaches on the

place, even during the days when they were at war with the whole world. They never bothered anybody much around here. I don't know what they might have gotten into, riding down into Mexico or over into Texas. No good, if the stories are true.

I sipped my coffee and watched the slow, nothing-special-to-do movement of the place through the window for a while, then called Peter Heilman in the city. Peter is an investment banker and my business manager. He keeps trying to make me rich.

"Peter, John T. *Qué tal, hombre?*" I said when he answered on the second ring. That's Peter—he probably had been in his office since six and already had two days' work done.

"Just fair, John T. How're things at Rancho Useless?" Peter doesn't like to see assets going to seed, and he never misses an opportunity to jog me.

"Well, it's one-millionth of one percent more of a liability this morning. There's another cactus flower blooming in the maid's quarters. Got a minute to talk?"

"Just about—I'm meeting with the people who're going to finance that new lake city up in the Guadalupes in about ten minutes. What's on your mind?"

"I'm coming to town for a couple of weeks, so I'd appreciate it if you'd have that beautiful secretary of yours rent me a comfortable apartment—ground floor, front and back entrance—and stock the kitchen and bar. Also rent me a couple of cars, Fords or Chevys. Park one at the apartment, the other at the Conquistador. Have her get me a room at the hotel, too. You know the one I like—it's on the second floor right next to the service stair. And I need a couple of thousand in cash."

"One of those weeks, eh? Working or playing?"

"This is work, Peter. For money."

"Then get on with it, podnuh. We need the gold; your account's getting anemic. Okay, we'll take care of it. We won't need to rent any cars—the bank has a lot full of repos, and there's a vacancy or two in that apartment complex I just bought. Your trust fund owns a slice of it, so you'll be at home, so to speak. When should we expect you in?'' That's why Peter is my business manager: he doesn't squeeze a dime—he milks it gently and gets a nickel on every stroke. I told him I would see him tomorrow and hung up.

I reread the dossiers on Cameron and his staff before I made the next call, and I had Sara Connelly's eight-by-ten glossy portrait in my hand when I dialed the number Senator Carlsbad had given me. The picture was worth looking at, and the voice that answered fit the photo. It was a rich contralto, pitched low but warm with the carefully rationed enthusiasm so necessary to anyone who works in politics.

"Sara, this is John T. McLaren. I've been talking with Senator Carlsbad, and he suggested I call you."

"Yes, Mr. McLaren. The Senator said you might call, and we've been expecting you. Are you going to help us?"

"Looks that way—and I'll need some help and advice from you. When can we get together?"

"You speak, I do, Mr. McLaren."

"Well then, why don't you hop into a helicopter and come on out to the ranch. We can have a bite of lunch and talk about things."

"Just a great big salad for me, please . . . with maybe some cottage cheese, and perhaps some trout and a steak; let's face it, Mr. McLaren, I'm a big girl and I'm always starved, so I have to warn people in advance that a plague is on its way." I looked at the photo again and hoped it wasn't lying to me. A girl who eats like that can put on a lot of war surplus in the battle of the bulge—or she could be like me and eat like a hay crew with no visible effect.

"I'll shoot you an elk. See you at lunch, Sara Connelly." She hung up and I looked at the photo again.

I'm a bachelor, but I know damn well I can't afford to

stay that way much longer because I'm the last McLaren. If I don't manage to get a male heir, Rancho Useless is sure as hell going to fall among strangers someday. That I won't have, so I spend a lot of time looking around. But you wouldn't believe what's happening to the female of the species. I haven't met more than two or three I'd trust to whelp a likable moron, let alone the kind of son who can grow up to match this place. He'll have to be strong enough and smart enough to keep it out of the jaws of some very hungry animals, the government included. I don't care what he does with it after I'm dead—he can raise goats, open a massage parlor, or even dam the end of the valley and flood it for a private bathtub, so long as he can hold it and pass it along to a son who can do the same. It would be a damn shame to lose this valley after five generations of McLarens have loved and fought and lived and died on it. So I'm looking for a woman with the qualities of heart and mind and body that will ensure the succession. That woman I can love forever.

Sara Connelly's biography suggested the possibility. She was a graduate *summa cum laude* from the state university, with a Master's degree in philosophy and political science. She was a natural athlete and an outdoor sportswoman when she had the opportunity. She had been Senator Cameron's administrative assistant for three years, since the day he had suddenly fired everybody for some mysterious reason and put on a complete new staff in Washington and in his home office in the state capital. According to the dossier, she was smart and efficient, and a charming hostess for the bachelor Senator's Washington home. I wondered if there was more between them. Perhaps, but I put her down as a possible anyway and looked forward to lunch. About then I heard a helicopter climbing over the lip of the valley, so I put on some clothes and went down to say good-bye to my guests.

Sam Price slapped me on the shoulder with his left hand while he shook my right.

"Damn good hunt, John T. Don't know when I've had such a good time. Don't you ever let this place turn into just another cow ranch, hear?" he said, and looked at Bill Arledge for confirmation.

"Second the motion, boy! Until I hunted out here with you, I thought deer had white and red spots and stood still while you milked 'em. Keep this place the way it is."

"I'll have to play a better brand of poker than I did this time if I'm gonna keep the tax man happy, Bill. That little wad I won from you and Sam will cover about three hours' worth, and it took me longer than that to get it off you. So bring more money next spring when you come after some of those big rainbows up at the falls. You too, Sam. Nothing like a certified mullet on a fishing trip—after you clean him, you can use the carcass for bait."

Sam laughed. "We'll be here, John T., but I can't afford many more contributions like this time or I'll have to move in with you."

Hector came out of the lavatory in the freezer plant and held out his hand. "John T. McLaren, you are the last of the mountain men, and it's a good thing you have your own private mountain. Not many left; hang on to this one."

"I'll hold it, Hector—tooth and toenail. I was just telling Sam and Bill to be here next spring for trout fishing. It won't be an organized party, so you fellows can come when you feel like it and stay as long as you like. Just give me a day's notice so my Apaches won't scalp you."

"These drug-store Indians? My grandfather—and yours —used to tell stories about some real Apaches. I won't worry about these until they start coming to town on motorcycles." He grinned and handed his sketch case to the helicopter pilot.

"John T.," he said, turning back to me, "I'm having an

exhibition of some new paintings in my gallery next week. Lots of champagne and pretty girls, so why don't you come if you can make it? Also Sam and Bill, although they have no use for pretty girls anymore. They can look at the pictures and drink my booze.''

"I'll be there, Hector. You just organize your girls the way I have my deer trained and maybe even Bill can make a kill,'' I said as they all started piling into the helicopter. There were more shouts of "See you in the spring,'' and "Good hunting, John T.,'' and then their voices were drowned in the helicopter's takeoff revs. I ran back out of the downdraught and dust and waved at them, then walked over to Con Enright's cottage to tell him to get the boys together for some instructions.

I lined out a couple of weeks' work for them, about enough to keep one working cowhand busy for a day, then went back to the house for more coffee. If you don't run cows and don't mess around with the country much, about all there is to do is to keep the wolves shooed out of the living room. Then I just sat in the sun on the long gallery that runs along the eastern side of the house and thought about the Senator's problem until I heard another helicopter waffling in over the valley lip. I went down to see if Sara Connelly had gotten fat.

She hadn't, and I don't suppose she ever will. The woman who stepped out of that bird was big, a couple of inches under six feet at a guess, and her shoulders weren't made just to hang clothes on. A deep chest with high breasts narrowed to a short, straight, flat waistline above an incredible abundance of hips. Her tapered legs were about a yard and a half long and looked strong and muscular. Long blond hair carelessly caught in a ponytail and serene blue eyes topped off more girl than I had seen in a long blue month of Sundays. She pushed out her hand to shake mine in a gesture that just escaped the masculine directness I half-expected in such a big woman, but her hand wasn't anything like a man's. I hardly noticed the man who had followed her out of the helicopter until she used her shaking hand to turn me toward him—a little trick of social judo that the politicians had to master long ago to keep the crowds moving past them.

"Mr. McLaren, I'd like you to meet Sam Anderson. He runs the Senator's home office, and I thought it would be a a good idea if he was in on this meeting."

"Nice to see you, McLaren," said Anderson, and I got the second surprise of the day. This man didn't look like anybody's assistant. He looked like a cross between an NFL linebacker, the restless hunter-killer type, and a professor of economics. He was an even six feet, with close to two hundred pounds of beef slabbed onto a square, flat body. His neck and shoulders were heavy and taut with muscle, and he stood easily on legs that looked like bridge pilings in the checked Bermuda shorts he wore. He had nondescript brownish hair, cut short, and wore black-rimmed glasses. His face looked sort of round and bland until you took note of the jawline and eyes. He was perfectly at ease, but with a hard awareness that made you want to look at your hole card.

"Welcome to Rancho Useless, Sara and Sam. Just leave your stuff here and one of the boys will bring it up to the house."

"I didn't bring anything but my purse, Mr. McLaren, and Sam must wear his briefcase on a handcuff and chain. I've never seen him apart from it—it's like a growth on the end of his arm," Sara said with a grin. "Now lead me to lunch; I told you I'd be starved."

"Why didn't you say you were hungry, Sara? I always carry a big pepperoni pizza in my briefcase," said Sam easily, and I suspected that communication between offices was not one of Senator Cameron's problems. These two had developed a working relationship that probably increased efficiency by forty percent.

"Okay, lunch on the patio in twenty minutes, tall cool drinks in three on the condition that you both call me 'John' or 'John T.'" He looked up. "Well, I can see that Senator Carlsbad is up and around. Do you folks talk to the opposition?"

"They do when we close ranks, John T.," said the Senator. "Sit down, Sara, Sam." He indicated the wood-and-leather chairs around the big redwood table. "We don't have all that much time for protocol and party politics. There's work to be done."

"Easy, Senator," I said. "There's no law that says we have to work on an empty stomach. Let's get these folks something to eat and drink before we start the heavy conversation." I went to the drink trolley in the corner of the patio. "What'll it be, Sara?"

"Some sherry if you have it, John T.," she said.

"I'll take a large glass of that orange juice," said Sam Anderson when I looked inquiringly at him—a normal choice for the most abstemious man I ever met. I never saw Sam take more than one light drink in all the hectic days that followed, and he ate just as sparingly. I served the drinks, with a light scotch and soda for myself and the Senator.

The Senator had elected himself chairman, and he proceeded to open the meeting with crusty dispatch, ignoring my request to wait for lunch. I decided that I had better take the ball away from him soon or he would become a pain in the ass.

"Have you and Sam read the brief I sent you, Sara? Are you both familiar with the police case against Senator Cameron?" He looked from one to the other impatiently. Sam Anderson answered for both of them.

"We had seen most of it before your messenger arrived, Senator," he said, and took a sip of his orange juice. One notch for Sam. "It's a strong case," he continued.

"The question is, do you believe it? Do you believe Latham Cameron to be capable of such an act?" The Senator acted as if he were cross-examining a witness before one of his committees and I watched Sam. His reaction to this would tell me a lot about his future usefulness.

"Of course I believe he's innocent, Senator. He's capable of it, of course—almost everybody is—but this is pretty far out of character. The police case is almost too perfect— as an inductive argument it's both consistent and complete, which just doesn't happen. But it's a waste of time for us to debate Senator Cameron's guilt or innocence. We all know that he has been framed, and that it's a good job as far as it goes. The question is, who did it? And why? And what are we going to do about it?"

"The motive first," said Sara. "Sex, religion, politics, or money? Or any combination of these?"

"The motive has to be political, of course," said Sam laconically. "They spent, as nearly as I can estimate, one hundred and eleven thousand five hundred dollars in direct cash expenditure to set this up, and that doesn't include bribes and payoffs which we can't know about. The Senator just isn't involved in any business ventures that would justify such an expenditure. If the purpose is just to eliminate him, he could be killed for a fraction of that amount. The only way this makes sense is to assume that they want both to eliminate him and to discredit him in politics. Then the money they've invested becomes a negligible campaign expense."

"Negligible?" I wondered what would be significant money to these people, and Sam answered without my asking.

"The Senator's campaign committee collected and spent over two million to get him elected. Senator Carlsbad spent about the same, give or take a hundred thousand—and both races were relatively unopposed. If the motive is to vacate the seat in preparation for a campaign two years from now, that's a small price to pay for the job. The question is: Who can possibly benefit from a vacancy in the junior senator's seat? It can't be Senator Carlsbad's party, because I rather suspect they were instrumental in getting Senator Cameron nominated and elected in the first place. Am I right so far, Senator?" I stopped worrying about Carlsbad steam-rollering the meeting—these kids could take care of themselves.

"You're too smart for your own good, boy," said the Senator. "You sure you don't want to come to work for me?"

"Not right now, Senator. I like this job. Now, back to *cui bono?* If the motive is political, and we eliminate the established parties as possibilities—although they will remain possibilities in the strict sense—that leaves the radical right, the radical left, and the lunatic middle. Which is a pretty broad selection."

"All right, Sam. You have the ball. What do you think?" The Senator sat back and relaxed for the second time in twelve hours, which might be a record for the breed.

"I'd like to hear what Sara and John T. think. Sara?" Sam turned to his teammate, and she pursed her lips thoughtfully for a moment.

"Political, I agree. Standard politics it isn't. But then there isn't much left of the old-fashioned Fourth of July politics, is there? The natives are getting restless, and we've seen a lot of things happen that weren't in the book. We've seen assassination come back into fashion as a political tool, with the addition of kidnaping, extortion, riots, open sedition, and anything else you care to name. And I think it's just beginning. We're in for some hairy times, political and economic. As for which of a dozen radical groups might be responsible for this—well, there are just too many possibilities."

"So where do we start? John T., that's your line, isn't it?" said Sam, and wham! the ball was in my court.

"Well, it seems to me there are two areas that call for action: the political arena, and the actual murder. I suspect that I would be lost in politics—that's your department—and I'm not that lucky kind of private eye who knows the underworld like the pattern on his drawers and can make a shrewd guess, pinpointing the likely culprits while he's strapping on his .357 Magnum. But my methods will be pretty much the same. While you, Sara, and the Senator handle the political aspects of the case, I'll stomp around and make noise with my number twelves. Even a case as well wrapped as this one will have a loose end somewhere. My guess is that our man will be watching to keep it from coming unraveled. When I find the loose end of the string, I'll just give a yank and see what happens."

"Are you a licensed private investigator, John T.?" Sam asked.

"Yes, and I am also a justice of the peace and a deputy sheriff. I decided to take out a license when I almost got thrown in jail myself for messing around in police business. As for the other, my great-grandfather went to some trouble to have this valley designated a precinct when the original statehood survey was made. We have held the magistrate's office since then, and we found being a deputy makes it easier to maintain a little law and order of our own. It's not unusual in this part of the country."

"Seems to me your method is a little haphazard, John T.," the Senator offered. "Seems to me you need a better plan than that. What if they just sit tight and don't take your bait?"

"Then we might elect a new senator next election. It's the only plan I have at the moment, and it'll have to do until I can think of a better one." I was spared further argument by the arrival of lunch, and I spent the next thirty minutes marveling at Sara's capacity to appreciate food. She stowed an enormous quantity, greeting each new taste with little grunts and cries and moans of sheer delight, and I decided she was a definite possibility. No woman who likes food that much can fail to measure up in other important moments of our animal life. So she's smart, tough, and lusty, and as beautiful as they come. Right on, John T.

When there was no more food in sight, Sara went to freshen up and the Senator said he wanted to walk a bit and ambled off. Sam sipped his coffee and looked at me in appraisal.

"Sort of ridiculous, isn't it?" I said.

"Ridiculous?"

"Everything about it," I went on. "First, the fact that somebody sees a way to advance his cause, whatever it is, with an expensive and elaborate plot to get a United States Senator hanged for murder. Second, normal law-enforcement machinery seems so useless that it could almost be a party to the plot, so you have to call on me. Then, when we try to figure out some likely suspects, all we can conclude is that it must be the work of radicals. Shades of Sacco and Vanzetti! The uptight establishment looking for anarchists behind every mulberry bush. But, most ridiculous of all, that's exactly the kind of world we're living in. A radical minority group can wreck a city and the police get blamed for it. A group of students can trash a campus and lay the blame on their parents' country-club activities, while on another campus a nervous army is massacring the same kids. There are so many public and private espionage, intelligence, and terrorist *apparats* even in Washington—or should I say especially in Washington—that they must stumble all over one another bugging and shadowing, breaking and entering. Okay, Sam, if I'm going to stumble around your woodlot looking for dry twigs to step on, you had better brief me on the tribes I can expect to alert. Who's on the program for this game?"

"Hell, who isn't, John T.? The capital of this state is a long way from hellholes like Detroit, Pittsburgh, or Los Angeles, but we have our share of social problems. Not an extremely large Negro population, but an extremely large Indian, Mexican-American, and Duke's Mixture of people. We have the remnants of the Spanish colonials, their mixed-blood descendants, and several tribes of Indians, on reservations and at large. We have an unguessable number of wetbacks from Mexico, many of whom speak not a word of English and some who don't even know Spanish because they grew up in some Indian dialect. Broadly speaking, the Spanish-Mexican segment has been disenfranchised since statehood, the Mexican-Indian segment were slaves to the Spanish for a century or so before that, and the Indian tribes have been dying like flies without power or hope. But you know all that as well as I do. What you may not be aware of is that they're waking up and have begun to listen to the people who want to organize them.

"So now there must be at least one political organization for each subgroup, and sometimes several. They have had some small success in electing state and local officials, and even a couple of congressmen. Which is all fine, well and good. You might say that's what this country is all about and that it's long overdue. But it isn't that simple. First, a politically naive and immature electorate, which is to say the very young and the very ignorant, are always most impressed by the arguments of socialism or statism or any damn ism that promises them a bigger share and less responsibility. Or in the case of the students, there's their natural idealism, which is subject to some pretty raw outrages at the best of times. We can say, I suppose, that the students, blacks, and Chicanos are pretty much to the left of center. On the right hand, we have damn near as many Protestant rednecks as Alabama who still think in terms of 'The Code of the West' and all the other clichés you can name, but it all boils down to rural ignorance as opposed to urban ignorance. So we have local chapters of vigilante groups such as the 'Minutemen,' the 'Jordan Association,' and of course the American Legion and half a dozen other legitimate but far-right organizations. If you sorted them all out you'd have half the population on one side and half on the other, and when you got them to the polls, one side would vote Democrat and the other Republican, unless the American Party could field a candidate. That is, up till now. I suspect the next few elections are going to be hummers."

Sam took the coffeepot and poured himself a half cup. "My honest opinion is that none of these are likely to have been responsible for killing Malena Vasquez and setting the Senator up. It's going to turn out a lot sicker than that would be, as bad as that sounds. Now, do you have any ideas where to pick up a loose thread?"

"Some thoughts I was rolling around while I waited for you this morning. One witness, the waiter Chavez, puts the Senator outside his suite when the murder was committed. That's one possibility. Malena Vasquez was an addict, which means she had a connection. That's another direction, right into the criminal segment. Third, if the Senator was asleep in the suite all night, and Chavez did see someone dressed like him and looking like him in the hotel, we have an impersonator. We have that anyway, at the apartment and at the banks. Fourth, there's the money. Large coarse notes of currency don't grow on any trees we have in this state, and there has to be a rattle somewhere in any financial machine. That gives me enough to work on for the time being."

"Ever walk the point, John T.?" Sam asked, and I identified the source of some of his hardness. It takes steady nerves, some guts, and a certain harsh realism to lead a platoon in hostile territory.

"A few times, Sam. Enough to know how I'm going to feel on this patrol." Yes, I knew that, remembering the feeling that every nerve end is exposed and freezing in a cold wind. If you do it often enough and long enough, you go one of two ways—you learn to like it, or you go quietly nuts. Two sides of the same coin.

"Okay, Sam, I'll be in town tomorrow and I'll get in touch. Now relax for a while and let's take a look at Rancho Useless." I took him for the ten-cent tour of the home ranch, and then we joined Sara and the Senator at the helicopter pad. The Senator had obviously changed his mind about staying over and already had his gear stowed. Sara was with the pilot, watching him make his check for the return trip. I told her when I would be in town and added that dinner wouldn't be too shabby an idea. She agreed and climbed aboard, and I wondered if I might rush things a little, marry her and get her pregnant before somebody blew my head off.

Chapter . 3

MY HOUSE NEVER FEELS EMPTY, even when it is. A vast stone rectangle, it's too solidly planted on a shelf of stone to ever creak or groan, but you can always feel the lives that have passed through it. Five generations of my family have impressed their personalities and their tastes upon it, but it is still the same Moorish fortress my great-great-grandfather started building six years after he married the only daughter of Don Alessandro de la Cruz y Velásquez, the common ancestor that Hector de la Cruz and I share. It took five years to build the house, and another twenty to furnish it. Much has been done to the interior since then, but the basic hollow square is still the same, blank fortress walls without, and very comfortable, not to say luxurious, living quarters within.

I spent the rest of the afternoon in the gun room, which is part of my second-floor apartment. Like any big old house where men who like and use guns have lived, there are weapons all over it, from the perfectly preserved Hawken rifle with the bird's-eye maple stock in the main hall, that had come into the valley on my great-great-grandfather's saddle, to the elaborately carved, engraved, and inlaid musket my grandfather had taken off a dead Moro on Mindanao. But the working weapons were in the gun room, and a warlike collection it is. The prospect of smoky days ahead had set my mind in that direction, so I laid out a selection on the long walnut table in the center of the room.

I supposed pistols would be in order, so I selected a pair of S&W .38's with the featherweight frame. They have quite a recoil, but that isn't much in my big hands. I skipped over the Magnums, which look more like small cannon than handguns. If I was going to carry heat, it should be something common and ordinary that I could get rid of easily. I added magnetic clips, some screws, and a screwdriver to the pile. I stowed these into my suitcase, with a box of cartridges, and called it enough. I was not likely to need more firepower than that, and even if I did, it probably wouldn't be convenient to my hand, so why load myself down? I put the suitcase outside the door to be loaded into the Cessna and went downstairs. Juana Sanchez stopped me as I started through the door to the patio.

"Juan Silva is on the long gallery. He asked to speak with you."

"What the hell does he want?" I asked her shortly, and got a shrug in reply, so I went to the gallery. Juan was leaning against one of the cedar posts that supported the gallery roof. He straightened up as I came through the door.

"Patron?" he said, with the expression of a coffee-colored clown.

"Patron, hell! What's on your mind, Juan?" I snapped, and wondered where my sudden bad temper had come from. Then I knew. I didn't want to go into the city and poke around in someone's garbage. I wanted to stay here where I belonged, read and loaf, maybe go to the mesa and light medicine fires—anything but a hunting trip to any city, which is where you find the really dangerous animals.

"I think you go to the city to do a job for the Senator, *de verás?*" he asked.

"So?" I answered with a raised eyebrow.

"So you need any help?" he answered, in a tone that suggested that the whole question and its answer were obvious and rhetorical, and why was I wasting his time.

"Why should I need any help, Juan?" I asked.

"Because, boss, you're about to step in shit. Maybe the Senator wants you to mess around because Senator Cameron gets busted for killin' Malena Vasquez. If that's what you gonna do, you gonna be messin' around in big-city Chicano business where you don't know much. You gonna need a guide, and that's me." Juana Sanchez, I thought. If she doesn't know about it, it didn't happen on this rancho. She still wanted to blow my nose and change my diapers, and in this case it wasn't such a bad idea.

"Okay, Sancho Panza. Go to town and be around when I need you. Get some money from Juana and leave today. I will be at the hotel tomorrow sometime." I didn't give him a lot of instructions, because if he was to be of any use, he didn't need any.

"Sí, patron," he said with a little glint of humor in his eyes, and spun off the gallery. He was heading for his pick-up at a high lope when I went back to the house to get myself ready to go to town. I didn't have any great enthusiasm for the trip, and I dragged around until a sudden memory of Sara Connelly started the adrenalin or some other secretion working. Then I got myself moving and had the Cessna off the strip in record time for me. I put down at municipal airport in plenty of time to take a short siesta before I changed for dinner, so I was caught up on my sleep when I took the short elevator ride to the Senator's penthouse suite where she was camped.

And a good thing it was. A weary man would have fallen to his knees and wept at his inability to fully respond to the Sara Connelly who met me at the door. The slightly angular, tough-minded politician with the careless ponytail was gone. Some mad genius with nimble fingers had turned the ponytail into a cascade of tinted ringlets that ignored the current fashion but somehow managed to focus all the light in the room on the woman who wore them. I could spend a month trying to describe the overpowering *gestalt* of long warm rounded color and light and scented softness that hit me like a rocket-propelled grenade. I know what the grenade feels like, and I can remember the warm flood of secret fluids that roared through my veins and charged my body with enough animal electricity to light a city. But I can't describe either of them. All I know is that if she had touched me then, I would have screamed. Instead she motioned me to a chair and went to the elaborate built-in bar. There was a small frosted shaker with two glasses already prepared, and she poured two martinis without asking what I wanted. I don't care that much for martinis, but I drank this one without ever tasting it.

"You're rather impressive in a dinner jacket, John T.," she said as she handed me the glass. "I hope that means you're going to take me somewhere I haven't been, and feed me food I've never tasted, and then maybe dance my shoes to shreds."

"Well, the choice is somewhat limited, but I do know a place that can do things with fresh trout and prime beef, and the orchestra doesn't depend too much on the amplifier. Are you hungry enough to do justice to that?"

"I told you—I'm always hungry. Why don't you pour yourself one for the road while I get my wrap?" She disappeared into one of the bedrooms. I decided against another martini and stood by the door until she came out and handed me a blue mink stole twice as long as she was. The soft fur in my hands brought immediate response to my overcharged nerve ends, and I sniffed deeply at her perfume as she wafted by me to the elevator. I decided to get a firmer hold on myself if there wasn't to be rape and red ruin long before we ever got to the menu stage. The elevator kept loading more people as we went down, and the lobby was full, so we didn't say much until the taxi was on its way up the mountain to the secluded restaurant I had chosen. Then we limited conversation to the commonplace remarks you make when you're not quite sure what you want to talk about.

The restaurant is a gaunt redwood edifice on a cantilevered foundation lipped out over the canyon. Half a dozen fireplaces and some big windows, with low tables cleverly arranged for maximum privacy and atmosphere, make it a very pleasant place on a cold bright evening. I was known, of course, and I had phoned for reservations earlier, so the Swiss maître d' led us to one of the choicest tables near a window that opened on to the lighted city a thousand feet below. There was a small fire in the rough stone fireplace; the logs were flickering with the colored flames you get when you soak them in a solution of mineral salts for a couple of weeks before they are dried and burned. Service there is always good, but I have never seen the waiters perform with the cheerful élan they displayed that evening. I suppose they knew a good thing when they saw it, too.

As the waiter left with our drink order, Sara calmly informed me that she had been stalking me, which came as no surprise. You always hunt the big predators on a two-way street.

"I spent most of the afternoon finding out a few things about you, Mr. John Thomas McLaren," she said with a grin.

"I spent it sleeping, and perhaps you would have used your time better doing the same. Anything you want to know about me, just ask. I'm all primed and ready to tell you the story of my life," I answered.

"What I learned just whetted my appetite, so say on, Macduff."

"Well, I was one of eight boys—see there, all it takes is a little attention from a pretty girl and I automatically start lying. As a matter of fact, I'm an only child. I was born on Rancho Useless, lived most of my life there, and I'm just about as useless. Twenty generations of McLarens are sitting around hell discussing my shiftless, soft and degenerate ways right now. Aside from the fact that I'm sound of wind, limb, and digestion, that's about all there is to tell. Now what do you fancy for dinner?"

"I want escargot, trout, Châteaubriand, and all the fixin's and trimmin's—and I want all the fixin's and trimmin's on your story, too. I've already learned more than that from the assistant women's editor at the *Herald*—who has been in love with you since high school, I might add. You were a fantastic athlete in high school, for example, and some of your exploits as halfback reminded a lot of people of Red Grange. You continued playing in college, and kept getting better until you suddenly quit playing in your senior year. Then you went into the Army and were all kinds of hero with the special forces, in Vietnam and elsewhere. You were horribly wounded when the VC overran the camp you commanded, and you came home with a purple heart and all sorts of medals for heroism. Now *tell* me!"

"Lord have mercy! You girls do carry on with the gossip, don't you? Angie always did tend to exaggerate things; that's why she went to work for a newspaper. What she really loves about life is the stories she can tell about it. And that's where most heroes are born, anyway, in somebody's typewriter."

"All *right*, then. Tell me about your ranch. Why isn't it stuffed full of cattle, for instance? With the price of steak these days, you could be far too rich to bother about mere senators and their problems."

"You wouldn't believe the number of cowmen going

broke these days. This twenty-dollar Châteaubriand we're about to demolish sold for less than thirty-five cents per pound, and it probably cost the rancher thirty-eight cents to bring it to market. It's so bad right now that the market is glutted with calves and breeding stock. If I had depended on cows over the past three years, I wouldn't own a foot of land.

"And besides, I told you I'm just naturally shiftless and a disgrace to the McLarens. When I got back from Vietnam, I just couldn't seem to work up much enthusiasm for raising cattle, so I let the place go to ruin. Now, I guess I just like it that way." The waiter had been and gone with our drinks, so I took a sip and wondered how much of that story would be of interest to her. More than I was willing to tell, at any rate.

"How does it stay so green?" she asked. "It's the middle of October, and the rest of the country we flew over this morning was dry and gray as an old bone. Your valley looks like spring all over again. Where does your water come from?"

"Now that is a story, and it's a few million years old. To make it short, the mountain-maker decided to play a little trick when he heaved that end of the plateau up on edge to form the Corazon Range. He double-faulted that long pie-shaped slice, and when the basic formation rose, it stayed where it was. That slice now forms the kind of valley they call a 'graben,' and a layer of porous sandstone about a hundred feet thick keeps collecting water up in the mountains and piping it down into my valley. I always have sub-surface water, even in the driest seasons, and a dozen or so springs keep the creek running the year round. The combination of water and the resulting greenery even give the valley its own special climate, from ten to twenty degrees cooler in summer and about the same differential warmer in winter. Some of the wildlife has evolved differently there,

and I have one species of sparrow that can't be found anywhere else on earth.''

"It sounds fantastic, John T.—a million-acre oasis. I
don't really understand the geology, but I'll take your word
for it.'' She sipped her drink and made the little motions
that said she was still all ears—all the little response reac-
tions that girl children learn at Mommy's knee.

"Whose word have you been taking for the size of the
place? It's not even close to being a million acres. A
hundred and eighty thousand, at most. The mountain itself
is more than a million, of course, but it's all government
land. I lease the slope that forms my watershed to keep
some cattleman from going up there with a bunch of scrubs
and using them as an excuse to shoot all the lions and
poison the wolves. They have enough trouble making a
living without having to dodge bounty hunters.''

"So you're an ecologist, too? Is that why you let the
range revert to wilderness? To protect the environment?''

I nearly choked on my drink. "No!'' I said angrily. She
looked a bit startled at my reaction, so I continued.

"I run my ranch to suit myself, and my motives have
nothing to do with the current maunderings about ecology
and the environment. I don't cry for starving wolves or
other so-called endangered species. There's a lot of truth in
what they say about the mess modern civilization makes of
any landscape, but I don't see any other way to have
achieved what we have in the way of a comfortable living
standard. I've done a lot of thinking about the subject, off
and on, but I don't have a solution. I certainly don't want to
join the ecology freaks who are yelling for government control of everything so the Tattooed Titmouse can feed and
breed himself to extinction.''

"Sorry I brought it up. I take it you don't yearn for the
socialist paradise?''

"There you go again! That's another red flag, if you'll

pardon the expression, and here comes dinner, so I'll just duck that one and go about feeding myself.''

The lusty girl who had done such a job on lunch hadn't disappeared completely, as Sara quickly demonstrated. She tucked into her dinner with as much or more enthusiasm as before. It was a natural response to a probable good provider, or at least I hoped she might harbor some such thoughts. The fact that she had gone to some small trouble to psyche herself up for the evening, including what I guessed was a brand-new dress, boded well. Also, Senator Latham Cameron's name had not been mentioned once, which was another good sign. The last spoonful of juice from Bananas Foster caused her to raise her eyes to heaven and just barely suggest the motion of a patted tummy as she leaned back in her chair and gazed dreamily at the fire. I decided that the preliminary capework was over and it was time to place a couple of *banderillas*, if it's proper to use a bullfighting metaphor when you're talking about prime heifer.

''So the girl is fed,'' I said. ''It's time you sang a little song yourself—about yourself. Tell me about Sara Connelly.''

''Surely you've read my dossier? It wouldn't be anything like Senator Carlsbad to send you to strangers,'' she answered, with a sudden return to the kind of awareness you develop when you work in Washington, which must be the world's meanest bear pit.

''Dossiers are dull documents. They only give you the low spots, the kind of facts that computers can read and understand. I want to get my mind around the girl—what she is, what she wants, what she thinks about herself.'' My mind, and then what? Foolish questions. . . .

''Well, I was one of eight girls—no, you are serious, aren't you? I'm not sure I want to tell you any more than you've told me, but I will. You know what I do, and it's exactly what I've dreamed of doing, at least for this stage of my life. I do important things, with and for and to important people. My work has a direct effect on the history of this world, to the extent that I help to make the Senator more effective in his job. He's a great man, I think, and he will do some great things if we can get him out of this mess he's in now. I want that more than anything in the world.'' The sudden earnestness of her response and her complete honesty were devastating. So dispensing with further maneuverings, I took the bull by the horns, to continue using the most inept metaphor I ever heard of.

"No thoughts of marriage? Children? Or are you personally involved with Latham Cameron?"

"Waiow! That one hurt. You *are* something of a bully boy, aren't you? Well, it's none of your damn business, John T." Her jaw came out, and she was ready for fight or footrace, but I had frolic in mind, so I put a more conciliatory note in my voice.

"Whoa, girl. That wasn't idle curiosity, and I wouldn't pry into your personal life at all if it weren't for the fact that I am uncommonly interested in you. You see, it is absolutely imperative that I get married fairly soon."

"Ooof! Talk about counterpunchers—what are you doing to me? You shouldn't hit a girl that low on a full stomach." I almost laughed at the consternation on her face, but fortunately my dearly won poker face kept me out of that trouble.

I told her, in bald terms, of my dilemma. Marry, get an heir, and keep the line going with a few hectares to its name. I told her of my high standards, and how close she came to meeting or exceeding them, in language that resembled a set of MIL SPECS for a weapons system.

"Oh, boy," she said at last. "Medieval McLaren! How absolutely feudal can you get? Tell me, John T., am I to take this as a proposal of marriage?"

"No," I answered. "Take it rather as formal notice that I intend to court your favor, with marriage in mind. With your permission, of course, in the absence of either parent, guardian, or duenna."

"I never heard such a pompous declaration in my life. But it's different, I'll say that for you. Especially after some of the pitches you get in Washington. Oh, permission granted, by all means. Pursue away, my lord! And that calls for a drink." Our fox-eared waiter didn't even need my signal; he was off and running before the period fell from her sentence, and the brimming cup was there to hand in thirty seconds flat. I raised my glass to hers and we drank. Little dancing lights shot rockets in my direction over the rim of her glass.

"Does that mean you expect me to fall into bed with you tonight, milord? If it does, then we need to look at your proposition with a more judicial eye." She could hook 'em in low, too. Another counterpuncher, with good recovery.

"That can wait. We have more pressing affairs to see to first—and besides, I'm looking for a wife, not a playmate."

"Un-huh. You're quite sure you don't want to find out if we're good in bed before you plight your troth? No trial spin to see if the wench is as advertised? You amaze me."

"We're not trying out for the Olympics, Sara. Sure, sex is important, and we might even get around to it one of these days. But there are many things that are more important. The life you live around your sex life, for instance. What you hope to achieve in bed, apart from the lovely tickle and the washing up. I repeat, it can wait."

"No talk of love? What happened to the old 'love and marriage' tradition? Or is that something that can also wait? Just what kind of marriage and/or courtship, etc., do you have in mind, John T.?"

"Love? We'll have to explore what we mean by that, won't we? That's what courtship is all about. Marriage is more than a gut issue, and the kind of love I hope you aren't thinking about—the kind they sing about in all the country-western discopaths—is a poor basis for marriage, or anything else. No, that can wait, too. Let's just play the hand as it's dealt and see how the cards fall.''

"All right, John T. We'll play it that way. And now we had better head back down the mountain. There's work to do tomorrow." We finished our drinks, paid the check and the fine on our coats, and rode in silence back to the hotel.

On the way up to the penthouse, I told her to get in touch with Sam Anderson and Cameron's attorney and ask them to come to the hotel as soon as they could make it. That was a waste of breath. When we walked into the suite, Anderson and Jim Cash were already there, in shirt sleeves, with papers strewn all over a long coffee table.

Sara excused herself and went to her room to change out of her evening clothes.

"About time you troops got here," said Anderson. "We have a little work to do. John T., have you met Jim Cash? He's the Senator's attorney."

"Shucks, we go back to high school, Sam," said Cash. "How are you, John T.?" I shook Jim's hand, remembering the time he lumped my head with that same right hand after a football game. I wasn't surprised to see him, although I had neglected to ask who Cameron's lawyer was. Jim Cash was another member of the club, and a ranking member of the minority party. He was the third generation of Cashes in the law firm of Cash and Carrol—inevitably referred to as "Cash and Carry." With good reason, I might add. Jim was big, smart, and aggressive, and liked nothing better than a good fight, legal or otherwise. He had flown an impressive number of combat missions in Vietnam, and his law record wasn't too shabby, either. We could use him on this one.

I sat down at the table with Sam and Jim.

"Have a nice evening, John T.?" asked Sam.

"Best in a long while, Sam. How about you?"

"Not as pleasant, perhaps, but Jim and I made a few numbers. He says he sees one or two holes in the case, and that we can make a fight of it if it ever comes to trial."

"That must not happen," exclaimed Sara, coming out of her room in a thick robe but barefoot. She began to pace the thick pile carpet, and I could see that she enjoyed the sensation of the rug under her bare feet, even in such a tense situation. "If the case ever comes to trial, the Senator is politically dead, even if he is acquitted. Voters are fickle, and whoever did this will have won whatever political advantage he is looking for."

"So we have to find a murderer and enough evidence to convict him before the case comes to trial. So what's our strategy?" I asked. I already knew what I was going to do, but it wouldn't hurt to let these people think it was their idea. Sam caught the ball on the first bounce.

"We make noise," he said. "That's what the opposition will do to capitalize on it, and I can already feel the rumbles starting all over the state. If we stay quiet, they'll win no matter what we do. We have to come out with a roar, and we're already late with it."

Jim laughed. "So pass out the noisemakers and let's get the party rollin'. How about a press conference?"

"Done and done," said Anderson. "We will win or lose the political battle on TV and in the papers, so I've got the staff roughing out a statement which we'll go over with the Senator later this morning. We'll call the conference for this afternoon, here in the penthouse. What do you think, Sara?"

"Schedule it for late afternoon, okay? About cocktail time? And if you'll get me a copy of that rough statement, I'll call Washington now, and New York. It's a funny thing—a lot of local newsmen don't know what they think about their own neighborhood until they read it on the wire. The Senator has a few friends in the media back East; in fact, they've been friendlier than the hometown scribes.''

''I hope that statement screams 'Frame' and hints at a lot of new evidence,'' said Cash. ''It won't make any difference in court, and it will help if we can create some doubts ahead of time. The papers will try the case in advance anyway, so we might as well start fighting there.''

''If you're loud enough, you just might drown out the noise I'll make looking around,'' I said as I went to the sideboard for coffee. ''But the man I'm looking for will hear me, and that's all we need. If he sits tight, we haven't a prayer. We have to roust him out of the brush and get him moving if we're to get a shot at all. So far as I'm concerned, you can go ahead with all the uproar you can make, Sam. You'll just be beating the bushes for me. I never did like still hunting, anyway.''

Which was not quite accurate as a statement of my hunting tastes.

Hunting comes naturally to me, as it does to all men. It's just that I grew up with plenty of opportunities to sharpen instincts and learn some skills. One of the things I have learned is that you hunt according to the nature of the game. If it's a timid, patient, secretive sort of beast, you wait him out. If he's a traveling type, you run him down. All you need to know to be a good hunter is everything there is to know about the game, his territory, and all his friends and enemies. With one exception: when you're hunting a man, you also have to know his name. You can hunt animals as a class, and shoot whatever comes along, but on men you have to call your shots. The application for the license has to be pretty comprehensive, too. And you can't ignore the fact that the quarry has a perfect right to be stalking you, and in this case that was part of the plan. I wanted that great big dangerous animal to break cover, and it would only work if he came right at me.

"All right. Is there anything else?" asked Sam, looking at each of us in turn.

"Yes, there's one more thing," said Sara. "If it's noise we want, we might as well get some people who like to make noise in on the party. It seems to me that we have a campaign situation. The Senator has to win a vote of confidence if he's going to survive, so why don't we treat it like an election? Put together a volunteer organization, raise funds, and canvass the state? The more people we get involved, the less chance he'll have of being bumped off when the clutch comes."

"Sara, you are a glutton for punishment. Do you have any idea how much work is involved in an all-out election campaign?" Sam was looking at her with an intent stare, as if daring her to defend the idea.

"I've been to a couple of fires," she answered evenly. "We lost one and won two, and I know exactly what hell we went through each time. But they were worth it, and so will this one be. Besides, it's part of the job." She wasn't chortling over broiled trout now, or curling her toes into deep carpet. Her fine square shoulders looked like iron, and I could see the heavy ridge of muscle along her jawline. So she loves to fight, too, I thought. I almost ended my suit with a proposal right there. Sam looked at her for a moment, then broke into a wide grin.

"Go to it," he said, and stuck out his hand. Sara took a deep breath and returned his hearty shake, and that turned into a good-night shake all around. We adjourned the meeting without further business. Ten minutes later I was in my own room with a drink in my hand, reflecting that I had seen the last of Sara Connelly until this thing was over. She was going to be one busy little girl, and I supposed I'd be busy too. I had started to undress for bed when there came a light tap-scratch on the door. When I opened it, Juan Silva glided into the room. I poured him a drink.

Chapter . 4

"Qué pasa, hombre?" I asked him when he had taken a deep pull on the straight bourbon. I didn't bother to dwell on the thought that the drink I had given him would have got me hanged in Judge Parker's Fort Smith court a couple of generations ago.

"I been looking around, talking to some people, boss. Do you know, this Malena Vasquez, she was a junkie?"

"The coroner's report said she had a fix just before she was killed. What about it?"

"I found her connection. He's my cousin. He said she was shootin' heavy." Paydirt, and I mentally hugged Juana for sending this one along.

"So what else? When can we talk to him, and where is he?"

"We can see him tonight if you want, boss. Only she don't buy that much from him the last couple years. And when she does buy, not regular. He figures she must have scored somewhere else, and only called him when there was a problem with the other guy. That's since maybe eighteen months ago." Eighteen months—one month after she had been installed in "Lawrence Calhoun's" apartment.

"Will your cousin talk to me, Juan?"

"Sure, if I tell him to. If he don't I break his head." My tame Apache was not a bit humorous when he made that pronouncement, and I suspected his cousin knew his temper well. He would talk to me.

"Let's go see him, Juan."

"Right on, boss."

"Juan, where in hell did you get that 'right on' shit?"

"Indians got equal rights with blacks, boss. Red's beautiful, too—and we didn't get carried here. Maybe I'm a Red Panther, boss." Maybe he was. His grandfather had been, without all the loud-mouth bragging philosophy that had to be imported, too. His red panthers had been all teeth and claws, as much a part of the desert as the rattlesnakes and cactus that had been food and drink to them—eked out with an occasional army mule. They had to be forced on welfare at the point of a rifle.

"One thing, Juan. Chavez, one of the witnesses against the Senator, is a waiter here in the hotel. Why don't you see if you can find out something about him while I change clothes? I'll meet you in the parking garage."

"Right on, boss," he said with a grin and left. I changed clothes.

Juan filled me in on his cousin as we drove into the hills south of the city where the bulk of the Chicano population lived.

"He's just a small-timer, boss, and he don't handle much of the heavy shit. Most of his customers stick to grass and hash, and a few pills. He don't have sense enough to score money for a big buy, so he'll stay small. His wife keeps after him to quit and get a straight job, but he likes the strange pussy he can get with plenty of dope."

"Where does he get his stuff? Is there a local distributor?"

"No, he gets it down South. He has a guy runs the border all the time, brings in a little every trip. Maybe another cousin makes the buys down there. They don't get busted if they don't get turned in on the other side. That's the only way that dumb Border Patrol ever finds any dope, except they automatically search anybody with a beard. Dumb kids try to bring it in all the time, and they get busted all the time."

"By the way, Juan, what did you find out about Chavez, the waiter?"

"I asked around the hotel like you told me, boss. The cops picked him up a couple of days after the Vasquez chick got killed. They ain't seen him since."

"Do you think they put him in jail?"

"Quién sabe? They don't need no excuse to put Chicanos in jail."

"Interesting. See if you can find out any more. We need to talk to that dude."

Juan's cousin's house was a small frame structure on a rundown street. It was neat enough, and it looked as if a room had been recently added to the rear. A light was showing through the draped front window.

"Looks as if he's home, Juan."

"I told him to stick around in case you wanted to talk to him. He's here." The flat statement didn't leave any doubt about Juan's relationship with his family. The door opened before we knocked, and a hand motioned us in. We stepped into a small living room past a short, round man with a long fat pistol in his hand. He held it beside his leg at arm's length, the muzzle pointed at the floor.

"Put that thing away, Memo. This is Mr. McLaren," Juan said. His cousin shuffled his feet in indecision as to what to do first. Finally he laid the pistol on a lamp table and held out his hand. I took it, feeling the clammy limpness of the brief contact. "This my cousin, boss—Guillermo Silva. He knows Malena Vasquez." Silva motioned us into chairs and asked if we wanted a drink. We declined, and asked him about Malena Vasquez.

"Sir, she just a junkie. I hear she dance pretty good, but I don't ever go to Cielo Azul, so I don't know. She used to buy all her stuff from me, until a couple years ago, then she don't buy so much." The words came in a rush, as if he wanted to get it all said as soon as possible and get us out of there.

"That's what Juan told me. I want to know more about her—everything you know. What kind of woman was she, whom did she know, where did she hang out when she wasn't working?"

"I tol' you, she just a *puta*, a whore. You say junkie; you say whore if she's a woman. Malena was no different. She danced at Cielo Azul, and she hustled for extra bread to feed the monkey. What more can you know about a junkie?" The contempt in his voice was so vast, so complete, that it made me wonder about his ability to continue in the business.

"Where did she come from? Around here? Was she local?"

"No, she was *pura mejicana*, from Chihuahua City. She come up here about five years ago and went to work at Cielo Azul. She was turned on already, but real light, you know? She started buildin' then, and in three years she was hittin' up three times a day. Then she moved into that fancy apartment on Guadalupe Street and I didn't hear from her for three, four months. Then she look me up with the runnin' trots at both ends, sneezin' her head off. I ask her why in hell I should sell her any shit, and she says she can't help it, her new connection had her locked in. I sold her a deck, and after that she buys a little from me ever' once in a while, enough for a couple of days. She was always in good shape after that, so maybe she knew in advance when she wouldn't be able to score from the other guy. Or maybe she was just buildin' a stash. Who knows what a junkie is doin'?''

"Did you ever see her boy friend, the dude who was keeping her in the apartment?''

"No, I just went there a couple times, and she was alone. You mean Senator Cameron, the big politico?'' I saw a small hint of the sly humor I knew so well in Juan Silva, a momentary glint in the flat, indifferent eyes.

"That's what they say. What about other boy friends?''

"She don't hustle anymore after she moved into the apartment; at least I don't see her around and I don't hear she's available. There's a whisper her new friend is heavy shit, and I guess he was.''

"Do you know any of her friends she might have kept on seeing, anything else about her? Where did she go when she wasn't working? What did she do?''

"Mr. McLaren, junkies don't have any friends. They don't do anything but hit themselves with the big stick, and whatever they have to do for more bread. Far as I know, she worked at the club and then went home and fixed herself and that's all. She wasn't around at all, not in this world.''

"All right, Memo. That helps some. Thanks.'' I put two twenties on the coffee table and started to get up. Memo said something with his eyes and shoulders to Juan Silva, then turned to me.

"You fellas wan' a number?'' he asked, and there was a sort of plea in his eyes that I couldn't read.

"Number?'' I replied, puzzled.

"Number one—a joint, marijuana. I got some good shit, *media y media.* You want to have one with me?'' I looked at him for a moment, then at Juan. Juan gave me the nod to go along. Well, what the hell—there was more to it than just smoking a joint together. I nodded, and Memo left the room for a minute and came back with a package of cigarettes in his hand. They were Pall Malls, machine-made with a cork-tipped paper twisted to a point at one end. He tapped one up in the pack and passed it to me. I took a cigarette and passed the pack to Juan. The taste was sharp and hot and reminded me of other times, in stranger places than this, when I had gone along with some quaint local customs.

"This is good dope, and it's mixed half and half with to-bacco. It will be maybe fifteen, twenty minutes before you're high, but it lasts a long time and no headache when you crash," said Memo, and took a long, sucking drag on his cigarette. We smoked in silence for a while, then Memo went to the kitchen. He came back with a bottle and glasses and a bowl of ice.

"Some people like to smoke and drink at the same time," he said, and I nodded. He poured straight whiskey for the three of us and then leaned back in his chair. He let a small flow of triumph show through the hooded eyes as he re-laxed for the first time since he had let us in. I could under-stand that. We were involved with him now; we were smok-ing dope; we were equally guilty. He could feel comfortable with us, at ease in his contempt for everybody who used his merchandise, including himself. Juan Silva finished his joint and carefully stubbed the roach, which he handed to Memo. Then he began to talk, slowly and confidentially.

"You wanted to tell us some more, didn't you, Memo? You know a lot more, don't you? Why don't you tell us who Malena's new connection was? Who was the boy friend who set her up and supplied her with shit?" There was no threat in his voice, no tension in his body, just a soothing, coaxing friendliness with a very slight undertone of silken hardness.

"I can't tell you who, Juan," Memo answered slowly. "Or anything about him except he ain't no senator and he's somebody that has to be bad news. The word was just a whisper, but it came down that nobody bother Malena Vasquez, nobody goes around her. Guys try to hustle her now and then, but somehow they get the word to cool it. *Quién lo sabe?* Maybe she belong to El Patron himself.''

"Okay, Memo. We gotta split now. You gonna gimme a lid of this for the road?'' I looked at Juan Silva and took command again.

"Smoke on your own time, Juan,'' I said.

"On second thought, this is all I need. Thanks, Memo.'' I reached over and took the unlighted cigarette from Juan's lips and passed it back to the pusher.

"We have work to do, Juan. Come on.''

"Okay, boss. Get 'em up, Scout!'' He jumped to his feet and trotted to the door, switching the side of his leg with an imaginary quirt as he played the childhood stick-horse game. Oh, well. Hi ho, Silver!

"I have a feeling we learned something back there, Juan,'' I said as we drove back toward the city. "Who is 'El Patron'?''

"We learned it all, boss—and we didn't learn nothin'. We learned that a lot of people are pretty sure the Senator didn't have nothin' to do with the Vasquez whore, but that's all. And you can bet that El Patron wasn't keeping her there, either. Who is he? Who knows? He's another whisper, boss, but he's a whisper Chicanos listen for. Somewhere, somehow, he's big medicine for Chicanos, Indios, and maybe even blacks. I don' know. Maybe he's God or the devil, maybe he's the ghost of Señor Jack. All I know is everytime one of La Raza decides to do something big, somehow he has to find out if El Patron likes it or not. If it's big enough, and he likes it enough, the guy gets help. If he don' like it, it don't get done.''

"For instance?''

"*Por supuesto,* a smart young guy works hard and gets

through school and wants to go to college. He gets help even if he don' play football. Then he graduates and maybe wants to go to law school. He gets more help. Then he's a lawyer, and it comes down that he's the man to go to if you're Indio and get in trouble. Then this lawyer goes into politics, and gets some more help. He might even make it into Congress, like a couple of guys already did."

El Patron. The Boss, Big Daddy, Godfather. The Man, who owns everything and everybody. Maybe. And maybe just another messiah rumor, another faith that says "Somebody up there likes me."

"What if he doesn't like it? What then?"

"Some guys found out about that, too. Like they wanted to get real big in the dope business, and gambling, and some whores. You know, the big mob stuff. They didn't make it."

"He discouraged them?"

"He killed them."

"How about Memo? He operates. And there must be whores and crap games and books operating."

"He lets them operate, boss. The whisper is they don't get trouble if they don't get big ideas, and if they don't squawk when somebody needs a contribution. Memo's a small-timer, like I told you, and he don't make any waves, so nobody notices him much. Maybe that's part of why he don't have no ambition."

"You mean El Patron controls all the action but doesn't have it organized for himself? Hard to believe, Juan." Damned hard to believe. Aside from that one little detail, it's a portrait of the big Eastern mobs with an Italian or Irish or Jewish or Greek *padrone*.

"How about the big mobs? Are they here? Mafia, Syndicate, Dixie Mafia, anything like that?"

"I dunno, boss. Maybe they try once. I hear a small rumor some guys out of Louisiana or Texas somewhere sent some dudes in to set up something with the gambling. You hear about them for a couple of weeks, and then nothing. They're gone, and nobody knows where."

"Where's headquarters for El Patron? Who works for him, and what do they get out of it?" That's the key question: the payoff. Organizations, from Sunday schools to the Pentagon, just eat money.

"No headquarters, boss, and I don' know anybody who works for him. Nobody goes around sayin', '*Yo soy el Segundo del Patron,*' and nobody sets up an office with his name on it and says, 'This is where you get the license.' Just rumors that if you talk a lot about a deal, he's gonna hear about it sooner or later. And if he likes it or don't like it, you're gonna hear about it sooner or later. And that's all I know, boss."

"How long have you known this much? And why haven't I heard about it before?" I thought I knew this territory pretty well, but you live and learn. It looked as if I had a lot to learn.

"Chicano business, boss. That's why you don't hear about it. Me, I hear stories about El Patron since I was a kid —ten, twelve years. Everybody at the rancho hears them, and sometimes they talk about them. You talk to Juana Sanchez. She knows maybe more."

And this is how revolutions get born, holy wars and bloody *jihads.* The first small whisper of "A Chosen One," a Mahdi, a Jomo Kenyatta, a Martin Luther King or Stokely Carmichael. Anyone with enough brains and balls and charisma to weld a mob with a grievance into a fanatic "wind of change." The history of this world is underlined in red with countless examples. And it *can* happen here. It *has* happened here.

"It's time we got some sleep. Where do you want me to drop you, Juan?" I had been driving steadily but very carefully since we left Memo's, but I still didn't feel anything from the *cannabis* I had smoked. I have heard since that the body has a brief natural immunity that is soon gone for good if you smoke enough. Maybe that was it, because my head was still clear and level.

"I'm a little high, boss, so I think I float around some more, maybe get some more ideas. Things just crankin' up down this part of town. You can unload me anywhere."

"Okay, Juan. Here's a cabstand. I'll put you down there and see you in a day or two. And maybe you better cool it with the shit. If you get in trouble, you can't help us any."

"*Sí*, boss. *La vista*." He got out of the car and stood on the sidewalk looking at me until I drove away. Long Juan Silva, Tonto, Sancho Panza. *Tonto* means "a little crazy," and aren't we all? I parked the car in the hotel garage and bribed the attendant to keep it parked by the exit on the ground level, instead of five or six floors up behind a Greyhound bus. He grinned as he took my ten, and I grinned as I went upstairs and crashed into my bunk.

The next morning, while I scraped my face and buffed the moss off my teeth, I planned a few calls to make. First on the list was Coley Brannon, chief of police and sometime hunter on Rancho Useless during the days when I took large parties hunting. I wondered how he had made it to be a top cop, since he had trouble hitting the same mountain a deer was walking on, and had never taken home a good head that I could remember.

The desk sergeant called my name to his office and told me to go on up to the third floor. I tossed him an offhand salute and stepped into the elevator, along with two Chicano cops in plain clothes. They didn't speak in the car, but I could feel them both memorizing my mug until they got out on the second floor. From what I hear, we have some good policemen on this force, and many of them are of Mexican or Indian or mixed ancestry. These two were big, clean-cut men, almost handsome, and they reminded me of the carefully chosen and trained policemen in Mexico City, every one of whom could give cards and spades to a lot of movie actors when it came to looks and charm and bearing. I might add that they are highly motivated and very tough.

The receptionist in Brannon's office was just getting ready to tell me to have a seat and wait when the door to his private office was thrown open and he charged through it, big smile and open arms giving the lie to any possible rumors that he was a hard, surly, difficult-to-know boss cop. Which is exactly what he was, big smile notwithstanding.

"John T., good to see you, boy! Come in, come in!!" He hustled me into his office with one big hand on my elbow while the other maintained a death grip on my eating hand, and I got a hint of the tremendous strength in his big body. I was glad he hadn't grabbed for a come-along and booted my ass in for "routine questioning."

"How's business, Coley? Are you managing to keep your little hotel full?"

"Pretty slow, John T., except for a few drunks and burglars and petty thieves. There's plenty of room left. Sit down, sit down! I'll have my girl get us some coffee. How do you like yours?" I told him, and he buzzed the receptionist on the intercom. The door opened immediately and she bustled in with pot, cups, and cream and sugar on a tray. I poured in cream and took a sip while I watched Coley wonder what the hell I was doing there.

"What can I do for you, John T.? I haven't heard from you in a couple of years, so I guess you have some business on your mind." So maybe a top cop doesn't have to shoot very straight with a deer rifle, I thought.

"Latham Cameron, Coley. He's on my mind. I'm sort of curious—it doesn't add up with what I know about the Senator."

"Latham? I guess that's the surprise of the year, John T. Imagine a man like that getting himself in that kind of mess. Just goes to show, I guess. . . . Well, we're treating him pretty well, considering. He has a comfortable cell, and his people brought some things in to make him more at home, so to speak. His meals are sent over from the hotel, so I guess you might say he's our star boarder. I guess he has about everything he needs, but I'll tell him you were asking about him."

"Well, I'm glad to hear you're not hosing him down every morning, Coley, but what I really want to know is this: Just what kind of a case can you really make against a man like that? There has to be a mistake somewhere, so where is it?"

"You'd think that, wouldn't you? But there's no mistake about it, as far as we're concerned. Looks like he killed that girl and there you are."

"Just where is that, Coley? Do you have some witnesses I haven't heard about? Has he confessed? What makes you so sure?" I would have been very surprised if he had answered that one, but I was even more surprised at the sudden anger that wiped the cordial expression from his face and flattened his voice into a snaky whip when he answered.

"The case is closed, John T. The DA has it now, and he has an indictment for murder one. Now, it was nice to see you again, but I really don't have any more time to talk about it."

"Why are you angry, Coley? Why don't you want to talk about it?"

"Why am I angry?" he snapped. "I'll tell you why, John T. I know all about your private license, and I know that Braden Carlsbad has hired you to clear the Senator. He gave you a pretty complete file on the case, including confidential police reports and other materials we don't like to circulate around. They leaned pretty damned hard to get them, and I don't like that. I also don't like private investigators wasting my time, and that's what you're doing right now. The case is closed, John T.'' He stood up then, and I was dismissed. Well, I could understand that. Nobody likes to be pressured. But I also thought he was a little silly to let his anger get the better of him. He surely knew he had nothing to gain by dropping the ax on Latham Cameron, and even mild encouragement and cooperation would have gained him more face with Cameron's party. As a professional politician, he should have known that. I shrugged it off and put him on the stupid side of my fecal roster.

Sam Anderson and Jim Cash were just leaving the sergeant's desk as I stepped out of the elevator on my way out. On their way to visit the Senator, I guessed, and Sam immediately confirmed it.

''Want to come along, John T.? You haven't heard the Senator's side of the story from him, yet. It might help,'' he said. I nodded and punched the elevator button again.

People who live in cities, smoke cigarettes, breathe carbon monoxide and other pollutants, and always suffer from some sort of sinus infection don't know what it is to smell. I suppose Coley Brannon's jail was as clean or cleaner than most, but when I stepped off the elevator into the jail level I began to regret my years of clean living and pure thoughts in the thin, dry air on my mountain. It was like being hit in the face with a wet mop full of vomit, fear, and disinfectant. It didn't seem to bother Jim Cash, who had a cigarette in his hand, but Sam, another nonsmoker, wrinkled his short, heavy nose in disgust.

''If you could bottle this and label it with a short, easy-to-read statement of the criminal statutes, the crime rate would fall by seventy percent,'' said Sam. ''I wonder why our lawmakers never thought of that.''

''You tell me, Sam. You're in the business of making laws,'' I said.

"Lawmakers are lawyers," said Jim with a laugh. "Laws are written to make work for lawyers, just as diseases are invented to keep the doctors in silk drawers. You know that nobody ever gets a disease until some doctor has written a paper on it and the pharmaceutical companies have a marketable specific remedy. Law is the same way; legislatures spend more time trading votes than they do reading the laws they pass, and it would take the entire graduating class and faculty of a new law school every year just to cope with the legal business generated by each year's legislation. Fortunately for the people, there just aren't enough policemen in the country to enforce the laws we have, nor enough courts, judges or lawyers to prosecute them. Your normal, law-abiding taxpayer's best protection is the inability of the republic to enforce its laws."

"The real criminals help, too," said Sam. "They keep the courts jammed and the newspapers busy making heroes out of them, so they don't have time left for the people."

We were getting VIP treatment, so the meeting was in a small conference room next to the jailer's office. A policeman ushered Cameron into the room and then left, shutting the door behind him. I shook the Senator's hand and sat down by the window. Sam and Jim opened briefcases and laid stacks of papers on the table while the Senator chose a chair next to the window. He had been in the slammer only a few days and was still insulated by his background and position, but the wall-awareness was already growing in his mind. I shuddered to think what a long stretch would do to him—or to me.

Any jail anywhere is the worst possible place for a man to be. The walls are no protection against hunger, cold, pain, or fear, yet they destroy the freedom to act against them and remove the dignity that helps a man to face them. A man in prison is reduced to a creature on all fours, crawling from one day to the next through endless agonizing minutes that steadily diminish him. Only a very large man retains any stature at all after a long stretch in the joint. Small men die there.

"I'm very glad to see you, John T. You're with Sam and Jim, so I assume you've come to help. Thanks." I could sense deep emotion in the man, though it was masked by the monumental dignity which he still retained. I nodded, and he turned to Sam with a decisive motion. He was still a United States senator and looked the part even here. He was tall and slender, in perfect health and with the grace of an athlete in his conditioned body. Generations of money and power had given him a lordly bearing, and a sense of command was part of his bone structure.

"What do we have, Sam?" The question was brusque but with no hint of impatience. He spoke to Sam as to an equal, with respect and affection in his voice.

"We've worked out a game plan, Senator, and I think we have a team to put it across . . ." Sam began, then paused to look around at the walls.

"We may or may not be secure, Sam. It doesn't matter. Just use your own judgment and tell me only what you wouldn't mind anyone's knowing. Anything else you can keep to yourself and I'll have confidence in you. After all, it's your game now." No man capable of that speech was likely to have done what Latham Cameron was accused of, so any lingering doubts I might have had were gone by the board. Sam just reached for the stack of papers from his briefcase and handed the top pages to his boss.

"This is a statement we would like to issue to the press this afternoon, Senator. Read it, please, and make any changes you see fit to make. If you approve, we will proceed from there." Cameron took the press release and began to read. Sam leaned back in his chair and started to click his tongue against the roof of his mouth, a controlled nervous reaction I was to become quite familiar with in days to come. Cash fiddled with some papers in his stack, then began putting them back in his case. The Senator finished reading the statement and looked up at Sam. He nodded once, then took a ball-point pen from his vest pocket and motioned Sam to sit beside him. He started again at the beginning, making small changes in the wording of the statement and looking to Sam for agreement after each revision. Sam would nod, and the Senator would proceed to the next. At one point, after an entire paragraph had been lightly marked through, Sam shook his head.

"Think again about that paragraph, Senator," he said. Cameron reread the passage and then went on without comment, leaving the paragraph intact. After revising the entire manuscript, they read it through again in turn and nodded to each other in agreement. Sam put the statement back in his briefcase. Cash looked at the Senator then and spoke for the first time.

"An attorney has the right to confer with his client without fear of eavesdroppers, Senator. If you are afraid this room is wired, then I am going to insist on a secure meeting place for our next conference. We can skip it this time, since I don't have anything very important to talk about, but you can bet that nobody is going to listen in on our next conversation." Jim had sat there and very quietly got mad as hell. I would have liked to be a mouse in his pocket at his next conversation with the District Attorney.

"It's only a possibility, Jim, but unfortunately a very real one in this day," said the Senator. "The men who put me here seem very determined, so we must assume they will stop at nothing to keep me here. They also seem to be capable and thorough, which is all the more reason for us to exercise caution. May I also suggest that all of you take some security measures in your homes and offices, and for your personal safety? Sam's football vernacular notwithstanding, this is not a game, and we are faced with some serious people." I had known Latham most of my life, but this was the first time I had seen him in a real clutch. He was coming through like George at Valley Forge, and I was beginning to think I might have been a little unfair to him.

"Latham," I said, "I have been blaming you for what some of your friends did, and it occurs to me that I was wrong. I want to apologize."

"They were never friends, John T., even though we were in close association for a time, and you were right to blame me for bringing them. I allowed a political expedient to abuse your hospitality, and, as usually happens, it went badly. I apologized for them, and I apologize for myself now. I hope you can understand, and forgive me for being a bad politician as well as a thoughtless guest."

"I'm no stranger to political expedients, Senator. I have to live with a few of them myself. Come catch some of my trout in the spring." I held out my hand and felt a lot better when he shook it warmly and patted me on the shoulder in *medio abrazo* with his free hand.

"You'll have to spring me first, John T., and I am confident you will," he said with a smile.

"Well, as Sherman's Yankee sergeant said to the Southern lady: 'You folks started this, ma'am, but we're gonna win it if it takes every pig and chicken you got.'"

"Then let's get started, John T.," said Jim Cash, waiting at the door. Sam motioned that he would be out in a minute, and leaned over to whisper in the Senator's ear. Jim and I went out the door, where the policeman who had brought the Senator was waiting. He started into the room, but I put out my hand and stopped him until Sam had finished his whispered conference. The Senator nodded to Sam and waved to us, and we left.

Chapter . 5

"ANYBODY WANT a cup of coffee?" asked Cash as we left the elevator. "There's a good place across the street from the courthouse." I nodded.

"Not for me, Jim. I have to get back to the office and get this statement ready for the press conference. Do we need to talk, John T.?" asked Sam.

"Not right now, Sam. I learned a few things last night, but I need to get a few ducks in a row before I tell you about them."

"All right. Shout if you need anything. I'll see you both later." He waved his hand and started across the street, ignoring the red traffic signal. I was never to see Sam pay any attention to traffic lights where there was no immediate danger from traffic. He was just as oblivious to all the other formal warnings and prohibitions that clutter the life we live.

The coffee shop was overflowing with the usual courthouse crowd, and most of the available booth and table space was full. Lawyers with briefcases, policemen, citizens with plastic JUROR badges pinned to their lapels, and a sprinkling of stenographers, secretaries and clerks mingled with truck drivers, barmaids, and sharpshooters on this busy fringe of the city's government. We threaded our way to the rear where a small booth for two had just been vacated by a young man in a business suit and a middle-aged black man in work clothes. Jim spoke to the man, who didn't introduce his companion, so I surmised that this was a lawyer and his client. We ordered coffee, and Jim fiddled with his glass of water until it came. While the harried waitress was slopping coffee into our saucers and snapping out a counter check, a bailiff came to the front door and shouted a jury call for the Fifth District Court. About a third of the people hurriedly left.

"Are we going to get the lid off this thing in time, John T.?" Cash asked, with a worried look on his face. "I could get the trial postponed, of course, but you know what that would do politically. We have to go ahead with it if we possibly can, so that means fast work."

"Who knows, Jim? If they lie low, we probably won't. If we can get them moving, we might get a handle on it. But one thing I know: a lot of people know where the handle is."

"A lot of people? You know something I don't, then. Tell me about it."

"Ever hear of someone the Chicanos call El Patron?"

"Hell, John T., they call everybody patron. Used to, anyway, before all this civil rights business got started. Now I'm not sure they'd give the title to God himself."

"Not patron, Jim. *El Patron*. The real cheese. Let me put it another way, Jim. Suppose there is, somewhere in the background, a real Chicano leader. Somebody with brains, money and a plan—a plan based on complete social, economic and political control of our Chicano, Indian and black population."

"What have you been smoking, John T.? Sounds like a James Bond thriller written by James Baldwin. I never heard of any such El Patron in this city, or anywhere in the state.'' I had been smoking Memo's grass when I first heard about El Patron, of course. He could have been born of the smoke—but maybe he wasn't.

"Know any young Chicano lawyers who came up fast out of nowhere and never seem to put a foot wrong? Know any Chicano politicians who made it into office without major party support? Hear any rumbles that somebody around here doesn't like big mobs, and that racket organizers have a habit of cutting their visits short?'' Jim Cash must be hell in a courtroom, because the flicker of amazement that flitted across his face didn't last long enough for a fly to land on it. He studied me for a moment and then went to work in the archives of his mind. When he finally picked up his coffee cup and took a sip, he had a brief laid out ready to present.

"I know two independent lawyers and a three-man firm that get all the business south of Guadalupe Street. The young independents have been ready to take in partners for a couple of years, and could afford them, but they haven't advertised for help. But one of them has leased space in that new office building on Guadalupe, with enough room for a couple more lawyers. There's a congressman from that district, and two more from districts along the border, and we have half a dozen Chicano state legislators with no visible means of political support. Now you want to tell me that the same man put them all where they are, and that they're all working for him?''

"Not working for him, per se, but indebted to him and probably loyal to him. That's the whisper, Jim, for what it's worth.''

"Bullshit, John T.!'' he exploded.

"Why do you say that, Jim?''

"Because it's fantastic! Sure, there could be a nice old man or a rich industrialist with a conscience who spends a little money helping young Chicanos realize their ambitions. He could even keep his philanthropy a secret, out of modesty or just to avoid the beggars. But to blow that up into a conspiracy directed at political control of the state, with no more evidence than a rumor or two, is ridiculous. I ask you again, what have you been smoking, John T.?''

''You jumped to the conspiracy conclusion yourself, Jim. As for its being fantastic bullshit, that's what J. Edgar Hoover kept saying about the Mafia. But if he's right, there has been a hell of a lot of conversation about something that doesn't exist. All the while, there's clear evidence of organized gambling, prostitution, narcotics, extortion and every other crime on the books. Just individuals, each doing his own thing? Small gangs that don't ever talk to each other? Jim, give me one example of a profitable enterprise that no one has ever tried to organize. Don't bother; you can't. Now think of the names you know of men who have been convicted in court of criminal conspiracy—we can both name twenty off the tops of our heads. Now think about a few familiar conspiracies that developed from no more material than we have right here in this city—just a few hundred or a few thousand people who think they're getting the shitty end of the stick. Do any occur to you? The American Revolution—conspiracy. The Russian Revolution—conspiracy. The French, the Chinese, Indian, Indonesian, African, Cuban, Argentine—all revolutionary conspiracies, and the list goes on. Want something a little closer to home? How many revolutions has Mexico had? Several hundred, and they all began with a small group of self-elected messiahs who raised the *Grito* and started blowing up bridges. Want some documented revolutionaries with branch offices all over the country? Black Panthers, SLA, Weathermen, Mau Mau, the John Birch Society, the American Nazi Party, to name just the blatant publicity hounds.'' Jim was listening seriously now, so I continued.

''So why not an attempt to organize the Chicano population of this state and several states around us? You've seen a lot of it happening in the open, aboveboard agitation for a fair shake for *La Raza*, so why not some people with less honest motives? They're second-class citizens of this republic, and you know it. They were slaves under the Spanish, and not much better off under the dictators who took over from Spain. And what better way to organize them than an image they already know and are used to: El Patron—which means a lot more than boss or leader or chief. The patron of a Mexican hacienda, which this whole state was a little over a century ago, owned not only the land but everything on it—houses, horses, cattle, dogs, and people. He even owned the mosquitoes and the tumble bugs, and as far as the peons were concerned, he owned the Apaches that raided, the government that taxed them, and the sun, moon, and stars that shone upon them. He was untouchable, omnipotent, and if not a god, then a devil. Do you think we've changed that view in the few years we've controlled the country? Hell, no, especially since we didn't change the system much. Big ranchers, such as I am, big industrialists, big politicians still own everything, and since they have remained relatively ignorant until last week, too illiterate to know that they were living in the world's greatest democracy, the old ideas still hold these stifled minds. Now, just suppose that their idea of El Patron has been that of a devil, and along comes one who acts like a benevolent saint? He helps them, protects them, encourages them. And like all effective gods, he keeps a secret face and a hidden name."

"All this from a whisper, John? One rumor?"

"To the wise, a wink is as good as a nod—and the whirlwind starts as a whisper. Dramatic, would you say? Sure, Jim, and I could be talking through my hat. But hear this: the whisper is there, and the realities it suggests are possible, even probable. And it fits the facts as we have them. If there is such a man, and he intends capitalizing on the potential of the situation, then he would have every reason to want his man in the United States Senate. His only chance of achieving that, given the political realities as they are, would be to vacate the seat in such a way as to discredit not only the incumbent Senator but also the party, and give his man an issue to run with. In this case, one that's guaranteed to get him every Chicano, black, and Indian vote in the state, plus a lot of white liberal votes. Maybe we're reaching with it, Jim, but it fits the facts, and *it's all we have."*

"So where do we go with it?" He still wasn't convinced, which is perhaps a good thing in a lawyer, especially one who will sooner or later be a judge.

"I was hoping you wouldn't ask me that question, Jim. I'm damned if I know." Some more bush-beating, of course. But in some unconventional ways that had occurred to me while the Senator was busy with Sam and the press release. But they weren't something I was prepared to discuss with Jim Cash, prominent attorney and officer of the court. I used to be, in my salad days as the saying goes, a specialist in unconventional warfare and expert in guerrilla tactics. Defining "expert" as a guy from out of town, my present problem was that I lived here. So, I was planning to call some guys from out of town.

"I need to think about this some more, John T., and dig around for some evidence a little more solid than your 'whisper.' For one thing, if what you say is true, the help he gave these lawyers and politicians should show up somewhere. I'll put some private investigators of my own to work looking for the connection. I have a couple of ex-clients who might give me a reading on the crime situation, and I'll check with them. They're professional thieves, and they keep me paid more or less in advance. One of them is up for one-to-three on a burglary and I can talk to him in the joint. I'll let you know if I learn anything." He took a sip of his coffee, found it cold, and stood up, reaching in his pocket for change to tip the waitress. I reached for the check and started to stand up, but he put his hand on my shoulder and pushed me back down again, then sat down himself.

"Speaking of devils, John T., there's one who just came in, and he's part of the case." I turned my head slightly and looked out of the corner of my eye. Two men were coming down the aisle between tables toward us. They found an empty booth about halfway down the room and signaled for a waitress. "That's Detective Sergeant Vittorio Sanchez and his partner, José Cuña. He came on the scene when the body was found and was assigned to investigate the murder. He and Lieutenant Allen made the arrest."

"Devil, you say?"

"I understand he's pure Apache and, according to those clients I mentioned, mean as hell. He has a reputation for being a good cop, and a lot of people are afraid of him." We left then, and I took a good look at Sanchez on the way out. He could very well be pure Apache. Short, blocky, smooth-limbed, with a slightly round belly that didn't look at all soft. His eyes were deep-set and slanted, and he wore his coarse black hair longer than is usual for a policeman in this town, almost mod. His clothes carried the mod suggestion even further. If our recent discussion of El Patron was close to the mark, this dandified Indio cop would bear some more thought. *Por supuesto* . . .

I left Cash then and walked a couple of blocks to the new bank tower that housed Peter Heilman's counting house and several hundred other enterprising firms. The express elevator took me to the thirtieth floor faster than I could have fallen the same distance, and I stepped out directly into Peter's reception room. He occupied the entire floor, which was only right and proper for the city's most successful investment banker. The receptionist, a slight, pleasant woman in her middle forties, had known me for years and didn't waste my time.

"Mr. Heilman is out of the office, Mr. McLaren, but Miss Conrad is expecting you. You can go right into her office. You know the way." I smiled at that, and her answering smile was a joy. I'd had a thing going with Miss Conrad once upon a time, but one or the other of us hadn't measured up, so we didn't live happily ever after—at least not together.

Julia Conrad, known to some as "Honeypot," was about as far from the average man's idea of honeypot as she could get. She was a flat six feet in her pantyhose, and looked, thought, and acted like some rare breed of racing animal. She was Peter's executive right hand, and a good part of the reason for his success.

"Come to town to raise a little hell, John T.? Or have you just decided to come courtin' again?" she asked with a grin as I came into her office. I gave her a hug and a peck on the cheek and told her I hadn't felt like courtin' since she had jilted me for a computer.

"It was a computer programmer, John T., and I jilted him in turn because he didn't have any staying power. Also, his personal life wasn't as consistent as his programs, which led me to suspect some of his programs. Anyway, he's long gone, so you can come home." Not bloody likely, I thought. She wouldn't be over the threshold ten minutes before she had Rancho Useless stocked with ten thousand head of whatever animal was selling best at the moment, and she would ride my shoulders until we became so damn rich we stank. I was under-gunned for stalking that sort of game.

"I think I'll stick to hell-raising, Honeypot. You got some walking-around money for me?" She took an envelope out of her desk drawer and handed it to me.

"There's two thousand in there, John T., in spendable bills. Also the key to apartment sixteen at the Second Coming apartments—two bedrooms, two baths, ground-floor entrance front and rear—'all mod cons,' as they say in the ads. The house is in with the swing set, so nobody will pay much attention to anything you do. The bar and refrigerator are well stocked, and there's fresh linen in both bedrooms. I spread enough ashtrays, books, pictures, and so on to make it look lived in, plus a few other amenities in case you actually spend some time there."

"The Second Coming? Sounds a little wistful, somehow. But I doubt if I'll spend much time there, so I won't have to live up to the name. Now, take the key back and get me a couple of copies made. Also, get me another five thousand in cash. I forgot about inflation, okay?"

"I don't think your special account has that much in it, John T."

"It does now," I said, and gave her the Senator's check. "I'll need that cash and the keys by tomorrow morning. Right now, I need to make some LD calls in private. Is there an empty office I can use?"

"Use Peter's—he'll be out for a couple of hours. And you might as well use the WATS line if you know the numbers; it's already paid for." Another reason why Peter will end up owning this end of the state—except for Rancho Useless. I went along and made my calls, and found the people I was looking for on the fifth try. We made a deal and they promised to be on the next plane in. I hung up and went back to Honeypot's office.

"Sugar, would you have one of your girls locate Juan Silva for me? Here's a list of places that might get a message to him sometime during the day. Make it casual, and if she can sound like a little Chicana chippie, it would help. Tell him to get in touch with me as soon as he can. You don't need to talk to him directly unless you actually find him, and don't leave a number. He'll know who's looking for him.''

''Sounds as if you're having fun, John T. Got a seat open?'' Do you see what I mean about this girl? If there's a game in town, she wants in—a born hustler in the higher sense of the term.

''Stick to the game you know, Honeypot. Here's a kiss, and one for Peter, and I gotta run. *Vista*.'' It was lunchtime by then, so I took the elevator to the plaza level of the building, which was built to resemble one of the seedier Paris boulevards, with shops, restaurants, and a couple of lunch-hour bistros. The shops had all been leased in anticipation of a three-tower complex that would house enough business tenants to make them all rich. There had been a hitch in the financing when a jealous wife had shot her financier husband, so the other two towers never got off the ground. These optimists were having a rough time of it in consequence. The restaurant was a different story.

Offspring of a better place with a famous name, McLaglan's was able to draw luncheon crowds from all over town, so they were busy and prosperous. I stopped at the bar while waiting for a table and sipped a scotch and soda to ward off the chill. I didn't get to town often enough to know many people, so I was left alone by the advertising crowd, the banking crowd, and the busy, busy crowd who were all happily entertaining each other. I spent the time fitting some pieces together and laying a few devious plots. It occurred to me that I am not all I seem from my frank, open, and honest-but-rugged exterior. In fact, I am one sneaky son of a bitch in many ways. I should have been born Italian—except for the fact that the Spaniard and the Scot have it all over the wop for really tricky business. Who but the canny Scot could maintain a thousand-year-old mystery concerning his underwear? As for the Spaniard, a lot of people speak his language, but damn few understand him.

Lunch was a minor disappointment, and I revised my opinion about wine being worth a damn, even for cooking. I paid the medium-high check, tipped the waiter and ignored the maître d', and headed for the next prospect on my call list for the day. He was still out to lunch, so I left my name and went back to the hotel. It was time for my siesta, a habit I had developed during my convalesence and hadn't been able to break.

A couple of hours after I went to sleep, I heard a tap-scratch on the door, and I opened it for Juan Silva. A faint smudge under his eyes told me he hadn't slept since I'd dropped him at the cabstand the night before.

"What's comin' down, boss? I hear you want to see me." He took a turn around the room while I was pulling on my pants, ending up at the bar tray on the dressing table. He looked at me and I nodded, so he poured himself a stiff drink and went over to stand by the window while he sipped it.

"Learn anything more, Juan? Or did you spend the night in the sack with some little *chamaca*?"

"Not much, boss. I figured I better keep my head down till we know who's got the bean. So I just played around and listened a lot, and I don't hear much. You got anything?"

"A direction, Juan. So I need some specifics, now. Can you get me the names of half a dozen pushers like Memo? Small guys who maybe want to get a little bigger?"

"*Cómo no,* boss? Memo knows them all, and he tell me if I ask nice. That all you need?"

"Not quite. I also want you to buy all the junk Memo has—heroin, grass, hash, pills—all of it. When you get it all together, bring it to me at this address." I gave him the apartment address and he grinned.

"I hear that's a swingin' place, boss. You got some action goin' for you?"

"That's our 'safe house' for the moment, Juan. And it looks as if someone did a good job of picking it. When do you think you can be there with what I want?"

"This evenin' sometime. You got some money for Memo's junk?" I gave him a thousand and told him to get Memo the hell out of town as soon as he made the buy, and to tell him to stay away for a couple of weeks. He said "You bet" and left. I finished dressing and went up to the Senator's suite.

The penthouse was already full of people drinking the Senator's liquor and eating up everything in sight. Sara, Sam, and two bartenders from the hotel staff were busy entertaining the fourth estate. I went to the bar nearest the door and asked the bartender for a scotch and soda. He poured out of a fresh bottle of Chivas Regal, and I wondered what the taxpayers would have to say about using Chivas for bar scotch. Well, I'm a taxpayer, and I just drank and said nothing.

Sara, circulating around the room, gave my arm a squeeze in passing, and Sam acknowledged my presence with a nod. A few more reporters came in, and a camera crew from one of the local TV stations. He had a helper with a heavy case full of lighting and sound equipment. The other TV station already had a couple of floods set up and aimed at the one blank wall of the room. The two technicians went into a huddle, made a few magic passes with a light meter, and decided to set one more light. When that was done, Sam, who had kept one eye on the process, came and stood in front of the lights and raised his hand with a release sheet in it. The reporters stood where they were, glasses and Swedish meatballs in hand. The cameras began to whir as Sam started to speak.

"Thank you all for coming here today. I hope you came

as friends. We seem to have enough enemies, for as you all know, Senator Cameron has been indicted for the murder of Malena Vasquez and is in jail awaiting trial for that crime. You have been waiting, more or less patiently, for the Senator to make a statement. You have copies of that statement in your hands, so it will serve no purpose for me to read it to you. But I will, with your permission, summarize the statement for the television audience." The cameras were up to speed by that time, and the cameramen had found their focus and adjusted the lighting to their liking. I had to admire Sam's sense of timing—this one would be a "take." He went on with his summary.

"Latham Cameron was chosen by the voters of this state to represent them in the United States Senate, in a general election held four years ago. Senator Cameron swore an oath to uphold and protect the laws of the nation. Nine days ago, Senator Cameron was arrested by the police of this city and accused of breaking that law by brutally murdering Malena Vasquez, a night-club dancer who is alleged to have been the Senator's mistress. I wish to read to you now the Senator's first public statement concerning this accusation. I quote:

" 'I have been accused, and indicted by the grand jury of this county, of murdering a young woman named Malena Vasquez. I am innocent of that crime. To my knowledge, I have never seen Malena Vasquez, alive or dead, and I do not recall ever having heard her name pronounced nor have I seen it in print, prior to my arrest for her murder. During the time in which she was supposed to have been killed, I was asleep in my suite at the Conquistador Hotel, and I had no knowledge of her death until I was arrested four days later. I am innocent of this crime; therefore I will fight this accusation to my last breath.'

"Those words were spoken by Senator Cameron from his cell in the city jail this morning. He intends to fight this accusation, and he will not fight alone. We of his staff will stand with him until he is again free, because we are convinced of his innocence.

"Since the Senator is innocent," Sam continued, "the murderer of Malena Vasquez is free to walk the streets, free to kill again. To clear the Senator's name, to see justice done, and to ensure the safety of the citizens of this city, that man must be apprehended. To that end we hereby offer, as a reward for information leading to the arrest and conviction of the murderer of Malena Vasquez, the sum of twenty-five thousand dollars." Sam paused for a moment and pulled a check from his breast pocket.

"This is a cashier's check for twenty-five thousand dollars, payable to bearer. On the day Malena Vasquez's murderer is convicted, this check will be given to the person responsible for his conviction." Sam paused again, and Sara put a printed card in his hand. He held the card before the camera and continued.

"Write this number down. This telephone will be manned twenty-four hours a day until the Senator is free. If you know or if you learn anything that might help bring a killer to justice, call this number. Any fact, no matter how trivial or insignificant, might be the information that leads to putting this brutal murderer behind bars, and it could earn you this reward."

Who knows?—it might work. Sam ended his statement and turned to face the reporters. They had already read the statement, so there was no surprise. They just had a few questions to ask. As they started asking them all at once, I left the room. Not my bag; and besides, I had a use for that reward.

Chapter . 6

I WENT TO MY ROOM and called Julia Conrad, on the off chance that she might have my keys and cash ready and still be in the office. She did, and was, so I went. She and Peter were in his office, working with a stack of papers, when I got there. As I walked in she neatly jogged the stack together on Peter's desk and turned with a smile.

"You guys start talking. I'll see about a drink." Which was no problem in Peter's office. His bar, a revolving affair that spent most of its time behind a paneled wall, would have put a lot of embassies to shame.

"So you've gone to work for Senator Cameron, John T. Glad to hear it. You need the bread," said Peter with a smile as I shook hands with him.

"How'd you find that out, Pete? I don't remember telling you or Honeypot about that." I made myself a silent bet and came up a winner.

"Joseph Shivers is controller for the bucket of worms Braden Carlsbad and his gang put together to run money through. Carlsbad was hunting at your ranch all last week, and it's to his interest that United States senators don't go to jail for murdering their girl friends. So he hired you to do a job on whoever did her in."

"You're a smug bastard, Peter. If you didn't take such good care of my money I'd take a contract on you. Or maybe just beat you up. I think I'll beat you up anyway," I said with a grin, cocking one fist in the general direction of his jaw.

"Honeypot does my fighting for me, John T., so watch yourself. You're overmatched."

"Canvasback Conrad to the rescue, fellows. Don't let's fight—let's drink instead." She put drinks in front of us and went back to get her own. I decided to pick Peter's brain a little. He just might know something. He usually does.

"There's an awful lot of money coming from somewhere, Peter. Sam Anderson says it had to cost a minimum of one hundred eleven thousand and some change to build the frame, with the possibility of quite a bit more. What do you think?"

"That's peanuts to the politicians, as friend Sam probably told you. A seat in the U.S. Senate is worth five million of any man's money, even if he's relatively honest. For a real crook, there's no price too high. As for any ideas that might help you, I don't have one. But I will keep my ears open."

"Well, then, I'll just take my money and go home. Got it for me, Honeypot?"

"It's in my office, John T. Come along and I'll get it for you." I said good night to Peter and followed her out. He had his hands in the stack of computer printouts before I reached the door. What a hell of a way to make a living—but then he makes a hell of a living, and I guess it's fun to him. When I got to Julia's office, she had another brown envelope for me, and she also had her hat and purse.

"Here you are, ducky. And don't come bothering me about your allowance again this week. Unless you run short, of course. And since you have all that cash, how about buying a girl a drink?"

"I'll even buy you dinner if you'll cook it. That is, if you weren't kidding me about stocking the larder in that apartment."

"Lead on, McLaren. Better yet, I'll lead on, since I know where the place is. My car's in the parking garage down below."

"Mine's at the hotel. Why don't you drop me there, and then go on? I can find the place."

I made a detour through the lobby of the hotel and picked up a Mapsco of the city. I looked up the address while the attendant was bringing my car around. The Second Coming was easy to find. Julia Conrad was waiting for me at the back door when I pulled into the parking lot.

"I could have used my key, John T., but, knowing how you feel about your old homestead, I thought I'd better wait."

"*Mi casa es su casa*, always. Next time, go on in, take off your shoes and girdle, and build yourself a drink. That goes for the old homestead, too. You are always welcome, for a drink or a week or a year."

"I'll keep that in mind if I ever have trouble coming up with the rent. Now, let's see what Mama can do about dinner while you build us a drink."

The apartment was fairly decent as apartments go. The rear entrance opened into a short corridor between bathroom and kitchen which led into a large living room with a modernistic steel fireplace and large plate-glass front windows. There was a built-in bar between living room and kitchen, open at the top for service between. I found booze and glasses, and Julia handed me a tray of ice through the serving hatch. I mixed a couple of light scotches with club soda while she rummaged in the big refrigerator-freezer.

"Steaks okay, John T.? If so, they'll need time to thaw out."

"Steaks are fine, love. How many do we have?"

"How many? Let me see—one, two, three . . . six. Big, thick ones. You won't starve if we get snowed in."

"Thaw them all out. There's a good chance we'll have company for dinner." I heard a series of clunks but no questions as she pulled the iron-hard beef out of the freezer and tossed it into the sink. I took a sip of my drink and inspected the apartment.

"Hey, you spent some money on this place—stereo, color TV—all the middle-class necessities. How come?"

"Why not? You're rich, and besides, they didn't cost anything. Those are repos from the finance company. We have a warehouse full of the stuff, so I called Saul and had him deliver them."

"Well, the price is right. Want to hear some music?" I took silence for assent and searched among a stack of records that must have come from her own apartment. Probably the only reason I hadn't married this girl. She's just too damned efficient in all the wrong ways for me. I prefer to be late for most of my appointments and to miss all my phone calls.

"Salad, steak, baked Idahos and hot bread in just about two hours, patron. How many potatoes did you say?"

"Six, I guess. And enough salad for about ten." I settled back into a big comfortable chair and waited for Honeypot to finish her fixing and preparing. It didn't take long; that girl never misses a stroke.

"All right, John T., what sort of convention do you have scheduled for this evening? Care to clue me in?"

"Just some old Army buddies, sugar. We'll play some games and have some laughs, and as soon as it gets cold enough we'll all go skinny-dipping in Guadalupe Creek."

"Sure, John T. Now the story!" She coiled her long whip of a body comfortably on the big white couch, took a sip of her drink, and waited with the expectant expression of a too-bright bird dog waiting for a slow hunter to kick something out of the bushes. I know it's *there*, boss! What do you suppose I'm pointing at? Now *come on!*

I told her the story to date, and of my theory about El Patron. Then I told her what I wanted her to do.

"Soon, sugar, I'll have a list of names. I want as much financial information on those people as you can get. The whole thing—retail credit, property held, money owed or in banks; the old financial statement, with as much as you can get on sources of income. There's a lot of money floating around in this case, and this could be one of the ways of opening it up. Can do?"

"Right girl, wrong reason, John T. That is, if you expect me to do it as a favor. Friends don't ask each other to do a lot of hard work for nothing."

"Speaks the pro, sugar. Sure, the fee's in cash, so much per name. Take the average cost of such a report from legitimate sources, double it, and that's the price. When I give you the list, you give me the price and I pay in advance for each name on the list. Fair enough?"

"Done and done. Now what if this claim doesn't pan out? Any other ideas? You don't have much time, you know."

"The old ESP is working, Honeypot. There's a pretty definite connection between the Vasquez woman and our shady mastermind. The whisper in Southtown has too much under it to be just an idle rumor."

"These people who're coming tonight—who are they?"

"They're specialists, and they're going to get that list of names for you. Just hope they do a good job, because the more names they get, the more money you make—and the sooner we finish the job."

"That's one of the things I like about you, John T. You don't work steady, but you always keep an eye on payday, as I do. So why doesn't it work for us?"

"You have everything I want, sugar, in abundance, but you're overendowed in one area. You have too much drive, too much single-minded devotion to the idea of using all the horses all the time, all pulling in the same direction. If you had been born a century ago, the robber barons would have had to sleep with their marbles, and you would have wound up with most of them anyway. And that's just too heavy for me. I have my toys, and I have my playground, and I just want to be left alone to enjoy them.''

"How wrong you are about me, John T. You missed me completely. That's not what I mean at all, at all.'' So who can ever know what anybody really means? We use language to dig a hole, then we get in the hole and pull it in after us. Of course I probably missed her a mile. I've probably missed myself a mile, and if you can't know yourself, who can you know?

"Sorry about that, Honeypot. Truly sorry, because to date you're the best I've found.''

"But not quite your cup of tea, eh, luv? All right, then, if you can't luv us, then knock us abaht a bit.'' She mimicked the accent of the old Cockney joke. "Pressures do build up in the banking business, don't you know—and we are good in that department.'' I was tempted, but the friendly friction between the sheets is a train that never gets there, no matter how earnestly the pistons pound, no matter how seriously the midnight whistles sound. It's still a lonely freight to nowhere, carrying too much private woe for casual conversation to unload. And like the ground-in grit of any train ride, the small smoky regrets for missed connections. But there you are again with the language problem. How the hell do you say that to a fine, clean, luscious girl who doesn't really want to settle for the casual romp, but does need to be held for a little while in friendly arms?

A cadenced tapping on the front door took me off the hook. I got up and started to answer the knock like any citizen, then had a second thought. This job was already two days old, and it was long past time for a few simple-minded measures for self-preservation. I pulled the .38 I had been carrying under my belt and motioned Honeypot to hit the deck behind the couch. She moved fast and was over the back of it in one serpentine motion. I flattened myself against the wall beside the door and twisted the knob, letting the door sag open under its own weight.

"Quién es?" I asked, and remembered that Billy the Kid is supposed to have asked that just before Pat Garrett blew his head off not too far from here.

"Kingfish," a deep, rumbling, laughing voice answered, and I relaxed a little, but not too much.

"Kingfish who?" I asked, in the honorable knock-knock formula.

"King fish for trout, Queen fish for fun," a second voice answered behind me. I turned head and gun to see Stone step into the room from the rear-door corridor.

"You're slipping, John T.," he said with a grin, but without taking another step into the room. His hands were open, palms up, and half-raised toward his shoulders.

"And you haven't changed a damn bit. You just scared the wadding out of me. Come on in, Kingfish, and I'll give you ten dollars to slap piss out of one Stanford Odum Stone. All clear, Honeypot."

The front door banged all the way open and the biggest Negro I've ever known came through the door, carrying three heavy cases as if they were a box lunch and a package of Kleenex. Arthur Andrew King, known in a lot of places as the Kingfish. I took one of the cases from him and damn near dropped it on my foot. It weighed over seventy pounds, and I was pretty sure what it contained.

"What you mean, makin' knock-knocks on my name, white boy?" he growled with mock severity. "You in trouble—and so is he, if that ten dollahs is in cash. I don't beat up nobody on credit."

"Honeypot, meet Stanford O. Stone and Andy King, sometimes known as the Kingfish. Gentlemen, Miss Julia Conrad." She put out her hand, and I looked with affection at these two men who had taken top honors in the smoke and fire test many times. Stanford Odum Stone, never called 'Stan,' was a slender man of medium height with long, carefully groomed blond hair and about three hundred dollars' worth of tailoring that looked as if it had still been on a top designer's manikin until five minutes before plane time. He wore the suit with enough natural presence to have daunted the most foppish Regency bucks, and was just as tough underneath as they were reputed to have been. King was overly large, dusty black, with a surface joviality straight out of the radio comedy that had given him his nickname. In the rare moments of immobility he allowed himself, he looked like a giant pagan god hacked out of a mountain of basalt. Together they were as unlikely and as deadly a team as you are apt to find in this day of medium men.

"Just tell me one thing, Mr. Stone," Honeypot was saying. "How did you get through a locked door without making a sound? John T. was concentrating on the front, so I bent my pink ear to the back, and I didn't hear a whisper—and I know the door was locked, because I shot the bolt myself."

"Locks, guns, engines and other simple mechanisms just roll over and beg for candy when Mr. Stone puts his hands on them, Miss Conrad," said the Kingfish. "And somehow he never gets a speck of dust on those aristocratic Southern pinkies. But he cheated this time."

"We arrived an hour before you did, John T. When there was no answer to our knock, we came in anyway and cased your pad. I fixed the lock, Miss Conrad, to yield to gentle pressure in a certain place, and oiled the hinges. I also memorized the squeaky places in the floor. I would be deeply ashamed if you had heard a whisper."

"Are you some kind of spook, Mr. Stone, or just a simple thief? Honest men aren't familiar with those techniques."

"Just a simple tradesman, ma'am, earning my crust of bread in the only way I know. Yes, among other things I am both spook and thief." And liar, killer, torturer, extortionist, pander, and everything else he had been taught to be by a paranoid government anxiously protecting its unofficial and unproductive colonies in the name of world peace. Kingfish and I had learned the same lessons in the same trade school, and we had retired to private practice at about the same time. And a precious lot of cutthroats we were. But, like the little hustler who wouldn't admit to being a pro, we only screwed for our friends and we tried to give value for the money. We didn't do government work anymore.

"Then if a scoundrel you must be, I hope you're a hungry scoundrel, Mr. Stone. Would a large steak and fixin's give you strength to continue your career?" Julia asked.

"Indeed it would, Miss Conrad. And might I suggest two or three of the same for this black rogue? His appetites are not as other men's, and he becomes surly and unmanageable when inadequately fed. And would it run to a drink or two while you're introducing the meat to the fire?"

"Indeed it would, Mr. Stone," Honeypot mimicked his casual Oxonian diction, "on the condition that you and Kingfish call me Honeypot. What's your pleasure? John T.'s wine merchant just delivered a fresh supply."

They both specified whiskey with a splash, no ice. Julia made their drinks and topped ours up. When we all had fresh drinks in hand, Stone looked at me.

"Are we in a tearing rush to get on with the job, John T.? Or is there time to relax for a small moment?"

"No rush at all. We're waiting for another man, and you can't move till he gets here. I'll just fill you in while we're waiting for dinner." I told them the story, in full detail, including my guesses about El Patron.

"And just what is it you wish us to do?" asked Stone.

"I want you to establish the connection. If there is such a man, he has an organization. The organization will be easier to find than he is, and if we behave in a certain way, the organization will find us. To find us, they have to move in the open for a moment."

"Say that again, Mr. John T., slow and easy so us practical folks can understand you," said the Kingfish. "Sounds like you want a prisoner. And you want that prisoner to talk to us."

"That's it exactly, King. Here's what to do. I will supply you with a list of pushers, and a guide, and a sack of merchandise. You two will make noises like out-of-town hoods who are here to set up a distributorship for the junk. If the rumors are true, El Patron has people watching for this sort of thing, and he'll send some boys around to give you your time. You rope and hogtie one, take him out in the country, and turn him inside out. You get the names, and then we have a handle. That's all I want from you, the names. Then you can go on about your business."

"Sounds simple enough. How long do you figure the operation for, John T.? We were packed and ready for a little trip to Uruguay when you called," said Stone.

"Minimum three, max five days," I said. "If you fool around more than five days and don't get a bite, there's probably nothing to it."

"You're about right, there. It'll take a couple of days for them to hear the rumble and sift it, then come after us on the third or fourth day. Now let's look at the territory." I started to get up to get the Mapsco I had bought, but King reached into his coat pocket and produced one just like it. I opened it to the fold-out map of the city and began to orient them. King used a felt-tip pen with transparent green ink to mark the map as we talked. When Stone folded the map and handed the book back to King, either of them could have parachuted blindfolded into the city and led a revolution.

"When we get our little bird, where do we take him for his singing lessons?" This from King, who probably knew more about general field intelligence and interrogation of prisoners than anyone else outside of China.

"Your guide, who will be here sometime this evening with the dope and a list of pushers, will follow wherever you go in a pickup truck equipped with a camper body. Carry your equipment in that, and if it works out that way, you can carry out the preliminary interrogation in the truck. If you decide you need more time, or a more secure and isolated location, my plane will be on ready alert at the airport throughout the operation." I reached for the Mapsco again and turned to the detailed map of the airport.

"The plane will be here, with the engine warm and ready to go." I turned to the overview map of the city, showing the entire county. "Fly on a heading of forty-five-degree magnetic for seventeen minutes at a hundred and twenty mph ground speed, then change course to two-hundred-sixty-degree magnetic for five minutes at fifty-four hundred feet. That will take you into a mountain valley with a short landing strip that very few people know about, some twenty-five miles from my Rancho Useless. There's a spring and a small cabin there, and I'll send a man to lay in some food for you. He'll be there to light the strip in case you have to land at night. If the strip doesn't warm up at this signal"—I wrote a recognition series of dots and dashes on the map—"with your landing lights, land by flare and go in ready to shoot. Although I can't see that happening at this point."

"Sounds simple enough if everything goes right. But there's always Murphy's Law." Murphy's Law: if it can break, it will break. If it can be screwed up; it will be screwed up. It's the basic operational creed of all government work, with the military adding its own imperative: If it doesn't screw up naturally, detail a man to see to it.

"Chance we have to take, boys. It comes with the territory—that's why I'm willing to pay the rate."

"Speaking of that, John T., it's only good business to ask for a little something on account. Expenses, don't you know?" said Stone in a parody of his own legitimate accent, which is strange enough as it is—Deep South mush-mouth clipped off with the very best English public school and university as a fitted overlay. As the man said, "If I were any more English you wouldn't understand a word I say." I pulled the brown envelope out of my pocket and counted out a thousand.

"You can check into the hotel and use that as a business address. This apartment is your 'safe house.' The dark blue Chevrolet outside the door is yours. Your guide will be Juan Silva, who works on my ranch and is completely trustworthy. He will go any distance you care to take him."

"Can he handle himself, John T., or do we have to look after him?"

"He's half Apache and naturally a mean fighter. He has handled weapons since he was born. I taught him a lot of hand-to-hand stuff, the way we learned it, so I would have somebody to practice on. He's good enough to catch me sometimes."

"That's good enough for me. Even I used to have some trouble catching you on your good days, John T.," laughed Stone. But he lied. I am adequate, but he is very, very good. He moves like a small bright lizard, and what he doesn't know wouldn't take too long to think about. If I could apprentice Juan Silva to him for six months and then bring him back to work out with, I could be a lot sharper myself. Oh well, I comforted myself, I can always wrestle with Honeypot. She must have had her ESP tuned in, because she chose that moment to call for help in serving dinner.

"Your second steak will be done as you finish the first, Kingfish," said Julia, "and I have a second loaf of bread baking now. So dig in.'' We dug in. We were all hungry, but the Kingfish was a scandal. He ate as if he were practicing deep breathing exercises, inhaling bread, salad, steak and potatoes like a big vacuum cleaner, washing it down with seemingly delicate sips of scotch and soda that steadily depleted the bottle. Stone ate with the perfect pacing that made it seem if if he hadn't eaten a bite, while the big steak disappeared by magic. I remembered the two of them in another time, chewing raw bloody hunks from a fresh-killed water buffalo that had blundered into our ambush on the Mekong Delta. King had killed it quickly and silently with his knife, and it had lain there while we waited for the VC patrol to come down the path. We cut up the patrol, and then cut up the water buffalo. That's called living off the country.

The conversation at the table was, thankfully, a long way from my thoughts. Honeypot and Stone talked steadily, covering a range of subjects from athletics to Zen. Stone was always at his best in such moments, keying himself for a coming operation, and with a beautiful girl to listen to him. His culture went much deeper than the skin. He came of a good family of career diplomats and statesmen, and his education had been the best available. He had been everywhere twice and done everything at least once, and he could talk about it all with charm and originality. Honeypot was entranced. She hadn't known such men existed, and she listened avidly to everything he said, interrupting him only to pour more coffee and to go to the kitchen to see to King's second steak. I somehow got the impression that she wouldn't be available for any wrestling while this hard ghost of Ashley Wilkes was on the scene.

As I was polishing off my own steak, I heard a tap at the door that was probably Juan Silva. The Kingfish froze, and a pistol appeared in Stone's hand. He hadn't lost any of that, either. I motioned for them to stay seated.

''It's probably your guide. I'll see,'' I said softly, and

started for the door. Stone and King looked at each other and shook their heads.

"Ol' John T. just don't take care of hisself none," said King, with a pitying glance at me. "I better talk to him about some assurance, soon as I get a minute." He got up from the table and went to stand by the front door, his back to the wall as I had done before. Stone motioned Honeypot into a corner and stationed himself by the corner of the corridor wall, then waved me toward the door. Could be they were right, I thought, and I slipped the .38 into my hand and went through the *"Quién es?"* routine again. Juan answered in Spanish, and I let him in.

"I got here early, boss. This stuff makes me nervous." He saw the Kingfish then and stopped in the corridor. His body tensed and his black eyes turned flat and opaque.

"Friends, Juan. Come on in." I introduced them, and Juan relaxed enough to grin. I told him to go ahead, that the stuff was for these men's use.

"Boss, that Memo's scared shitless. He gave me this stuff and headed for the border. He's afraid of El Patron, and he's afraid of gettin' busted, and he's afraid of me. You want some names now?"

"We want you and the names, Juan. I understand you're to be our guide," said Stone.

"Suits me, if it's okay with you, boss."

"I want you to go along with them, Juan, in your pickup. They'll tell you what they want done. They're going to pick up one or two of El Patron's enforcers and wring them out."

"Okay, boss. We goin' now?"

"After you've had a steak, if you're hungry. Okay, Stone?"

"Eat, Juan, and have a drink. There isn't that much hurry. It's only eleven o'clock, and if this town is like most, it's just beginning to come alive," said Stone easily. "In the meantime, I'll help Miss Conrad with the dishes." He went into the kitchen and took up his conversation where he had left off. Juan took a couple of flat packages out of his coat and handed them to me.

"Three decks of shit, some pills, and half a brick of hash, boss. That's all he had. He sold out of grass yesterday except for the lid he gave us the joint from, and he wanted to keep the rest of that to calm his nerves."

"It's enough, Juan. Did he say how much the heroin has been cut?"

"Not too much, boss. It's cut in half when he gets it in Mexico, and he stomps it again. I hear they do it three or four times back East, till a fix don' last no time."

"It'll do, Juan. Now fix yourself a drink, and eat when it's ready. You've got work to do tonight." I shook hands with King and went to the kitchen.

"I'm leaving now," I told Stone. "Will you be all right, Julia, or do you want me to take you home?"

"I'm fine, John T. I have my car, and I don't see any way I can get into trouble. Unless I'm already in trouble with the company I keep."

"You're in trouble, Honeypot. Keep an eye on these thugs. They have an insatiable appetite for little girls. Good night, then, and take care." I went out the back door, stopping for a moment to see what Stone had done to the lock. I might want to use that one myself sometime.

Chapter . 7

ANOTHER IDEA OCCURRED TO ME on my way downtown, so I stopped at a drive-in grocery store and used the phone. I called Jim Cash and found him at his office, working late on the Cameron brief. He probably had half a dozen clerks on overtime, too.

"Jim, have you done anything about those people we discussed this morning? The lawyers and politicians?"

"I got my investigators started, but it's too early for them to have anything. Why?"

"I have some people working from another direction, and it might help if I could throw those names into the hopper. They might be able to spot a connection from where they sit." I took a notebook and ball-point pen from my pocket and held it ready.

I took down the list of names and then called the apartment. I gave the list to Julia when she answered, and told her to add it to the list of financial reports I wanted and to pass it on to Stone for reference when they found a prisoner to interrogate. I hung up then and continued on my way downtown. Reviewing the campaign in my mind as I drove,

I decided that we were doing all we could at the moment. Snapping dry twigs. A splash of bright blue neon a couple of blocks ahead indicated a veritable forest of dry twigs, so I pulled into the parking lot of Cielo Azul and went to work.

Cielo Azul was a converted Victorian mansion in which extensive remodeling had been done. It was a huge place, and clever planning had resulted in two completely separate dining rooms, each with a character of its own, and a small, intimate club behind the larger of the dining rooms. The entrance was from an old-fashioned porch, through stained-glass double doors. The night club was reached by going through the large dining room. It had its own bar and an upright piano on a dais to one side. Malena Vasquez had danced in the main dining room, but the club was where the action was. I went straight in and found a small table by the piano.

As I had expected, Sylvia was perched on the piano stool, rippling the keys and crooning a ballad into her microphone. Sloppy piano, a small and unimportant voice indifferently trained, but the skin of a child on the face of a decadent angel. Sylvia was the most completely corrupt woman I had ever known, and the luminous rot of her soul added the necessary something to her singing that made it entertainment. She had obviously just completed a set, because she turned off the mike and stepped down to my table.

"Long time no see, John T. Where's your girl?"

"Lost but not forgotten, Sylvia. You can be my girl now. Care to join me?"

"For one drink, at least. Joe!" The bar waiter brought a daiquiri for Sylvia and a tall scotch and soda for me. I complimented him on remembering what I drank.

"You always drink the same thing, Mr. McLaren, so what's to remember?" he said. He remembered my tips, of course, which are nature's best mnemonic.

"What brings you to town, John T.? I didn't think you ever left that weed patch you call a ranch." Nasty little bitch. I'd like to take her out there and turn her loose in that weed patch for about a week. No, that would be cruel, and a waste, and I couldn't take the chance that someone would see the opportunity, fly in a piano, and build a night club around her in the middle of my deer herds.

"I'm looking for the dude who beat Malena Vasquez to death, Sylvia." If I expected to surprise her, which I didn't, I had come to the wrong store. Sylvia pursed her lips, whistled soundlessly, and then grinned.

"You come on strong like a bear's breath, John T.—but then you always did. Now I thought they had Senator Cameron wrapped all nice and cozy for that." Laugh, laugh, laugh in the eyes that never smiled, but a bored and lazy droop to her bare white shoulders. I wondered what it would take to interest her in anything. Then I gave it up; I don't have that much imagination.

"You know the Senator, Sylvia. Do you think he was keeping Malena? In a three-hundred-dollar apartment, with five hundred a month allowance?"

"Latham Cameron? You're kidding, John T. Of course he wasn't, but if they can prove he did, what difference does it make? Oh, boy! Latham Cameron spending a round one a month on a little chippie anybody could tumble for the price of a fix. I heard she needed three a day to keep the worms out of her eyes by the time she was killed. But why ask me, John T.? I don't know anything." Of course she didn't know anything, but she knew everybody and didn't give a damn about any of them. She would drink on this story for a week. She finished her drink, tapped me on the cheek with one finger, and went back to her piano. I signaled Joe for another and sipped it slowly while I looked around the club. I didn't see anyone I knew, so when I had drained my glass, I left.

The three big Chicanos who closed in around me in the parking lot all had guns, so I didn't argue when they asked for my car keys. I produced them, and they hustled me into the back seat. Two of them got in front, and one drove while the other pointed his pistol at me over the back of the seat. The third one followed us in a compact sedan as we drove down a side street toward Southtown. I spoke to the man in front of me, ignoring the gun he kept pointed at my head.

"My wallet is inside my coat. I don't have a lot of money, but take it and leave me alone, okay?"

"Shut up, Mr. McLaren. We don't want your money."

"What do you want with me, then?" I asked.

"I said shut up!" he repeated. "You're going to school." After that I shut up. Somebody had reacted, so I should have been happy. I wasn't, particularly. This wasn't quite what I had in mind.

The driver turned into an industrial area a few blocks south of Guadalupe Street. It was a new development of single-story brick and concrete buildings, all constructed to a single pattern: office space in front, and warehouse or manufacturing in the rear. He stopped in front of a long, narrow building with a "For Lease" sign in front, and the car following pulled up behind us. There was one other car there, a late model LTD.

"We get out here, Mr. McLaren. Carefully!" said the *pistolero* in the front seat. The others were already on the pavement, one on either side of the door I was to use. I didn't want to start any trouble right then, so I got out carefully. They searched me then, for the first time, with my hands up against the car and legs spread, like on TV. They found my .38, of course, and one of them tucked it into the waistband of his trousers. I didn't argue when they hustled me into the building. There was light shining through the gap around the metal door, and I expected to be welcomed when we got inside. I had no idea what was likely to follow.

The large room I was pushed into had a row of metal shelves along one wall, five or six unopened crates without shipping labels or other identification, and a dapper, brown-faced man with a small moustache sitting on one of the crates. He got up as we came in, and I saw that he had spread a handkerchief on the crate to protect the seat of his pants.

"Come in, Mr. McLaren," he said, and motioned toward one of the crates. "Have a seat." I remained standing and looked at him for a moment. Medium height, straight black hair that had been styled to fit the round smooth face, and the droopy moustache that framed his straight, thin mouth. I had never seen him before.

"What the hell is this all about?" I asked with all the righteous indignation I could muster.

"Forgive us the unconventional way we brought you here, Mr. McLaren. We felt it necessary to talk to you, and we had no assurance you would be willing to come. We only want to talk, and you will not be harmed if you are reasonable."

"Reasonable? About what, for Christ's sake?" I didn't think it would do me any good, but this seemed to be the time and place for a little blustering. "I don't know you, and I don't have anything to talk to you about, so you just tell these thugs to give me my car keys and I'll be on my way." In a pig's ass. I wanted to hear anything he had in mind to say.

"All in good time, Mr. McLaren," he said politely. "Now, as you say, you don't know me, but I believe you do know a man named Guillermo Silva, called Memo? A man who deals in certain narcotics, in a small way?"

"Who the hell are you, and what's this all about?" I blustered some more.

"Just answer the question, Mr. McLaren. Yes or no?" I had him taped then. This nice little man had to be a lawyer or the equivalent. He had spoken the jargon too long to be comfortable in any other language.

"No, I don't know anybody called Memo. I don't know anybody who has anything to do with narcotics. Are you a federal officer?" Funny as that might sound, he could be. He fit the pattern. He was polite, he spoke legalese, and they hadn't tried to slap me around. I could have stumbled into an operation by the federal fuzz, and they were naturally curious as to how I fit into the picture. But somehow I didn't think so. The three shitheads who had picked me up weren't feds.

"No, Mr. McLaren, I'm just a private citizen like yourself. Now, about Silva. We know you visited him last night, and that you sent your employe, Juan Silva, who is Memo's cousin, to buy his entire stash of drugs earlier this evening. We want to know why, Mr. McLaren. Are you an addict?"

I started to say no, but he nodded to his henchmen. One grabbed me on each side, and the third came up behind me and peeled my coat down over my arms. Then, one at a time, they rolled up my shirt sleeves and looked at my arms. I could have taken the four of them then without working up a sweat, but it wasn't time for that.

"No needle marks," said the one who held the gun on me. None inside my thigh, either. Also no irritated mucous membranes in my nasal passages from snorting, and no screaming nerves from popping pills. I had almost been addicted to Demerol once, when the surgeons were patching enough of me back together to send me home without a scandal, but I rode that nightmare out on my own stone patio, cold turkey, with the ghosts of five generations of McLarens to keep me company.

The gunman was looking at my arm, and he suddenly became more wary. "*Cuidado*," he murmured to the other two, and they tensed a little. They had more reason than they knew from just looking at my arm. A careful program with the weights had packed a lot of muscle on my big bones, and hand-to-hand with Juan Silva, plus a lot of riding and hiking around the ranch, keeps me supple. He had noticed that, like Mickey Mantle, the more clothes I take off, the bigger I look.

"Why are you buying narcotics, Mr. McLaren? Tell me, now!" The little man wasn't completely silly. There was a hard edge to his voice now, and he was poised on the verge of some violent action. But the situation was becoming funnier every minute. I had gone to no small expense to import a team to find El Patron's narco squad, and here they were, dandling me on their laps. I had been afraid that all the bait I was strewing around had set me up as a target sooner than I had expected, but all they wanted to know was why the hell I was messing around with dope. All I had to do now was to gather them into my arms and welcome them to a little session with King and his black box.

"Guillermo Silva didn't go to Mexico, Mr. McLaren," the interrogator continued. "He came to us instead. So we know that you were interested in his merchandise, and we know that Juan Silva bought his stash tonight. What we don't know is why. Are you thinking of going into business? Do you have some rich junkie friends you wish to supply? Or do you have larger plans?" He nodded to the *pistolero,* and my head exploded. I fell to my knees, supported by the two men who held my arms. I shook my head to clear it and watched the blood spatter on the concrete floor. The two thugs lifted me up, and the dapper inquisitor asked me again.

"Are you going into the drug business, Mr. McLaren?" I raised my head and looked at him. The pistol hadn't made much of an impression on my thinking. My head is pretty hard, and I have as high a threshold of pain as any pro guard. The blood didn't mean anything. Scalp wounds bleed a lot for no particular reason, and it doesn't hurt to bleed unless you try for records. But the dapper little man was green in the face. There was pity in his voice, and he almost retched as he asked the question. *The little bastard couldn't stand the sight of blood!* I put a little moaning whine into my voice when I answered this time, a little more eagerly than before.

"I don't know anything about it," I said, letting my shoulders droop. I grunted and went to my knees again as the *pistolero* hit me in the kidneys. I stayed there, rocking back and forth a little, until the two pulled me upright by the arms. Still the dope, so Memo must have neglected to tell them that my main interest had been Malena Vasquez. Maybe Juan wouldn't quite kill him the next time they met.

"Why are you doing this to me?" I whined, pitching the fear a little higher. "I don't know anything about narcotics. I only smoked one marijuana cigarette with Memo and Juan, to see what it felt like. I didn't feel anything. I sure don't sell drugs, and I didn't send Juan Silva to buy any. If he bought some, it must have been on his own." The words came out in a rush, as if I just wanted to tell it all and get them off my back. Well, I did. I wasn't really hurt yet, but if they kept it up long enough, they could knock all my inner moorings loose.

The little man was even greener now, and I wondered what he was doing there, handling a job he had no stomach for. Then he told me.

"Narcotics are a very serious thing, Mr. McLaren. Especially for my people who have been vulnerable to drug abuse for centuries. Too many of them are addicts, and many more destroy their lives with milder drugs and hallucinogens such as mescaline and peyote. The police aren't able to control the drug traffic, and it grows under their very eyes, until even the grammar schools are filled with users. Some of us don't like that, Mr. McLaren, and we're doing something about it. We keep a close watch on the drug business in this city and in the state. We can't stamp it out completely, but we have managed to keep it small. We can keep the big organizations from getting a foothold, and we can keep the local dealers small and insignificant. That's why we were concerned when someone like you seemed to be buying drugs in quantity. A man like you wouldn't be content to stay small. You do understand, don't you, Mr. McLaren?''

How sweet it is to be slapped around by thugs who call you ''Mister'' and tell you it's all in a good cause. Takes the sting out, it does.

''And you think you have a right to beat people up, just on suspicion? There's such a thing as laws to protect people, you know!'' I let a little of the indignation creep back in, as a leitmotif to the whining fear that threatened to break my voice each time I spoke. I don't know whether it was my magnificent acting or just his amateurism, but the little creep bought it. He nodded to the gorillas—or maybe they were just chimpanzees—who were holding me. They let go of my arms and stepped to the side, still watching me warily. I did the same with them. Even a chimpanzee can tear a man's arm off and beat him to death with it.

''We might have made a mistake, Mr. McLaren. If so, we apologize. But we may have been right about you. If so, we will know in time and make you very sorry. This is a warning, Mr. McLaren. If you are innocent, stay that way. Don't try to do any business here. We will know about it if you do, and we will eliminate you from the scene.'' He looked at his minions again and they took another step to the side.

''You may go now. It wouldn't be wise to go to the police. They can't help you, especially if we plant a few things in your car and let them know about them. And don't try to find out who we are. It would not be good for your health." For a little man who couldn't stand the sight of blood, he talked a very ferocious game.

But the main thing I had learned, aside from the fact that they had had no instructions about me, was that they were part of something big. The other thing, equally important, was that they were probably honest. Not leaning over backward to do things legally, but honestly concerned about a real problem for their people. It occurred to me that that was the way it would have to be if El Patron was doing what he seemed to be doing. The rank and file of any army is usually honest, as far as that goes. The real atrocities come from the top down and are performed by specially chosen troops that don't have much to do with the organization as a whole. So "the Man" would have some black shirts around somewhere. After all, the pattern had been perfected and well publicized to the last period in this century, and anybody setting himself up in the business would have read the literature on the subject, from *Mein Kampf* to *The Thoughts of Chairman Mao*.

I managed to sneer and look grateful at the same time as I put my coat back on and headed for the door.

"Hey!" said the big *pistolero,* and tossed me my car keys as I turned to look at him. I caught them in one hand, and then decided I had overplayed the Little Boy Blue part a little. I walked back to him, feinted a right at his head, then decked him with a left hook to the jaw. It hurt my hand, but it was a nice gesture which suggested that I didn't know enough to kill him with one finger, which I fully intended to do if he ever came at me again. The other two jerked out their pistols and aimed them at me, but the little man stopped them with a word.

"That's enough, Mr. McLaren. Maybe you had that one coming. But go now." I was beginning to think of him as a real little gentleman. I hope the next hardcase he pulled in here for questioning didn't pull him through a knothole just for fun.

I got in my car, turned the lights on, and backed it past the LTD. I memorized the license number, then burned a little synthetic rubber getting out of there. I hoped I could get to a phone fast enough to alert the boys to this new development. There was no answer at the apartment, so I assumed they were already out on the tiles, doing their work like good little terrorists. I drove to the apartment. Tomorrow might be interesting, but tonight had been one hell of a drag. I debated getting my skull patched but decided against it. I cleaned it up as well as I could, wrapped a towel around it like a turban, popped four aspirin and went to sleep.

The sun was bright around the edges of the drapes when the phone pulled me out of sleep the next morning. I let it ring a couple of times while I looked at my watch. When I grunted into the receiver Stone's cheerful voice finished waking me up.

"Rise and shine, comrade! Old rosy-fingered dawn has come and gone and we have a fistful of shining hours to improve."

"What's going on, old buddy? Where are you?"

"Having breakfast at the airport. Your job is done, we think, and we're ready for further instructions. What is your pleasure, sahib?"

"How the hell did you get it done so quickly? Are you sure you have what I want?"

"You're running on a fast track here, John T. We just peeled the first apple that dropped off the tree. Want us to come along to the apartment?"

"Yeah, this is as good a place as any. See you when you get here." I felt fairly well except for a slight headache, but when I started to pull the towel off I discovered that my wound had bled some more during the night and the towel was glued to my hair. I turned the shower on hot and stepped under it, and after a while I was able to peel it off. I used a shaving mirror to get a side view of the cut. It wasn't enough to worry about, so I just put some disinfectant on it and combed some hair over it. I was dressed and having a cup of coffee when Stone and King knocked on the door. I poured coffee for them, and we sat at the dining table in the bright sunlight from the window.

"You've got a very, very funny situation here, John T.," King said. "We started at the top of Juan's list, and it didn't take thirty minutes for three guys to drop on us. They hit us when we stopped to say hello to the second pusher outside a bar where he had agreed to meet us. But *schoolchildren*. We laid them out the easy way and flipped the biggest one to see who would be 'it.' He came up heads, so we bundled him into the truck and started cruising around. He woke up after a while, and I just started talking to him preliminary-like, you know—advising him of his rights, of which he didn't have any—and he came apart like a cheap watch. Get him to talk? I had to give him a dollar to shut him up. The guy was a pure john, John T., and that makes us even for that 'knock-knock.' He was honest, and just doing a little vigilante work around the narco scene. Him and his two buddies. The three of them just happen to report to a single guy, who is the only man they know higher up. And each of these guys just happens to have three little helpers under him. Only this guy don't know any of the guys working for his two buddies. They keep their crews separate. Which tells you what, John T.?" Kingfish looked at me with his great big watermelon-and-pork-chop-eatin' smile, and I let him say it. After all, it was his specialty, and he knew it better than I ever would.

"It tells you about a fairly sophisticated cell-type organization. Not just the old three-man bit, but a little geometrical solid called a tetrahedron, which adds up to four points.

Four men in each cell, with two-way communication in a lot of different directions. We got seven names, includin' his—the guy over him, his two buddies, and the three under him. And I'll bet my polygraph they're all honest johns, as far as any major conspiracy is concerned.''

"You're perfectly right, as far as it goes, King." I told him about my little fiasco, and my conclusions concerning it. "How many people do you think are involved? That makes a difference, too."

"The john we picked up is pretty far down the pole. He had one level under him, and that's the bottom. That sort of structure, with the interlocking tetrahedrons, fits inside an open triangle. With seven levels it would add up to a thousand ninety-three people, which is one hell of a bunch for a clandestine operation. I figure maybe five levels, which would give us a hundred and twenty-one, or six for a total of three hundred and sixty-four. And that's still a big organization."

"Not if everybody below the second level is honest, King," said Stone, pulling out a ball-point pen and writing some figures on a napkin. "The three top levels add up to thirteen, which is a damn fine number for a conspiracy. The cells from there down could be perfectly honest citizens, interested in civic reform, public safety, and free breakfasts for hungry schoolchildren. And there's nothing to stop any of those thirteen from having two or more cells under him—say one honest and one strong-arm squad complete with black shirts hidden away in the attic."

"That's it, then," I said. "Give me the names and I'll at least have a direction to work toward. And that wraps it up for you, fellows. You did a good job, as advertised, and I thank you. How much do I owe you?"

"Hell, John T., you have change coming from the thousand you gave us yesterday. Suppose we just take out three hundred for expenses and call it even? Glad to do you

a favor for old times' sake.'' King looked a little embarrassed to be taking money for the short night's work. ''Besides, we didn't even work up a sweat. Sure you don't want
us to stick around and finish the job with you?'' The
thought had occurred to me, but I didn't think I really
needed them.

''Thanks for the offer, King, but I think I can handle it
from here. All I have to do is find one man. I'm not interested in smashing the whole organization. That wasn't
ordered.''

''Well, then, John T.,'' he said, putting on his dialect
voice like an old, well-worn sweatshirt, ''I think I better
talk to you about some *a*ssurance.'' He had gotten hold of a
complete tape of the Amos 'n' Andy radio programs years
ago and had memorized most of the Kingfish routines. At
his best he was a black W. C. Fields. Many men had taken
this to be the real Andy King, without the perception to see
where the act ended and the black rock of the man began.
To their brief sorrow.

''We'll be around for a couple of days anyway,'' said
Stone. ''That is, if you have no objection to my getting to
know Honeypot a bit better?''

''Not at all, Mr. Stone. Honeypot and I were more than
friends once, but that was a long time ago and in another
country, as the saying goes.''

''And speaking of Honeypot, tell me something, John T.
Last night, when Juan Silva did his little tap-scratch on the
door, I motioned her into the corner out of the line of fire.
She went quickly and without question. When I found time
to look at her again, she was standing ready, shoes off and
her skirt tucked up around her waist in an oddly familiar
position—without reference to the immodesty, of course.''

''It's her hobby, and according to her it beats joining
Weight Watchers,'' I said, deliberately letting him drag it
out of me.

"Is she any good at judo, John T.?" he asked gently. "Does she have any rank?"

"Second *Dan*," I told him, my face in guileless repose. The rank wasn't valid at the *Kodokan*, of course, but she might give a moment's pause to the black belts there because of her strength and speed.

"She must be quite a person, then," Stone said with a thoughtful expression on his bland face. "Yes, I think we'll stick around for a day or two, then on to Uruguay."

"What's the action in the Banana Belt?" I asked.

"They have always had some odd political customs, but some chaps who call themselves 'Tupamaros' have been making it hairier than usual. They were roundly defeated in a recent election, and their strength broken in a determined effort by army and police, but many survived and are still at large. The government, which is fairly decent as South American governments go, doesn't want it to happen again. I believe they're interested in building a small but effective force to combat terrorists with their own weapons, in a quasi-legal manner. We promised to go down and talk to them about it."

"I'm almost tempted to go along. Sounds like the old days."

"Glad to have you." Stone answered. "How soon can you be ready to go?"

"I said 'almost.' I think I had better stick around here. I'm too lazy for that sort of work these days. Thanks again for helping out, and have a good time in Uruguay. I can see King now, with a little brown harem fanning him and feeding him so he can perform his once-a-week duty."

"No, man, those little brown Indian girls can't handle me. I break 'em just as fast as they come at me. I tried it in Mexico last year, and they're just too tiny for this black man." Which was probably quite true. They aren't large girls in any way.

I told them to take the Chevy they had been driving, and

to leave it at the airport when they were through with it. Stone went to the phone extension in the bedroom, and I heard him making a luncheon date with Julia Conrad. Kingfish said he would just mess around town for a while. I went to work with the list of names, trying to plan a way up through the levels to the top thirteen.

Five names from Jim Cash, seven from the Kingfish. None from me, but a connection, maybe. My little green man was almost certainly a lawyer, at least an educated man, and far too civilized for the role he had been playing. A john, as King had called his honest but unlawful citizen, playing at vigilantes to keep our city clean. I could find out who he was soon enough. The license number of his shiny new Ford was at the top of my list.

And it was pretty obvious that he was my only way to the top, at this point, at any rate. The cell King and Stone had burned out was already isolated and by-passed. The little lawyer hadn't known he was blown last night, and he hadn't been briefed on me, either. He had been acting under standing orders, and my little session with him had nothing to do with the Cameron case. It was past time for a call to Jim Cash.

"Jim," I said when he came on the line, "that's a 'go' list you gave me. We got some confirmation last night and the organization I described to you does exist. Now do you know this guy?" I described the man who had questioned me in the warehouse, emphasizing that he seemed to be an honest man involved in something he didn't understand, and probably a lawyer, from his language. I gave him the license number also.

"Sounds like Rafael Muñoz," he said. "He's the youngest of the two independents on the list I gave you. He's the one who has leased the big offices, and it looks as if he's ready to take in a partner or two. How'd you get on to him?"

"I'll tell you later, Jim. Right now I have to get a look at

Muñoz, and I'd like you to continue with the rest of the list. See you later." I hung up and then dialed Peter Heilman's office and asked for Julia.

"Hi, sugar. Got your pad handy?" I gave her the list from King and told her to ignore all but the top name, and never mind digging too deeply into his finances but to concentrate on his associates. The same for Muñoz.

"That really isn't my thing, John T., but I'll do what I can. Now you can do me a favor. Tell me more about the beautiful man I've agreed to have lunch with!"

"He is a serpent, without morals and without conscience," I said. "He is also one of the best friends I ever had, and I owe him my life a dozen times. We dropped into a lot of places together, and the two of them are as complete a pair of rogues as you will find. They are also absolutely honest in their personal relationships, and they never tell lies on their own time. Go ahead with Stone if you wish. You're a big girl and you might even be able to cope with him. Just don't get in his way when he's working."

"Are they still working for you? Stone sounded as if they are finished here and are getting ready to go on to something else."

"Yes, they finished my job last night. He's on his own time, so live it up, sugar." I laid the receiver back in its cradle just in time for it to ring. Sam Anderson's voice answered my hello.

"What's going on, John T.?" he demanded.

"Just the rent, Sam—plus a few other developments it's time for me to tell you about."

"Yes, Jim hinted that you were onto something. In the meantime, the proverbial 'possum's loose in the henhouse down here. Why don't you come downtown? We can have a bite of lunch and talk."

"Where would you like to eat?"

"McLaglan's all right?"

"Fair enough. I'll see you there about twelve-thirty. I have one stop to make before I get there." I rang off and left the apartment, after looking up Rafael Muñoz's office address in the Yellow Pages. I had tried to find a classification for "Conspirators," but Ma Bell wasn't up to that yet. I amused myself on the way by making up a list of classifications the phone company would have to include in their directory if they were completely honest. I handicapped myself by limiting the list to those enterprises which were totally dependent on the telephone, but that wasn't much weight. "Assassination" and "Armed Robbery" were doubtful for the A's, but "Bookmaking" was a sure bet for the B's. "Call Girls" headed the C listing, with a cross reference for "Prostitutes." Communications is everything these days.

Chapter . 8

THE RECEPTIONIST IN MUÑOZ'S OFFICE could have been chosen by a really hip industrial psychologist. Pretty and placid, content to spend her days answering other people's phone calls, opening their mail and smiling at strangers, fixing her hair and nails, and letting the innumerable small tragedies of a small law office flow through her without once disturbing anything real in her mind. Her plastic smile flickered on when I came through the door, persisted through the statement of my name and business, and disappeared as if it had been wiped off with a washcloth when she heard Muñoz's reaction to my name. She listened for a moment, then turned to me.

"You—you can go in, Mr. McLaren. That door." She indicated his office door with enormous eyes and the beginning of wonder. Something had finally touched her.

Muñoz was at his desk, leaning forward with both elbows planted in the middle of the green blotter pad. Clasped tightly in both hands was a large automatic pistol, with the simple eye of the muzzle centered between my own eyes.

"Put the gun away, Mr. Muñoz. I didn't come here to beat you up."

"How did you learn my name?" he asked. "How did you find me?"

"I know a lot of people, and a lot of people know you. You talked like a lawyer, so I called a man who knows a lot of lawyers. Besides, I had your license number, and that would have been my next call. In short, Mr. Muñoz, it was ridiculously easy to find you. Now put that gun away—or keep it, if it makes you more comfortable, but point it in some other direction. *Now, Mr. Muñoz!*" I put a parade-ground snap in my voice, and damned if he didn't obey me. He let go of the butt with his left hand, and pointed the muzzle at the wall. I sat down in the straight chair in front of his desk, the one he used to make people uncomfortable and nervous. I'm sure it worked beautifully. The front legs were a full half inch shorter than the back legs, keeping me tilted forward in a position of respectful, alert attention. The lawyer, on the other side of the desk, was in a position to relax and issue calm pronouncements from the majesty of the high-backed, luxuriously upholstered swivel chair. However, *el Abogado* Muñoz was not so calm as he could have been.

"I just want some information, Mr. Muñoz, and I'll try to get it without beating you on the head. I am investigating the murder of Malena Vasquez. You, whether you know it or not, are involved in her killing. So I want the answers to a few questions."

"Malena Vasquez? You can't be serious, Mr. McLaren. I have never had anything to do with Malena Vasquez, before or after her death. And besides, I thought Senator Latham Cameron had been arrested for killing her. Is that not true?"

"Arrested, yes. Guilty, no. You probably know the guilty party better than I do. After all, you are involved with a secret vigilante group concerned with narcotics, and the Vasquez woman was an addict and a member of *La Raza.*"

"Yes, of course we're trying to do something about this

shameful narcotics business, but we don't kill addicts. We don't kill anyone.''

"You just pistol-whip them, is that it? In deserted warehouses, with a bunch of thugs holding their arms while you sit there and enjoy it?" I said with disgust.

"I am sorry about that, Mr. McLaren. It was unforgivable, of course, but it seemed to be the thing to do at the time."

"You're sorry. Well, that makes it all right, of course. And you don't think an organization that sends honest men out with guns is capable of killing—if it 'seems to be the thing to do at the time'? You're even stupider than I thought, Muñoz!'' It was time to drop the Chinese smile and shake this little fascist up a bit. "Let me tell you a few things about this pleasant little marching society you have joined. First, the majority of its members are no doubt honest citizens like yourself. But I don't think you've paid enough attention to the way it's organized. Now, correct me if I'm wrong. You have three men under you, all recruited by yourself and answerable only to you. Is that correct?" He nodded, and I went on. "Depending on the level at which you were recruited, each of your lieutenants will have a group of three, recruited by himself and unknown to anyone but you. Is that correct?" He nodded again and I continued. "You, in turn, report to one man above you, and that man is the only man you know. Am I right so far?" I had him nodding, and that's a good sign with a sales prospect.

"Doesn't that seem like an unusual way to organize a civic action group?" I didn't give him a chance to answer, but rode right over his attempted response. "It should, because it is a well-known method of guaranteeing the anonymity and security of clandestine and criminal organizations, dedicated to whatever interests they might have—

espionage, sedition, revolution, whatever you wish. Doesn't that make you think a little?'' He nodded again, thoughtfully, and I mentally pulled out an order blank and a ball-point pen. ''So who is El Patron?'' I asked.

''I don't know El Patron, Mr. McLaren.''

''You don't know the man who put you through law school? The man who set you up with an office and started a stream of clients to your desk? The man responsible for so much business that you can afford to rent this big suite of offices and start interviewing prospective partners? Stop putting me on, Muñoz! Give me his name, Muñoz!'' I hope I never have to depend on this little lawyer to defend me against anything hairier than a traffic ticket. He hadn't really thought about any of it, and his honest consternation was a complete admission of the truth of my guesswork.

''Sure, I had some help in school. I couldn't have made it on my own. But the money came from the man who started me on this 'vigilante' thing. He has told me that there is a 'Patron,' a very wealthy man who wishes to help his people. But I do not know his name or anything more about him. I know the money came from him, and that my clients came to me because of his influence, but I don't know who he is. When I asked my friend, he told me that the man wishes to help without being known, because if it is known what he does, he would have no peace. People would be after him for money all the time. Would they not? Beggars would fall out of trees to pick his pockets.

''A strange thing, as you say, Mr. McLaren. But not really so strange when you think about it. We keep our activities a secret because it is in a sense illegal to do what we're doing. It is also wise to stay hidden from the people we combat, because they are sometimes violent men, and there could be danger if we were known. But to think of us as criminals, as people capable of murder? No, Mr. McLaren. Mistaken, perhaps, in some of our methods—and I will have to think about that before I continue my association with this thing of ours—but we are not murderers."

"You, perhaps, are not a murderer. The six men you know, your cell, the cell under you, are perhaps not murderers. But what do you know of the others, Muñoz? They could be eating babies for breakfast and you wouldn't be aware of it. They could plan to burn the city and you wouldn't know about it until your own roof fell. All right, I'll leave your own involvement up to you and your conscience, but I want you to tell me two things: How many cells are there under you? And who recruited you? I don't need the names below—just the name of the man who hinted that there is a Patron with a great big heart and bottomless pockets." He took a deep breath and looked around the office, then exhaled slowly. He seemed to notice the pistol he was holding for the first time and laid it on the corner of the desk with a small, embarrassed smile.

"All right. I can tell you that much. There are three 'cells,' as you call them, under me. The man who recruited me, who helped me with money in school, is Teofilo Gonzales, congressman from the third district. I believe him to be an honest man and a good congressman. He has represented our people well." But one of the top thirteen if Kingfish's analysis was correct, and one of the men who must know El Patron and his three colonels.

"One more thing, Muñoz," I said, reminded of my own by the pistol on his desk. "Give me back my thirty-eight."

"I don't have it. There is a place where we are instructed to dispose of these things—a Salvation Army collection box in a shopping center near here. I put your pistol there on my way to the office this morning."

"I suppose it's gone, then," I said. "I'll take your check for seventy-five dollars in payment for it, Muñoz."

"You're right, of course, I owe you a pistol. Will you

take mine in lieu of the check? I somehow think I have no
further use for it." I nodded and picked up the weapon from
his desk. It was a .38 Colt automatic with plain walnut
grips, and clean on the outside at least. It wasn't shiny from
use, and in fact still had the matte-blue finish of a new gun. I
slipped the clip out and jacked a cartridge out of the
chamber. I sniffed the barrel, and there was no smell of
recent firing. I reloaded it, put it under the waistband of my
trousers, and started to leave.

"Before you leave, Mr. McLaren," Muñoz said with a
slight frown of worry on his face. "I expected trouble from
you when the receptionist told me you were here. I instructed her to call for help, to a number we have for
emergencies. Some people are probably on their way, and
it's too late to call them back."

Stone had said I was getting old, fat, and careless. Maybe
he was right. I started out of the offices, but I didn't get far.
I heard the elevator door open as I started to open the
reception-room door into the corridor, and footsteps
started toward me. The riot troops had arrived, and I was
fairly caught. I wondered where the receptionist was, and
guessed that someone had told her to get out of the line of
fire. I looked quickly around the room for a way out.
Muñoz's office door was closed, and there was nothing
there anyway. I went down the short hallway between his
office and the two vacant spaces reserved for his new partners. My feet made no sound on the deep pile of the carpet,
and I reflected that there must be some good money in the
lawing business. The vacant offices were open and empty
of anything but furniture. One closed door opened into a
conference room with a long walnut-veneered table and
upholstered chairs. No more doors, so I stood where I was
with the door slightly open to the hallway. I heard the outer
door open, and then the door to Muñoz's office. I took the
Colt out and slipped the safety. I could shoot my way out if

necessary, but somehow I didn't like the idea of wasting some possibly honest citizens. No way out—so how about up?

The building was new and was equipped with a suspended ceiling—a grid of light metal strips with two-by-four-foot tiles laid loosely on the flanged strips of metal. Above that would be a two-foot space between ceiling and roof, carrying electrical wiring, air-conditioning ducts, and a mat of insulation on the ceiling tiles. I decided to take the chance and looked for a ladder. The built-in bookcase that formed one wall was made to order. I slipped my shoes off, put one in each side pocket of my jacket, and went up the case. The ceiling tile yielded to a slight upward pressure, and I lifted it up and out of the grid. There was a steel roof truss directly above the bookcase wall, so I muscled my way up into the crawl space and replaced the tile. I got a lot of dust from the insulation down my neck, but so far, so good.

Suspended ceilings aren't designed to carry any weight. I had to move along the roof truss hand over hand like a big foolish monkey on a welded tree until I could put my stockinged feet down on the top of the hall partition wall. It almost gave way under me, and I held on to the truss until I figured out how it was constructed. It was nothing more than a framework of thin sheet-metal studs and headers, with sheets of gypsum wallboard screwed to them. Quick and cheap to erect, easy to finish with texture and paint, but not exactly the Great Wall of China when it came to carrying a load. But it would serve, I thought. Until those Chicano commandos start pumping slugs up through the ceiling. I squatted there like Humpty Dumpty, my head brushing the underside of the roof and my toes curling over the sides of the partition, and waiting for the balloon to reach my monkey level. There was no place to go unless I could duck-walk the top of the partition until I was over another space, but that wouldn't get me anywhere either. So I waited.

The conference room adjoined Muñoz's private office, but I was about fifteen feet from his ceiling. I could hear a faint murmur of conversation from that direction, but I couldn't distinguish voices or understand anything that was said. Muñoz telling the rescue squad about the bad man, no doubt. Then there was a loud noise, and I told myself that it had been a shot, no doubt. But no slugs came ripping up through my flimsy cover, and I was at a loss to figure out who was shooting at whom. So I waited some more. After a long slow minute, I heard the outer office door open and close, and the faint clatter of footsteps in the tiled hallway outside the suite. After another minute or so, the elevator machinery went to work, and I heard the car come up and stop, the doors open and close, and then down it went again. I waited some more, but nothing happened. No sound. No light. No movement.

After about two weeks of that silence I decided to move. I didn't fancy any long duck walk down that partition, and there was nothing for me in that direction anyway except the hallway outside the suite, so I simply went back down the way I had come. There was nobody waiting for me in the conference room, and nobody in the hall. I tiptoed toward the front, but I might as well have turned cartwheels. The vacant offices were still vacant, as was the reception desk. Muñoz's door was open, and from his position, sprawled across his desk with one suppliant hand reaching toward me, I suspected they would be vacant for quite some time. No new partners, no prosperous law firm, no career on the bench or in politics for this young man who believed in direct action, no matter how misguided. El Patron had wired around another burned-out cell. But a little late, if the information I had was any good. I rather thought it was, even if it had been fairly easy to get. Except for him.

I could have saved myself a lot of trouble by taking a closer look at that corpse and searching around the office, but I was a little sick about Muñoz. He hadn't really deserved that sudden hole in the head, especially not from people he had summoned for help in an emergency. But the Fool Killer is always on the job.

Nobody bothered me as I left the building and got into my car. I was probably followed downtown, but I didn't spot the tail if there was one. I didn't particularly give a damn if I was followed. I wasn't keeping a low profile, anyway. In fact, my head was up like a rubbernecking tourist looking for celebrities. I just hoped nobody would take a shot at it before lunch, anyway.

I heard sirens coming toward me from downtown when I was about halfway there. I wondered if it was police on a serious call, or just on their way to lunch at whatever restaurant had the best free-for-cops special today. The car passed me going in the opposite direction, lights flashing and siren wailing, with a white ambulance half a block behind, making the same hideous noise, so I guessed it was a genuine code three. I figured I knew the address, too.

Sam Anderson was already at a table in McLaglan's when I got there, an empty glass with orange juice flakes in front of him. The table was spotted with scattered crumbs and the bread basket was empty, so I guessed he had been there for a while. I sat down and motioned a passing waiter. I needed a drink of something stronger than orange juice.

McLaglan's may not serve the best food in the world, but they understand thirst and they run a good saloon. My drink arrived in record time and it had some guts to it. I downed half of it without saying more than hello to Anderson, and told the waiter to bring me another.

"If you don't mind my saying so, John T., you look like hell," said Sam.

"I also feel like hell, Sam. I have had little sleep, which is not my habit. I have been beaten up, which is even more of an event in my young life. And I have been looking at a corpse, which I probably helped to make. You may well say that I look like hell.'' I took a more controlled sip of my drink and started to tell the story. I was fairly launched into my tale when the Kingfish walked into the room with the most beautiful woman I have ever seen. I stopped dead in the water and just stared.

She was magnificently tall, splendidly regal, and a hell of a lot of other adjectives you could pile around her and the stack wouldn't come up past her hips. I guessed she was about five-ten, give or take a millimeter, judging her in relation to King, who tops six-five. A perfect blue-black Afro halo added six inches to her height, and two-inch heels jacked her up level with him. Equal in height, but not in solid bulk, she was slender as a wondering breath, but with a solid, big-boned frame that could carry one hundred and fifty pounds. Her face was beyond description, but I'll try it anyway. Nilotic. Thin, curved, insolent nose, high-bridged between oval slanted eyes . . . I gave up. Black Nefertiti? Who is to say that Nefertiti wasn't black? But this girl wasn't, either. The deep, rich brown of dark chocolate, with the high translucent gloss of burnished leather, like a dash of cream in black coffee from the upper Nile. She didn't walk like mortals walk, but moved between the close-packed tables in a gliding, arrogant stalk, flexing and relaxing the long muscles in her endless legs. One and only one sure conclusion: this woman had been born of a proud and insolent tribe and had lost nothing to the erosion of generations.

I was staring without shame and was already bunching muscles to stand when King gave the signal that said ''I require no assistance.'' The black bastard. I relaxed into my chair and took another sip of my momentarily forgotten drink.

''You were saying, John T.?'' asked Sam, with a smile of amusement. I shrugged my shoulders with a little shudder and picked up the dangling thread of my report. I told Sam the whole thing in detail, up to the moment I had left Rafael Muñoz bleeding on his new desk. When I finished, Sam leaned back, rocking his chair, and I heard the click-click of his tongue against the roof of his mouth.

"That's a pretty fantastic story, John T.," he said after a moment. He started questions then, taking me back through the whole affair with searching skepticism, probing the areas of uncertainty with a surgeon's ruthless skill. After we had gone through it twice, he leaned back again. Click-click, click-click.

"It's really just a lot of guesswork," he said finally. I nodded. "Propped up with a surmise or two," he continued. I nodded. "And a few thin slices of evidence." I nodded.

"If such an organization does exist, which is possible and even probable, given the story from Muñoz, it could be nothing more than what he thought it was."

"Except for the fact that someone shot Muñoz dead through the head," I countered.

"There is that, of course," he admitted. "Which may or may not have anything to do with the other thing. He could have had other enemies."

"You're perfectly right, Sam. I could be completely spaced out, but I don't think so. It feels right; and besides, it's all I have. It's the only thing that's happened that fits the situation. Hell, it's the only thing that's happened, period."

"No, some other things are happening. The political scene, for example. Things are beginning to happen there, too. First, there's the matter of someone to fill out the Senator's term if he is convicted. The constitution of this state specifies that in case of death or disability, a replacement will be appointed by the state legislature. The infighting has started, and it could get bloody, because there are some unexpected elements that seem to cut right across party lines. That might indicate a strong independent movement.''

''Who are the independents pushing?'' I asked, flashing the list Jim Cash had given me on a little screen behind my eyes.

''Teofilo Gonzales,'' said Sam flatly. I looked at him through my little list. ''Yes, it's another slice of evidence. A connection, at any rate. But not conclusive. Gonzales is a strong congressman, and very popular. He's also ambitious, and this would be a natural move for him whether or not he is involved in the plot to knock off the Senator. He has just finished his third term in Congress, and the Senate is the next logical step, given a vacancy.''

''What else?'' I asked.

''Sara leased a vacant store for a campaign headquarters and moved in yesterday with a crew of volunteers. Pickets showed up this morning, mostly Chicanos with a few blacks and white kids with long hair.''

''Peaceful?'' I asked, with a little stab of fear for Sara. I felt a little guilty that I hadn't thought of her since the press conference.

''Placid, you might say, just like the assortment in front of the jail. Except for the signs they carry, of course. The gist of them is 'Hang Cameron.' They accuse him of everything from genocide to mopery, and demand the extreme penalty for each offense.'' He sipped a fresh glass of orange juice and click-clicked a couple of times.

''So where does that leave us?'' I asked, with that feeling you get when you're way out to the left and the play is breaking to the right.

''Get your ass in gear and find El Patron!'' he said with a laugh.

''I thought you didn't buy the theory,'' I said.

''Didn't say that. Just said 'Not proven.' But I have the

same feeling about it that you do. The only thing that worries me is time. The sort of organization you describe is just the sort the FBI, Treasury, and IRS take years to crack. You have a little more than a week.''

''And as of this minute, very few ideas about where to start. I can't grab Gonzales and start pulling his fingernails out. Congressmen are a little hard to lean on—and as you say, he could be honest. So where do we go from here?'' As Sam had said, this was the kind of puzzle it would take the FBI years to crack, and they would think they had done well if they got fifteen percent profit in terms of convictions. Hell, they still won't even use the word ''Mafia.''

''I think I'll pass on lunch,'' I told Sam. He agreed that he wasn't too hungry, either, and I could see why. He had cleaned out the bread tray and four or five pats of butter, and he never ate much more than that anyway. We got the check and were on the way out when I literally bumped into Hector de la Cruz as he was coming out of the men's room.

''Hey, John T., happy to see you. Have you had your lunch?''

''Yes, sir, yes, sir, two glasses full,'' I answered, putting an affectionate hand on his shoulder. ''Why don't you buy me another? I have a little time to kill.''

''It's in your hand, John T.,'' he said, leading me to his table, which was around a corner and at the other end of the room from where Sam and I had been sitting, which was why I hadn't seen him before. Sam went on out, probably on his way to an office that would be slightly insane by now. I sat down and wrapped my hand around the third tall scotch in an hour.

''I had heard that you were in town, John T. Did you come in for my show?''

''To tell you the truth, Hector, I had forgotten all about it. When are you planning to open it?''

''Well, the printer made a mistake on the date of the invitations, so I sent them out ahead of time,'' he said. ''It opens in exactly two hours, at four-thirty. Can you make it?'' Hector owns the gallery where he exhibits his paintings, but he doesn't take it too seriously. There isn't enough commercial demand for his stuff to pay for his paints, let alone support a gallery. Not that he needs it. He still owns a respectable slice of the family grant, although it isn't more than a small slice of the original family estate, which included a dozen ranchos larger than mine and including mine. Time and Yankee imperialism had eroded the de la Cruz holdings to the home hacienda which Hector now occupied. It was twice as big as Rancho Useless, but less than half as fertile, so they were roughly equal in value. Hector ran a fair-sized herd but was much too old-fashioned in his ranching methods, so they didn't pay as well as they should have. His outdated methods and the current market notwithstanding, he had enough money.

"Wouldn't miss your show for a new saddle," I said. "Do you have a lot of new stuff?"

"Quite a bit. I've worked pretty hard for the last couple of years, and I haven't bothered to sell much. I have twelve new canvases, and some old stuff that was on consignment to other galleries when I had my last show. This will be my biggest showing ever, John T. I'm glad you won't miss it."

"I might even buy something, Hector; you never can tell. I would buy one right now if you would do me a triple nude on commission."

"How's that, John T.?" He leaned back and looked interested, so I told him my little dream.

"Did you see a Sudanese empress walk in about an hour ago, on the arm of an enormous black man?"

"Beulah Johnson. Yes, she is splendid, isn't she? I know her well."

"Who is she, Hector? I haven't been the same man since she walked in."

"She's the executive secretary of the local chapter of NAACP. She's proud, serious, and dedicated, and has quite a bit of ability. Her boss is rather ineffective, so she runs the place. What about her?''

''Well, you know her, and you know Julia Conrad. I don't think you've met Sara Connelly yet, have you? No? Well, you have another treat coming. Now, if you can get the three of them to pose together in the nude, I'll buy it no matter what the price.'' And hang it where? In my private room to gloat over, or in the main gallery of the ranchhouse for everybody to enjoy? Never!

''If the third girl measures up to that pair, I wouldn't trade the canvas for Rancho Useless, John T.—assuming I could do them justice. Which I seriously doubt. No, I think I'd better stick to cowboys, desert rats, and politicians. It would drive a sensitive artist like me mad to know that no matter what I did, and how well, it would still miss. Smart artists stick to the easy stuff like battle, murder, and sudden death. They're easy to paint.'' That was a thought about Hector that hadn't occurred to me: he never painted women, unless they were Indian squaws or *mestizas* in his big canvases, part of the crowd. That hadn't been true in high school, where he had been as girl-curious as any of us and had drawn them with considerable skill. But after graduation, when most of us went on to the state university or to A&M, he had gone to Spain for his education, following a tradition of his family. The years I spent in the Army saw him touring Europe like the grandee he was. He returned when his father died and left him all his property, but I'd never heard anything about women in his life. I had heard nothing to the contrary, either. As far as I knew he wasn't queer, but then who knows anything about anybody when it comes to sex?

''You don't even have to mix red for the blood, do you?'' I said, continuing in the vein he had opened.

''Ketchup right out of the bottle, John T. No self-respecting artist uses conventional materials anymore. Haven't you heard of Andy Warhol?''

"Yeah. And Ponzi, Goebbels, Barnum—they were great swindlers, too, but they mystified people with an original idea. Warhol has contempt not only for his audience but for himself, his materials, and the whole concept of art."

"But you like my stuff, John T.? According to the critics, it stopped being art a hundred years before I was born. Earlier, maybe, when they invented the camera obscura."

"Who listens to critics? They're worse than the con men; they fall for their own pitch. Hell, they even listen to one another, and if that isn't incest, what is?"

"More like mutual masturbation, John T. They sit around and finger each other's ideas. If by chance an artist happens to be present, he has to keep his mouth shut. Nothing he has to say about art or his own work is valid to them. Well, why don't we toddle along to the gallery? You can drink my scotch there as easily as here."

"I'll be along later, Hector. I need to talk to a couple of people." Hector left, and I sat there wondering why I had lied to him. I didn't need to see anybody—or if I did, I didn't know whom to talk to next. Go find El Patron, said Sam. Ask anybody. I wondered what the waiter would say if I asked him. I wondered what cell he fit into, and on what level. I wondered how long it would take him to bring me another scotch and soda. It took forty-seven seconds. I decided he was not El Patron. He was too nice a guy, and too fast with the drinks. I wondered if I went back and smiled real nice at the Kingfish, would he introduce me to his black empress. And maybe he would hand me my head.

"Another?" asked the waiter as I tipped my glass up. I decided against any more and asked for the check. I might as well run along to Hector's party while I felt like it.

"Mister de la Cruz signed the check before he left, sir. Will there be anything else?" I left a tip, the waiter, and the restaurant, and went out into the cold.

A front had moved in while I was inside, bringing clouds

and a cold drizzle, and I shivered in my light sports coat. I debated going to the hotel for a change of clothes, but went on to Galeria de la Cruz instead.

I was still early, and the place was empty except for a couple of early birds like myself and a Negro in a white jacket setting up a bar at the far end of the room. I started browsing among the pictures in the big front room. There weren't too many, and Hector had cleared out everything but his new work. If what he had told me earlier was true, there would be paintings in the other rooms, and I suspected the best would be there.

Hector and his gallery manager came through a door at the rear, carrying another giant canvas in an ornate frame. Hector nodded, saying he would be with me in a minute, and went on to hang the picture in the front of the room.

"You're early enough, John T., so I will give you the tour myself. Let's start down here." I liked Hector's way of guiding a tour. He stationed himself at my left hand and we started on the wall to the left of the door. He said nothing as we went from picture to picture unless I asked a question. He was just there. He didn't point, gesture, comment or sell. He didn't have to. Each picture was absolutely self-explanatory, telling a chapter out of a dark and bloody history. These weren't self-indulgent daubs, subjective guesses, or experiments in paranoia. They were history, in the heroic mode, re-creating long-dead moments of time out of the imagination and scholarship of the artist. When Hector painted an eagle feather in an Indian's headdress, it was an eagle's feather. If the Indian was a Crow, the feather would be painted in colors and patterns peculiar to Crow tribalism. If he painted a Walker Colt in a scout's holster, you had the feeling that a magnifying glass would show you the armory stampings on butt and barrel.

He painted more than physical details, of course. His eye saw deeply into the souls of his subjects, which was why he always used living models for every character in each painting. He chose them well, for they looked completely alive and perfectly fitted to the scenes in which he placed them. Some of them fit the picture better than their own lives and skins. That was brought home to me when we got to the final picture in the third and smallest showroom. It contained only one canvas, but that one held more of life than most painters can encompass in a life's work.

The subject was a trappers' rendezvous, an annual event in the days when men wore beaver hats and the Rocky Mountain fur trade boomed. Each year the mountain men—free trappers, company men, traders, Indians, all the roistering crew that lived on the flat side of a beaver's tail and the edge of a Green River knife—came together in some chosen place at the end of the long winter season. There they traded their furs, drank, gambled, fought, bought and sold squaws, raced their horses and killed their friends until it was time to move on. Hector had painted a scene at such a rendezvous, at the split second in time when the event was at its peak. A meadow cupped in rolling hills, a quiet stream, and in the distance ragged foothills leading to the Grand Tetons. Within the golden triangle bounded by the stream and a grove of trees, pandemonium.

I stood flat-footed in the middle of the room, empty except for the vast canvas, spellbound by the insane ferocity of my own face. I was the focal point of the picture—the apex of a triangle within a triangle within a triangle. Stripped to the waist, long Green River knife in hand, I was locked in combat with a bearded giant of a man. My feet were planted solidly on the trampled ground. Lines of inhuman stress ran up my legs, visible through taut buckskin, and continued through the bulging tortured slabs of muscle on my torso, ending in the knife. The knife was held point forward, my thumb flat along the hilt, poised inches from my opponent's throat. But the eye was drawn inexorably to my face, by straining shoulders, corded neck, tilted head. Lips drawn back from shining teeth in a snarling smile of hatred. Nose questing, pointing at the vulnerable throat before me. My one visible eye was a window into hell.

My opponent leaned slightly, subtly backward. You could feel the creak and groan of his gigantic muscles as they went one point beyond the point of cracking, feel the sure knowledge of his body that there was no more to give, no reserve, no future strength. The eyes held the knowledge. The first faint flicker of awareness was about to stir, the shadow of the dark horseman wavered within the slitted eyes, and in one more microsecond we would see the other side of darkness.

I didn't see the other details then. I had seen too much. I had seen myself as few men have ever done, perfectly executed through the vision and the omniscient hand of the man who stood beside me. I knew one thing—that Hector was one of the truly great artists of all time. And that he had been born too far out of his time and place ever to receive the recognition he deserved. I had to clear my throat before I could speak.

"I must have it, Hector. How much?" I finally said.

"You like it, then?" he asked, with something of a smile in his voice, a tiny twinkle of smug wisdom that he could not resist.

"I hate it. I would give anything never to have seen it. But now that I have seen it, I have to have it. How much?" I snarled the last request for price.

"If you really want it, John T., it's yours. I'll have it crated and delivered to your rancho, under one condition. Will you let me come and look at it from time to time? This is the best I've done. I'll not paint a better one."

"Any time, Hector—that's a deal. And there's no law that says we can't go fishing when you come."

"Come along, then, John T., and let me buy you a drink."

It was almost five then and the gallery was beginning to fill up, with most of the crowd clustered at one end of the big room near the bar. I passed up the drink, and Hector soon wandered away with a couple who wanted to dicker for one of the pictures. I stood there a minute, didn't see anyone I knew, and decided to leave.

The rain had increased while I was inside and the heavy clouds promised early darkness. I walked down the street for half a block looking for a cab, then on an impulse went into a department store and bought a raincoat with a zip-in lining. My gray ranch hat, a permanent fixture on my head, was sufficient protection for it. I went outside into the gathering darkness and started walking. I didn't see the rush-hour crowds leaving offices and stores, lined up in parking garages waiting for their cars, crowded bumper to bumper on the wet streets on their way home to wife and kids and warmth.

My mind was filled with a mountain valley, with a triangle of grove and stream within a triangle of mountain and blue sky, and within these, the pyramid of men near death. It was as if the whole painting were there, projected on the sheets of rain. I kept seeing details I had not paid any attention to in the first viewing. The bank of dark clouds boiling down from the Tetons, promising rain within the hour. A Crow buck and his squaw, bargaining for whiskey with a small, dark man in buckskin britches and bright blanket coat. The trappers, Indians, and traders ringed around the arena, eyes bright for the spectacle, making bets of gold and furs and weapons on the outcome. The lone buck on the Appaloosa stallion at one side, his dark face impassive as he watched from his seat on the fifty-yard line. The long knife-cut on my bare chest, shallow but bloody, with the white lips of the wound at the deep end pouting open. I had a knife scar on my chest in exactly that place, and I felt a twinge of remembered pain from the dark jungle night when I had gotten it.

I had fallen into the old route march cadence and was stepping off a steady three miles an hour down the dark streets. As I walked, leaving the downtown area for the decaying belt of old houses, small businesses, used car lots and gaping holes where new developments were reclaiming the valuable real estate of the central city, the vision began to fade. I became aware of growing hunger, and stopped at the first sandwich shop I found. They served me dark bitter coffee out of a Silex pot, and small chopped barbecue sandwiches dripping with sauce. I ate four of the small sandwiches, drank more coffee, and started thinking about the work again. Going over the information I had, I could see it wasn't nearly enough. Not only was there no obvious direction from where I stood, I wasn't even sure about where I had been. The tired-looking waitress came back to my booth for the fourth time with the half-empty Silex to warm my coffee, and I asked her to call me a taxi. She came back a moment later and said that, because of the weather, there would be a twenty- to thirty-minute wait. I didn't want to walk any more in the cold rain, so I waited there, letting the coffee grow cold in my cup while I gnawed the cold facts of the case again. Nothing, and nowhere to go.

Chapter . 9

IT WAS NEARLY EIGHT O'CLOCK when the taxi finally came. I told the driver to take me to the hotel and settled back for the ride. I was beginning to be a little tired. I hadn't had my siesta that afternoon. When the hotel came in sight, a small instinct of caution made me stop him two blocks from the entrance. I paid him off and started to walk the rest of the way.

As I was passing the darkened doorway of a clothing shop near the hotel, I heard a hoarse voice whisper: "Boss?" My hand moved to the Colt under my belt as a small hunched shadow detached itself from the darkness in the doorway and started toward me.

"It's me, boss. Blue." The little rider was blue, all right, with the raw cold of the wet evening, which had seeped into his stove-up body through the heavy mackinaw, leaving him hunched and shivering.

"What is it, Blue?" I asked.

"Come on, boss, let's get in the truck over here." He led me to the pickup parked against the curb halfway down the block.

"What's going on, Blue? I was on my way to the hotel. Let's go in there and get you warmed up."

"Let's get in this truck and get your ass off the street, boss. We got some trouble, and I don't think you want to go to no hotel." I got in the truck without further argument, and Blue started the engine and drove away. He fiddled with the heater control, then turned the radio on.

"All right, Blue, let's have it," I said impatiently.

"Just listen, boss," he said, indicating the radio. I listened as the announcer finished a commercial and introduced the eight o'clock news. The national disasters came first, then a half dozen commercials, then Blue's blockbuster.

"Police are still searching for John T. McLaren, wealthy rancher wanted for questioning in the pistol slaying of Rafael Muñoz, attorney, in his Guadalupe Street offices today. Police were called to the scene of the crime at lunchtime today by the victim's secretary, who said that McLaren was in the office and that her employer expected trouble with him. When police arrived, Muñoz was dead from a gunshot wound in the head, and his secretary had disappeared. A thirty-eight-caliber pistol registered to McLaren was found near the body. One shot had been fired from it. A ballistics report comparing bullets from McLaren's gun with the bullet in Muñoz's body indicates that it is the murder weapon. Sources close to police headquarters have indicated that investigating officers found evidence linking McLaren with Muñoz in the wholesale distribution of narcotics in this city. Wait a minute . . . wait a minute—here's another late bulletin from police headquarters: The secretary, Alicia Torres, who called police to the murder scene, has still not been found, and it is assumed that the murderer might have taken her hostage. Police have asked us to warn citizens that McLaren, a war hero and experienced hunter, is an expert with weapons. He is probably—no, surely—armed, and is considered extremely dangerous. Stay tuned to this station for more news as it happens—'' I snapped the radio off and cursed.

First Muñoz and now his girl. But why take her hostage? Why take her anyway? Unless they figured taking her back to the office was too much of a risk, in which case letting her live would also be too much of a risk. So she would be dead by now, and the hunting season on me was officially open. Well, I had a hunting license, too.

Blue just kept driving, looking straight ahead at the cold rain driving into the headlights. After a few minutes of silence he spoke. ''There's another thing, boss.''

''What else?'' I snapped.

''Juan Silva. Somebody just beat the holy shit out of him about dark, and threw him in a ditch outside of town. I was driving along and saw his pickup parked by the side of the road. He's in pretty bad shape.''

''What hospital did you take him to?''

''He wouldn't go to no hospital, boss. He told me to find you.''

''Blue, goddamn it, where is he?'' I yelled.

''He's in back, wrapped up in my sleepin' bag. Bleedin' all over it, like as not.''

''Can you get us somewhere safe where I can take a look at him?''

''Yeah, boss. But don't worry about Juan none. He's had worse just fightin' for fun. He'll be all right.'' He drove in silence for another five minutes, then pulled into the driveway of a small house on the outskirts of the city. He drove the pickup straight back to the detached garage and got out. He opened the garage door, drove the pickup into it, then clicked a light switch after he had closed the door.

I went to the back of the truck and opened the camper door. Juan was sitting up in the sleeping bag, spread out on top of half a ton of canned goods, looking at me with one eye. The other was swelled shut, and a slow trickle of blood was seeping out of his matted hair and down his jawline.

"Where are we, Blue? Can we get him inside?" I asked.

"This is my woman's house. She's still at work, but I got a key. Come on, Juan, we'll get you out of there."

"Let the tailgate down and I can get out by myself," he said. "Hi, boss. I been lookin' for you."

"Join the crowd, Juan. Here, let me give you a hand." Juan was holding one arm tightly across his stomach, pushing himself along with the other. I got hold of the sleeping bag and pulled him bodily to the rear, bag and all. He put one arm over my shoulder, and Blue got on the other side. We lifted him out and he put his feet to the ground. He tried a couple of steps and said, "Okay, let's go," and we walked him into the kitchen of the house. We put him down in a kitchen chair by the small dining table, and Blue started searching the cabinets for first-aid materials. It didn't take him long to find the most important remedy. He handed Juan a pint bottle of blended whiskey with the cap off. Juan raised it very carefully and took a long swallow, wincing when the alcohol bit into the cuts inside his mouth.

"That's the first drink you bought me in a long time, Blue," he said.

"Indians ain't supposed to drink whiskey," Blue said with a grunt. "Makes 'em undependable. You shut up now and let me get you cleaned up." He had run a pan of hot water, and he started on Juan's face with a dish towel. With the mud and blood cleaned off, he didn't look as bad as I had feared. But he still had his arm locked over his abdomen, so I suspected some internal injuries. I took a swig from Blue's bottle and recapped it. Blue promptly uncapped it and took a long swallow himself, looking at me with one indignant eye, then he turned back to Juan.

"Who did it, Juan?" I asked.

"Cops. Lookin' for you, boss. I told 'em I was just a

dumb Indian and don't know nothin'. So they beat hell outta me.''

"Anybody you know?''

"Yeah, that Sanchez and his partner. They worked me over with slapsticks and kicked me in the guts a few times. Boss, that Sanchez is one mean son of a bitch. I'm gonna have to talk to him one of these days.'' He grunted when Blue put some disinfectant in the cut on his head.

"Better stay away from him, Juan,'' I ordered.

"He told me to stay out of town or he'd kill me next time, boss. He's *puro* Apache, and I guess he would do it. But he just half-killed me this time, and he made one mistake. He didn't kill the Apache half.'' I let it drop. Juan Silva would just have to take care of himself. I had problems of my own.

"Blue, I have to find someplace to hole up for a few hours until I can figure this thing out. Any suggestions?''

"Stay here, boss. My woman won't mind. I'll get Juan fixed up and take him back to the ranch. You can stay here. I'll stop by the club where she works and tell 'er you're here.'' I agreed. This was as good a place as any. All I needed was a phone and, later, a bed. I added another category to my underground Yellow Pages. F for "Fugitives.''

I went into the small, neat living room and found the phone. I dialed Sam Anderson's office and got no answer, so I tried the Senator's hotel suite. Still no answer, so I looked up his home number and tried that. He answered the first ring. He knew my voice so I didn't mention my name.

"Looks as if you found yourself a little trouble,'' he said. Calm and reasonable, he sounded as if I had told him I had a flat tire across the street from a garage. "Can you talk?'' he asked.

"Go ahead, Sam. What's on the menu?''

"Well, for one thing, I'm a lot more ready to buy your

theory on El Patron. You must have been getting close to something or they wouldn't have gone to all this trouble to take you out. It doesn't pay to blitz unless the other team is close to pay dirt.''

"Yeah, I figured the same, Sam. I also figure we had better treat these dudes with some respect. When they take out a linebacker, they really take him out. But they sure make it hard on their friends. First Malena Vasquez, now Muñoz and probably his secretary.''

"Like who needs enemies, hey? So where do we go from here? I imagine we can get the police off your back with a little pressure. Jim Cash called and said those radio reports are grounds for a criminal libel suit, and you can sue the stations, the city, and probably AT&T. All you have to do is give yourself up and let Jim work on bail for you.''

"Like hell. You just haven't thought enough about that, Sam, nor has Jim. Whoever leaked all that shit to the press was just declaring open season on one John T. McLaren. Anybody can shoot me on sight now and get away with it. No, there's only one way to go, now. We have to find them before they find me, or you will be short one senator and one bully boy.''

"Maybe you're right, John T. So what are you going to do?'' I heard the click-click start on the other end of the line.

"It just occurred to me, Sam, that we have a lot of man-power working on this thing, and we haven't been together to compare notes since the first evening. Do you think it might be worthwhile to get everybody together for some idle conversation? Including Senator Carlsbad and a couple of guys I called in from out of town?''

"That might help. So far, only you, Jim Cash and I know anything about the El Patron angle. Give me the number there and I'll call you back in a few minutes.'' I gave him the number and hung up. Blue, who had been pacing nerv-

ously around the house after finishing his patch job on Juan
Silva, was standing by the front window looking out
through the lace curtains and drawn venetian blinds.

"Boss, come here a minute," he said. I went to the window. "Look across the street and about halfway down the
block. That car wasn't here when we drove in, and it
doesn't belong here. There's a couple of guys in the front
seat, and they kept the motor runnin'. You can see the
smoke from the exhaust." The car was a nondescript
sedan, four or five years old. I could see the driver indis-
tinctly, and then a small red dot glowed in the passenger
seat as someone took a drag on his cigarette. I wasn't surprised. Considering the manpower available to El Patron, it
was a foregone conclusion that they would find me sooner
or later. The only question was, what did they intend doing
right here and now? The answer wasn't long in coming. As
we watched, two more cars came slowly into the street and
coasted past the first one. One stopped on the other side of
the street, about the same distance from the house as the
first car, while the other continued to the corner and made a
turn. Going around to cover the rear, no doubt.

"Blue, we have maybe three minutes before those guys
get in position behind the house and they're all ready to
move. I'm going to use one of them, hoping I can get lucky
on the phone. You get Juan back into the pickup and get out
of the garage. Hold there for me unless they move in faster.
If they do, leave me and get the hell out. They mean business."

I grabbed the phone and dialed the apartment. It rang
four times and was picked up, and I heard the Kingfish's
rumbling voice. I told him the situation in short sentences,
and that we were going to make a run for it in the pickup,
then described the route we would take.

"We'll appreciate any small assistance you might render,
King."

"Well, it's nice to have steady work, John T. We're on our way." He hung up the phone and was probably already on his way. They might even get there—wherever there might be—in time to help a little. I suspected we might need it.

I checked the cartridge in the chamber of Muñoz's automatic and flipped the lights. I bailed into the rear of the pickup as Blue backed it out of the garage and slapped the front wall of the camper twice. Blue gunned the engine, and we shot down the driveway into the street. Blue drove a pickup the same way he rode a horse.

Both cars in front of the house were on the opposite side of the street heading west. Blue backed into the street in a sliding turn to the east, shifted gears, and gunned the engine straight toward them. The cleated snow tires spun for a moment on the wet pavement and then grabbed, almost tossing me out the back door of the camper.

The second car was already in motion, backing across the street in a fast turnaround, when we passed the first one. The first car could have blocked the street if the driver had thought fast enough, but he didn't start moving in time. The second car was almost through his backing turn to put the car crossways in the street, but Blue cut behind him anyway. The heavily sprung truck bucked and fish-tailed as he hit the grass verge and mowed down a couple of shrubs on somebody's front lawn. He straightened the truck out and rode the sidewalk for about ten houses, then took a driveway back into the street. I saw a gun wink out of the side window of the following sedan, and then we were around the corner.

I opened the sliding rear window of the pickup so I could talk to Blue, and suddenly I felt a lot better about the situation. The gunrack in the back window of the truck was just full of beautiful weapons. We keep a rifle and a shotgun in every vehicle we use on the ranch, and nobody bothers to take them out when we go to town. I told Blue the route to take back to town, and pulled the twelve-gauge Browning and the Winchester lever-action carbine back into the camper with me. Somebody was in for one hell of a surprise if he got too horsey. Juan Silva saw the weapons and grinned, reaching for his share of the tools. I gave him the shotgun and kept the rifle for myself. I doubted that his marksmanship would be up to snuff, considering his condition. He would do better with the scattergun, although it would probably rock hell out of him every time he fired it. I checked the chamber of the rifle for a load. Five shots in it if the magazine was full, and five in the unplugged shotgun. Enough, I supposed. If we got into an extended firefight we were in bad trouble anyway. Somehow I didn't think we were. The characters following us didn't look all that formidable to me.

Telling Juan to roll over, I stacked some cases of canned goods behind the tailgate, then looked out through the small gap between the camper door and the tailgate. The first car was about a hundred yards behind and coming up fast. The second was another hundred yards to the rear, also closing. I opened the camper door, which is hinged at the top with a stop-bar, and took a good look. It was safe enough. They were well out of pistol range, and I doubted that they would have long-range weapons in the car. City folk don't often think in those terms. Even if they did, it would take better shooting than they had done so far to hit anything. I expected them to overhaul us and try to shoot us at short range, as quickly as possible. That's why we were headed back into town. They were handicapped if we could get into the city.

The lead car was pulling up on us fast, so I took careful aim with the carbine and put a neat star in the center of the windshield, right between two heads. They didn't seem to be too discouraged by it, which convicted them of recklessness if nothing else. The heavily loaded pickup made as good a gun platform as I could have wished for under the circumstances. I aimed at the driver's head and was taking up the slack in the trigger when a snarling vision came between me and the target—a vision of my own killer's face with my knife at a man's throat in Hector's painting. I eased off the pressure and laid the rifle aside. I motioned to Juan and he handed me the shotgun.

They were within forty yards when I put three blasts of number-four shot through the windshield. Point-blank for a rifle, but far enough for the shotgun pattern to spread pretty wide and lose a lot of force, so those fools would have at least a chance to live. The windshield disappeared in three sections, right to left, as the shots smashed it in like a big fist hitting a speed bag. I had a brief glimpse of the driver's bloody face as the car went out of control and spun on the pavement. It turned over three times and ended up on its wheels again beside the highway. They were out of action, and they might even be alive, so I switched my attention to the other car.

It didn't even slow down as it passed the dead vehicle, which told me a couple of things about my opponents. One I knew already: they weren't too interested in their friends' well-being. Second, they wanted me very badly. They didn't make the mistake the first car had, and they hung back out of shotgun range. That was still a mistake, considering the rifle, but I had made up my mind not to kill anybody unless I had to. I was kicking myself for a sentimental jackass as I made the decision, but I had to draw a line somewhere. The image of myself as a hired killer wasn't too appealing, and I was in no mood for sitting ducks.

We were in the city now, barreling down a well-lighted street. Too soon for a lot of traffic signals, but there was more traffic. I started watching the road behind our pursuers more carefully, and in another three blocks I saw what I had been waiting for. The Chevrolet I had given Stone and King pulled out of a side street and fell in behind them, keeping a fifty-yard interval. I crawled forward to the window and told Blue to pull into first big parking lot he saw, and why.

"Okay, boss," he said, and skidded the truck into the alley behind the next big shopping center. He pulled alongside a big steel trash container, leaving the metal barricade between us and the street. He bailed out of the cab then, and I tossed him the reloaded shotgun. He took up a position between the steel dumpster and the brick wall of a drugstore. I stayed where I was and traded the pistol with Juan Silva. I told him to stay put on the floor of the truckbed.

The pursuit car had gone past the alley entrance but had pulled into the parking lot at the next street entrance. They stopped there, looked over the situation for a long minute, then started easing the car forward. They were a good hundred yards from the alley entrance. The parking lot between street and building side was about fifty feet wide, and they were completely in the open, with only the car for protection. Considering the microscopic thinness of the steel they had to hide behind, I could understand their cautious advance. When they started easing toward us, Stone and King made their move. They had slowed to a crawl when we pulled into the alley, and then come to a stop at the alley entrance, forming the third corner of a triangle with a fifty-foot base. The pursuers hadn't noticed the Chevy until it stopped and Stone and King fell out of the other side and leveled weapons over the hood. They stopped dead when they saw the flankers out, then went into reverse with a crunch of gears. We didn't fire as they got the hell out of there.

I tried to find some saliva in my mouth with which to moisten my dry lips, then gave it up as a bad job for the moment. I told Blue to watch down the alley in case the boys got their nerve back and came at us from another direction; then I walked over to Stone and King. Stone was back in the car, stowing a couple of nasty-looking machine pistols into a fitted leather case. I gave a little nervous giggle in my mind as I thought of the firepower leveled at the carful of thugs in the few seconds they had taken to make up their minds. They would have lasted through one series of four bursts, plus what was left in my carbine and Blue's shotgun. I was glad they had packed it in. I could see the headlines the next day, about "Mad-Dog McLaren" and the machine-gun war he had started.

"Man, man, I thought you needed help," said King, shaking his head from side to side. "One little old car full of rank amateurs, and you sittin' in a steel bunker all ready to cut 'em down. How come you wastin' my time, John T.? You know what I left to come down here and watch you make a fool outta yourself?" He looked at me with a mixture of affection and disgust, much as a parent would look at a backward child, and turned to appeal to Stone. I cut him short.

"King, I am very glad to see you, believe me. And if you left what I think you left, I appreciate it even more. I hope you never put me to the same test. I'm just glad you were at the apartment when I called. It could have been a mess otherwise, and I'm in enough trouble as it is. You've heard, of course?"

"Yes, we were in the airport lounge when they announced it on television," said Stone. "We thought it might be a good idea to stick around for a while until you get it sorted out, so we went back to the apartment. The girls came over to help us wait."

"If you don't mind a fifth wheel, I'd like to ride back to the apartment with you. I have to send the truck back to the ranch with an injured man, and I don't think this is quite the time to be calling taxis. Also, since you're still here and my situation has changed somewhat since we last talked, we might discuss extending your engagement a bit, at least until the air clears.''

"Consider it extended. We weren't all that interested in Uruguay. If it won't wait, it probably isn't worth doing. Shall we run along, then? The girls will be getting worried. We told them we were just going for a haircut.''

I told Blue to take Juan back to the ranch and to get Doc Maldonado over to take a look at him.

"Yeah, boss, but I better stop by the club and tell my woman not to go home tonight. Those guys might go back there and give her some trouble.''

"Take her to the ranch if you want to, Blue. It wouldn't hurt if she stayed there until this is over. Tell Juana Sanchez to make whatever arrangements seem to suit. I'm going along with these fellows, and I don't know when I'll make it back. You and Juan stick close to the ranchhouse, and keep your eyes open. I don't expect any trouble there, but you never can tell.''

Blue said, "Sure, boss," and got back into the pickup. I saw him open the glove compartment, take out a flat bottle, and take a long pull of the liquor. Then he passed the bottle back through the window to Juan Silva.

"Here, Indian. You might as well get stoned. It's a long ride back to the ranch, and it's getting colder.'' Then he slammed the truck in gear, put the spurs to it, and steamed off toward the night club where his woman worked. I got in the front seat of the Chevy with King and we started back to the apartment.

"Now, Mr. McLaren, sir," said King, "just how did you get yourself in the shit again—before lunch, at that?''

"Luck and natural ability, Mr. King. Just following the Yellow Brick Road. But a much more important question. How did you manage to find a woman like that before lunch, when I would have sworn you were a stranger in the city no later than last night?''

''Same answer, John T.—luck and talent, plus five hundred dollars of your money which I took down and donated to the NAACP this morning. She turned out to be the head nigger, and we just naturally found we had a lot in common.''

I filled them in on the day's events as we drove. Stone asked a few questions, which I answered, then we fell into a comfortable silence for the rest of the drive. By that I mean I damn near went to sleep. I woke up when King braked to a stop in the apartment parking lot.

Honeypot answered the door to Stone's knock. She smiled with relief when she saw me and closed the door behind us quickly.

''I hope you didn't get too bored waiting, Honeypot,'' Stone said.

''You were gone long enough,'' she said with mock severity, ''but we weren't too bored, really. The fellows who came to peek in the window kept us in stitches. See? I'm still wearing all my stitches.''

''Window peekers, is it? Could it be some of your playmates, John T.?''

I allowed as to how it could, and felt my fatigue vanish under a new flood of adrenalin. Stone looked around the apartment but didn't comment on the pistol he saw on the low table beside Honeypot's drink.

''These fellows are getting to be something of a nuisance, Mr. King,'' he said, with small fires beginning to smolder in his cold blue eyes.

''They are indeed, Mr. Stone,'' said King with a judicial air. ''Do you think we should remonstrate with them?''

''I do indeed, Mr. King,'' Stone answered, stooping to open the case of pistols he had carried with him from the car.

"Hold it, fellows," I said. "You're still on half-cock. I don't think it's really a good idea to start shooting a bunch of people. And besides, this is still my show. Let's talk some instead."

Stone continued opening the gun case while he answered me. His back was turned and I couldn't see his eyes, which was just as well. I knew that if they matched the tone of his voice, they wouldn't be a pleasant'sight just then.

"Very well, John T. It is, as you say, your show. But you have brought us into it, and I for one am just a bit tired of the clumsy way you have directed it to date. You started out to do in a murderer, for the purpose of clearing a politician's name. But all you've accomplished so far is to get a couple of other people killed, yourself set up for the long fall, and a nest of thugs milling about with guns in their hands. And you still haven't the foggiest idea of the murderer's identity. You are working with a fairy tale about a criminal mastermind who may or may not exist. It's time you pulled up your socks, John T. If you had stumbled around like this in the jungle, you would have gotten us all killed years ago. We have kidded you about getting old and fat, and I'm beginning to believe that that might be the case. If it is the case, then King and I will make our most graceful bows and leave the scene, because there isn't going to be any applause." He turned to face me then, and my surmise about his eyes had been right. They were not a bonny sight. I could meet them, but just barely. I held his glance with mine while I took a long look at my hole card.

"There's a lot of truth in what you say, Stone," I admitted. "Yes, I have been stumbling around—deliberately. When you don't know who the enemy is, or where he is, that sometimes is the only way to make him break cover. Perhaps I have been clumsier than usual. Peaceful living has a way of doing that to a man. You tend to forget what it feels like to walk the point. But it's like riding a bicycle,

Stone. You don't ever completely forget, and it comes back very quickly. If you wish to bow out, however, leave whenever you like.'' I went to the bar and mixed a drink. When I turned with it in my hand, Stone was closing up the pistol case, and King had plopped himself down beside his dark empress with a look of contentment on his broad face.

''El Patron is no longer a myth,'' I continued. ''He went to a lot of trouble to frame me for Muñoz's murder, and started his storm troopers after me fast. That means I'm getting close to him. I still don't know who he is, but I know what he is, and I can guess what he is after. We all know how he'll go about it. Every visionary thug since Attila the Hun has used it, and recent history proves it still works. I think he made a mistake with the Cameron move. He wasn't really ready for that, and his people have made mistakes because they're amateurs with not much experience. But that won't last, because they will get more work to do, and they will learn fast. But we can find him, now.''

''*Who are you people?*'' I had forgotten all about Beulah Johnson. She was sitting on the big couch with King, looking at the four of us with shock and disbelief on her face. No wonder. What she had just seen and heard was enough to make any girl ask a question or two. We had been talking as if she didn't exist.

''We're the good guys, sugar,'' King chuckled. ''Haven't you figured that out from what you just heard?'' He grinned at her, and his expansive good humor flooded the room. ''Let me introduce Mr. John T. McLaren, one of the 'gentry' hereabouts, and justly famous for his deeds. You no doubt heard his name taken in vain over the radio this evening. The story is not true, of course, and some people will be highly embarrassed when we point out that fact to them. John T. is trying to help a friend of his, Senator Cameron, beat another bum rap. Mr. Stone and I are old friends, and he asked us to come and help with the harvest, so to speak.''

''I also heard the name El Patron bandied about,'' she said with a sarcastic smile. ''I just wondered how the 'gentry' happen to be talking about such things.''

''That's right, you know what's comin' down around Guadalupe Street, don't you, sugar?'' said King. ''Why don't you tell us what you know about El Patron?''

''Why don't you go and bugger yourself, Uncle Tom?'' she asked with sudden venom. ''What the hell do I care what happens to these people? And right now I'm getting the hell out of here.'' She jumped up and took two long strides toward the door. King didn't seem to move at all but he was there before her, standing relaxed and easy in her path.

''Now you just calm yourself, sugar, and give us half the chance you would ask for yourself. You're just too pretty to get yourself all uptight when you don't have a program.''

''Don't call me 'sugar,' '' she snapped. ''I don't know anything about El Patron except that he has helped a lot of people, including black people. That's more than can be said for Mr. Murderer—Pusher—Mother-Jumper McLaren. He's one of the 'gentry,' as you say, and that's enough to convict him in my neighborhood. Get out of my way, Tom!'' She was vibrating like a battery of shrill drums. I started to speak, but Stone beat me to it.

''Will you listen to us for a few minutes, Ms. Johnson? With an open mind? I think I can show you where your interests are not identical with those of any organization such as the one we have been discussing. Rather the opposite, in fact.'' Then he turned to King. ''If she won't listen, King, I suggest you let her go. She could be as bigoted in her own way as any redneck sharecropper in Alabama. Unless she has a reasonable mind, we could argue till doomsday and never be closer to agreement. What about it, Ms. Johnson?'' The girl stood poised for flight for one long moment, then looked at King. Finally she spoke to him.

''Do you really think you people have anything to say to me, Mr. King?''

''I really think we do, Beulah,'' he answered, with no trace of humor.

''All right, then. Let's hear your story, Mr. Stone. And you might begin by explaining why it's so important to convince me that you're right.'' She sat down in the big armchair, as far as she could get from King, with all the dignity and lack of expression of a Supreme Court justice. I gave a little snort of disgust and took a sip of my drink. Then I wondered why I didn't like the idea of her sitting in judgment on my values. Stone sat in the chair next to hers and leaned forward.

''You are Mr. King's guest, Ms. Johnson. That in itself is sufficient reason to clear up any misunderstanding. In addition to that, you have called him a name considered vile among your people. That was unjust because it is untrue. I have been his friend for many years, and I consider him the equal of any man I have ever known. He has earned my respect and affection many times over, and never have I seen him back down or bow before any man, white, black, brown or yellow. The name you called him implies the opposite of every quality I know him to possess. If you should be so fortunate as to come to know him as I do, you will bite your tongue a thousand times for calling him 'Tom.' Now, as to the matter of your interests as opposed to those of El Patron and his organization, that should be self-evident to you.'' Stone stood up and went to the bar for a drink. He continued from where he stood.

''To begin with, if our judgment is correct, his methods are not only illegal, but directly opposed to the personal rights of every man, whatever his color. He is willing to lie, steal, and kill to accomplish his purpose. He is willing to use whatever tool comes to hand, and his methods of disposing of people who are no longer of use to him are summary, to say the least. Rafael Muñoz, whom Mr. McLaren is falsely accused of murdering, was a member of his organization. Muñoz was killed by another member he had called for assistance when McLaren came to question him about Malena Vasquez.''

"How do I know McLaren didn't murder him?'' Beulah interrupted. "The police think he did, and they have evidence, according to the radio.''

"You don't know that—but I do. I have known John T. for the same number of years as I have known the Kingfish. He is capable of killing, and it wouldn't make any difference to me if he had killed Muñoz. We have killed a large number of people together. But he has told me that he did not kill this man, and that is enough for me. To continue about El Patron. You say he has helped some black people. No doubt he has. Black people are justifiably angry at the treatment they have received and continue to receive in this country. That makes many of you willing tools of any unscrupulous man who promises to change things for the better. El Patron needs strong and angry people to carry out his plans, and he will no doubt use anybody who comes to his hand. But how much will he need you when he has succeeded?''

Beulah started to speak, but Stone held up his hand.

"Please let me finish. Will El Patron need his faithful black troops after he accomplishes his purpose? I think not. In the first place, all the evidence points to him as being more closely allied with the Spanish-speaking people of the state, which is perfectly logical. They are the majority, and the first line of offense. It is they, not the blacks who help them, who will be in command. It is they who will reap the first fruits. After all, racism is not limited to the white race—you will find it in China, in India, and even in black Africa.

"In the second place, El Patron himself is probably white. The fact that he is so well hidden indicates this, as well as the methods he has chosen to use. I have studied revolution throughout my adult life, and the patterns of conspiracy are quite familiar to me. El Patron, when we find him, will turn out to be a highly sophisticated man, a man accustomed to commanding respect from every level of society. The subtlety of his mind is European in nature, or Oriental, and this is not to imply any racial superiority. It is just that different cultures have different ways of thinking, even when they're plotting a revolution. I will wager a considerable sum that El Patron is white, an aristocrat, and probably a racist.

"So what will be the fate of the black people who help him achieve his ambitions here? It will be the same as that of the Jews who helped Hitler to power, the same as that of the anarchists who fought with the communists in Spain. When they were no longer needed, it was 'Up against the wall, Comrade Anarchist!' and they executed several thousand of them in a bloody purge. What makes you think a criminal organization headed by someone styled El Patron will be any different? It will be 'Sorry about this, Comrade Black Man, but after all, you are not a member of *La Raza!*' "

"And you really think that's the way it will be?" asked Beulah Johnson without heat.

"Do you really think the Chicanos here identify their interests with those of your people?" Stone answered in rebuttal.

"No, damn you, I don't! They should, but they don't. They're just as much against blacks as the whites are, and just as racist in their thinking. Oh, hell, what is the answer?"

"If there is one, it will be somewhere within the

framework of constitutional republican government such as we have," said Stone. "Here, and only here, has there been a serious attempt to recognize the rights of all men. The problem, of course, is to make it work."

Beulah sat in silence for a moment, then smiled tentatively at the Kingfish. "I'm not sure I buy it, but I can at least apologize for calling you 'Tom.' "

King answered her with a broad smile and walked over to take her hand without speaking.

"Would you like to tell us about El Patron, Beulah?" asked Stone.

"Well, to start with, you didn't have to argue very hard to convince me there's something funny about him. I've felt that all along, and I've had my doubts about how much real help he can give black people. I just hadn't thought it all the way through so I could put it into words. What you said about him maybe being white fits in with my own suspicions, and I don't think he is the same kind of white as John Kennedy was. But that's all I know about him. I know a few blacks who are supposed to work for him and pass down news from him, but they don't seem to know much about him either."

Stone explained the cell structure of the organization, and the girl nodded her understanding. "You're right about that being European thinking," she said. "We blacks have to feel close to each other or we can't work together at all. We sort of huddle together for warmth. No, I can't tell you anything about him, but I can tell you this. There's going to be hell to pay in the next few days. There's a lot of talk about demonstrations in front of the jail, and at the Senator's new headquarters. And there's whispers that these demonstrations won't be all that peaceful, either. *La Raza* has been looking at Watts and Detroit, and they think maybe they learned something from that."

"Do they think they can force his conviction by rioting?" I asked.

"No, but they can make a lot of headlines, and maybe push some politicians into a panic decision when they appoint a man to fill out the term. With one of ours in the Senate, and a lot of publicity showing racial solidarity, it wouldn't be too much trouble to get him re-elected." And that was the whole thing in a nutshell. Once he's in, it's hell to get a man out of office, which explained the drastic measures to unseat Latham Cameron.

Honeypot, who had been silent throughout the argument, spoke then.

"John T., I have some information that bears on this political thing, information that came out of the financial investigations you asked me to do. Do you want to hear it now?" I started to tell her to go ahead, but just then the phone rang. When I answered it, Sam Anderson's voice exploded in my ear.

"Where in hell have you been?" he snapped. I told him about the business of Juan Silva, and the thugs at the house, and he just grunted. "Well, I've talked to Jim and Senator Carlsbad. The Senator's in town and wants to get together tonight. Is that all right with you?"

"Sure. Where?"

He told me the Senator was waiting at his town house.

"All right. We have a little cleaning up to do here, and then I'll be along. I have a couple of people I'd like to bring with me."

We arranged to meet at the Senator's house in an hour. I hung up and turned to the others.

"Save it for a little later, Honeypot. There's a little prayer meeting scheduled at Senator Carlsbad's house, and everybody might as well hear it at once. Right now, there's a little matter of some window peepers. If we leave here, we'll have to take care of them first." Stone and King nodded and the three of us went into a huddle. We decided that they would scout the premises while I held the fort with the girls. They slipped out of the apartment after I flipped the light switch, and I heard the car start. They planned to drive off and come back on foot. If there were any strangers in town they would find them.

I took one of Stone's machine pistols and told Honeypot I was going to shower and change. "Don't try to do anything if there's a problem. Just scream like a banshee and I'll come in and shoot the place up."

She grinned and curled up on the couch as if she went through this kind of flap every day. Beulah Johnson did the same.

I went to the bathroom and scraped my body. It was about time. I stank of stale sweat and fear and excitement, and only now was the saliva starting to flow again to lubricate my dry mouth. I used a double ration of spray deodorant and gave myself a close shave.

Honeypot had been busy in the kitchen while I was in the bath, and there was a large platter of sandwiches on the bar when I came back in. The barbecue I had eaten earlier was long gone and I was hungry again. I had wolfed down two of the sandwiches and a cup of coffee when there was a tap on the door. I went through the identification routine and then let Stone in.

"We didn't find anybody," he said, and I took that to mean there wasn't anybody to find. "King is still out there, but I don't think they had a team on the place. If it was the enemy, they scouted the apartment, saw only the girls, and tucked it in. They will probably be back if they have a firm line on it. Is everybody ready?"

We piled into two cars and moved out. Stone, driving the lead car, went to the end of the alley and stopped. King stepped out of the shadows and got in the car. The courtesy light didn't come on, so I guessed one of the first things they'd done when they took over the car was to disconnect it, as I had done with the Ford I was driving. I took the lead when we hit the street, and they followed me to Braden Carlsbad's big town house.

Chapter . 10

I DROVE ON IN through the big brick gate and up the wind-
ing drive to the house. Stone stopped a moment at the gate,
and I caught a glimpse of the Kingfish slipping out of the car
and into the shrubbery. He would scout the grounds and
then join us if the place was clean. It would be after his
survey. Nobody cons the Kingfish in the dark. I grinned
when I thought of all the "nightfighter" jokes Negro troops
have had to endure. They were true in King's case. His big
body moved like a deeper shadow, and when he was still,
he was just another giant of the forest. Birds would nest in
his kinky hair and enemy snipers try to climb his legs when
he wanted to be really still.

The Senator answered the door himself and led us into a
big library, crammed floor to ceiling with the accumulated
reading tastes of several generations. Sara, Jim Cash and
Sam were already there, sitting in big leather chairs, balanc-
ing coffee cups. I waved to everybody and went with Stone
and Beulah to the sideboard, where the Senator was offer-
ing coffee and sandwiches. I introduced them, and the Senator almost but not quite raised an eyebrow at Beulah. I
was sure this was the first time a black had been introduced

as a guest in his house. Senator Carlsbad is not a racist, in the bad sense of the term, but he is old-fashioned and tends to move very slowly when there are important decisions to be made. He shook hands with Stone, and a smile of recognition lit his face when I pronounced Stone's full name.

"Stanford Odum Stone. You're not the first to bear that name. I know your father well."

"Yes, sir," Stone replied. "He has spoken of you many times."

"We've gone to the wall together many times," said the Senator. "If you're anything like him, and I suspect you are, I'm glad to have you here. Now, you, John T., seem to have gotten yourself into one hell of a mess." He gave me a questioning look and waited for my explanation. I decided he could get in line. I'm not really long on explanations.

"Or you got me into one, Senator. This is your chestnut, as I recall. But I promise you I'll be clean when we hang it all out to dry."

"As you say, John T.—my chestnuts. So let's take a look and see if we're going to get anything fit to eat—and I don't mean Joshua's sandwiches. I need to know what's going on."

"Let's wait a few minutes if you don't mind, Senator. There's another man. He will be here shortly, and his contribution might be worth something," said Stone. The Senator nodded, and we all sat down and chatted amiably while we waited for King. I used the time to wrap myself around another sandwich while I got as close as possible to Sara Connelly. We waited about ten minutes, and suddenly King was in the room. The Senator nearly spat out his teeth when the giant black man materialized in the library, and the others were no less surprised.

"Who are you?" the Senator asked, with more calm than I had expected. "How did you get in?" He jumped out of his chair, then relaxed when Stone laughed.

"I got in the same way anybody else would who wanted to storm your castle, sir. These big old houses are all alike. Lots of windows and doors, and servants are a little lazy a lot of the time. You ought to be more careful, times like these."

King looked serious, but I could feel the chuckles rumbling deep in his massive chest. The Senator's house was probably a lot more secure than King implied, but that would present him with few problems. None to Stone.

"I would like you to meet my partner and very good friend, Senator. Arthur Andrew King, known to many as the Kingfish. King, this is Senator Carlsbad, an old friend of my family." The Senator shook King's hand and motioned him to a couch by the door. Then he went to the sideboard and poured a cup of coffee. He put the coffee on a tray with cream and sugar and took it to King. He was learning. King took the coffee as if he had been served by senior senators all his life, but with a subtle set to his shoulders that indicated his appreciation of the situation. From that moment, he gave the Senator his undivided attention, and more respect than I had ever seen him demonstrate to a new acquaintance.

"Now, John T., about those chestnuts," the Senator prompted. I briefed him in short choppy sentences that would read like a combat report, bringing him up to date on everything we had learned and everything we had guessed, without editing anything.

He considered what I had told him for a moment, then turned to Sam Anderson.

"Anything you'd like to add to that, Sam?"

"Nothing you don't already know, Senator, except that I think John T. is probably right so far. But we still don't have a direct line to the Vasquez killer and nothing that would be of much help to Senator Cameron. Unless Jim has seen something I haven't." He turned to Jim Cash, who shook his head.

"Then, as I understand it, we are faced with a rather elaborate conspiracy to gain control of this state by a well-organized and ruthless group which is capitalizing on economic and racial unrest among minority groups," summarized the Senator. "They seem willing to kill to gain their ends, and I suppose they will not stop at lesser crimes such as extortion, bribery, kidnaping, and other acts of terrorism as they feel the necessity. Am I correct?"

"With the additional thought that the terrorism seems to be one method among several in what appears to be a basically political campaign," said Sam. "The organization is using honest people in conventional ways to control the votes of Chicanos, blacks, and Indians, and using other means to accomplish what overt political action can't. Such as beating an incumbent senator at the polls, which is not an easy thing unless you have some hard issues."

"Well, this is nothing new in American politics," the Senator growled. "Nor in any other country, either. We have cities and a few states that are run that way. There's only one thing that's different here. As I understand FBI reports I have read, attempts by organized crime to gain a foothold here have failed."

"But you have everything necessary for the nurture of a home-grown product, Senator," Stone remarked. "You have a poor and ignorant, racially homogeneous group, united by the bonds of another language and skin color, who feel that they have been denied what is rightfully theirs. They are numerous enough to form a substantial power base, and the political and social climate is conducive to their effective use. I'd say you are as ripe as an August plum. El Patron sees this also, and is in the act of plucking it."

"Then the problem is somewhat more complicated than simply finding one murderer," said the Senator. "You've given me a lot to think about, and not much time for deliberation. I assume that if they are successful in getting our junior senator convicted, they will have achieved much of what they intend. And we'll be in trouble." He settled back in his chair and seemed to go to sleep, but nobody thought for a second that he was napping. The Senator was looking at his hole card and adding up the odds against tomorrow.

"And we have the job of stopping it, don't we?" he said finally. "I know, of course, what I must do. The fight that is shaping up in the state legislature is the political pressure point, and it will take the full weight of leadership in both parties to resist the demands that are going to be made. But I think I can assure you that Teofilo Gonzales will not be appointed to fill out the term, no matter what happens to Latham. Now, what is your plan?" He looked directly at me.

Sensing something that had been growing in me all day, he had put me under the gun instead of Sam or Jim Cash. The thing he sensed, I think, was that I was no longer just a hired gun. It had become a personal thing with me, and not just because El Patron had put the frame around my shoulders. That was part of it, of course, but I was also wondering what would happen to a great big beautiful piece of property like Rancho Useless with tigers loose in the state. How long before they saw how vulnerable I was and came snarling in from all my flanks? The frame was more or less in the line of business, but these people were also threatening me where I lived.

"You can't score without ball control, Senator," I said. "It's time for a little offensive action, and I intend to make it as offensive as I can. I explained the cell structure before. Now, the thing to do is isolate the action arm of the organization, the black shirts. They'll be a lot closer to him than the honest citizens, and we can get to him faster by wringing a few of them out. The place is crawling with his troops, all of them after me. I intend to grab one and work my way up through the cells to the top." I was stopped in the middle of my brave little speech by the Kingfish's rumbling chuckle and a sad, wise smile from Stone.

King laughed, "Honey, you been gone too long." I swore that if he said I was getting old and fat again, I was going to bounce the coffeepot off his skull.

"You applied the cell theory too liberally, John T.," Stone said seriously. "The 'action arm' won't be organized that way, but will be the conventional line organization with a definite chain of command. It will be a lot easier than you expect to get to the top of that."

"You should know that line troops don't function well in isolation," added the Kingfish. "It ruins their morale. They have to feel like they belong to something big, and they have to know who their buddies are. They have to have a captain to follow and a general to cuss, and some guys just like them to get drunk with. So, somewhere you're going to find a paramilitary organization, probably with a perfectly legitimate front that lets them get together and socialize, something they can belong to and brag about. They will have a headquarters, and printed literature, and a program of social reform that nobody much can quarrel with. That's where you'll find your 'action arm.' " Honey, I *had* been away too long.

"Sam," I said, "what do we have in the way of groups like that? You've been doing some research, haven't you?" Sam started the old click-click, and then answered that there were half a dozen possibilities.

"No! Just one," said Beulah Johnson, and all eyes turned to her. It was the first time she had spoken, but her hot black eyes hadn't missed a thing. "The group you're talking about has to be El Sociedad de Simón Bolívar. They wear berets and black leather jackets, and they swagger around a lot and talk about 'Power to the People' like our own Panthers do. Membership is limited to Chicano veterans with combat experience or training. They have a headquarters in a big old store south of Guadalupe Street. Their leader is a Colonel Gutierrez who's retired from the Army."

"You seem to know quite a bit about them, Miss Johnson," said the Senator.

"Colonel Gutierrez likes black girls, Senator. I went out with him a couple of times, but he comes on too strong. He spouted some about his 'fine young men and the great work they're gonna do.' I decided I couldn't stand him, so I stopped seeing him."

"Would that be Colonel Ramon Gutierrez, Beulah?" asked Stone, with a glance at King.

"None other," Beulah answered. "Do you know him?"

"Very well," said Stone. "Colonel Ramon Gutierrez commanded the Fifth Ranger Battalion in Korea. He was operating in conjunction with a ROK Ranger outfit when the Chinese started their offensive. He held back and let the ROKs get cut to pieces, just to suck the Chinese in. When they overran the ROK positions, he turned his mortars and machine guns on them. He wiped out a Chinese brigade, but he also finished wiping out the ROKs. The Koreans raised so much hell that he was relieved of field command and sent back to run a supply depot. He was a light colonel then. He got his chickens out of the action, but he lost any chance of ever commanding line troops again."

"So now he has formed his own army," I said. "How does Gutierrez stack up as El Patron?"

"Could be, but I doubt it," said King.

"I also doubt it," Stone added. "I don't think he is the political mind behind this. He's just a butcher, and his treatment of the ROKs indicates that the man is a political Neanderthal."

"How well do you know Gutierrez?" I asked Stone. "And does he know you?"

"I helped train that ROK battalion," he answered.

"King and I were with the military advisory group that helped set up the Korean Rangers. He knows us."

"Think you could get next to him?" I asked, thinking of a possible infiltration operation. I dismissed it immediately as a long-range project.

"We'll get next to him, but probably not in the way you're thinking. We want Gutierrez as our own little project. Right, King?"

"Right on, baby," King answered with a smile. "I just got a feelin' he's up to his pension check in this. He's ours, John T."

I nodded to him and turned to Honeypot. "Speaking of pension checks, Julia—have you made any progress on that list I gave you?"

"I have something, but I don't know what it is. I went off on a tangent. The thing is, John T., as far as the politicians are concerned, their financial records are supposed to be almost an open book." She glanced at the Senator, and I thought of the cashier's check he had given me. Catch him opening his books to anybody. He could be relatively transparent to a financial tiger like Peter Heilman, but it would probably take an army of accountants and Univac to unscramble his finances.

"But everywhere I turned," she continued, "I kept running into this campaign fund thing. You see, politicians get elected these days only if they have a lot of money to spend. But most of the money they spend is not their own, and they never see a dime of it. They are required to report campaign expenses, of course, but only what they spend out of their own pockets. That's coffee money, and wouldn't get them elected dog catcher." The room was full of politicians, and they all knew this, but they still gave Honeypot their full attention.

"Major political campaigns are conducted by volunteer committees, who collect money from private contributors and spend it on whatever is needed. Advertising, mostly, a lot of which is nothing more than open bribery. They collect the money, and it usually goes into a special checking account, opened for that campaign and closed out the minute it's over. No accounting is ever made to anybody for this money. It just gets spread around. As I said, I kept running into this, so I got copies of the account statements for the last three elections—never mind how—and called Hugh Brainerd. He's the ad man who handled Senator Latham's campaign, and we've been friends for a long time. He took one look at those accounts and came unglued. He spent most of the day talking to media people and filled me in late this afternoon. The gist of what he told me is this: The finance committees for the five politicians involved—and some names kept appearing on all the committees—collected several times the amounts needed for normal campaign expenses. He showed me a breakdown of the money each of them spent to get elected, for radio, TV, newspaper, outdoor and other advertising. He had to do some guessing on the printing and specialty advertising, but he does a lot of that sort of thing for political campaigners and said it's no trouble to guess pretty close. The media records are public, of course, and all he had to do was ask. But, he pointed out, after all provable expenses, and making very liberal guesses as to other expenses, there was still over three hundred thousand dollars left. This surplus had been withdrawn *during* each campaign, not after it was over, in the form of checks written to 'Cash.' ''

''I didn't get a nickel of it,'' interrupted Jim with a laugh.

''You said certain names kept cropping up on the finance committees, Miss Conrad. Do you remember what they were?'' asked the Senator, not at all disturbed to hear the citizenry discuss the various kinds of chicanery the poor politician must navigate in order to serve the people.

''The one that comes immediately to mind because it was

on all of them is that of Colonel Ramon Gutierrez," she announced.

"I don't doubt that a minute," said Beulah, laughing. "That man not only served on committees, as you say, but he sent his black berets out collecting from everybody. I even contributed fifty dollars myself, when I was going out with the guy."

"Those black berets, Beulah," said King suddenly. "Does this look like one of them?" He reached inside his coat and pulled out a piece of headgear. He spun it several times around his index finger and then tossed it onto the coffee table. The group sat in stunned silence for a moment, then Stone spoke.

"Holding out on me, buddy? Where did you get that?"

"Found it hanging around outside a while ago. I didn't think it should be left out in all that weather, fine cap like this, so I brought it in." His big square face was as solemn as a preacher's, but the roaring of his inner laughter made his body shake.

"Any sign of a man under it?" Stone asked gently.

"That dude? He was too heavy to carry around, so I just gave him some sleepy stuff and stuck him under the back porch out of the rain." He couldn't hold his laughter any longer, and it exploded among us like a mortar barrage. When he got himself under control, he slapped Stone on the shoulder. "I was so happy to hear you put in a reservation for the colonel, pardner. I don't think we goin' to have any trouble pinnin' him to the wall, at all, at all."

Nor did I. What King couldn't get out of a prisoner just wasn't worth listening to. Intelligence had been his function on the A team, with heavy weapons as his second specialty. As far as his prisoners were concerned, he was the big artillery when he began interrogating them. The small, wiry VC, who wouldn't average five-five and a hundred and thirty pounds, thought he was the living devil come to collect for their sins. His size, his blue-black color were enough to terrify most of them. They would start spewing at both ends when he gently hooked them up to his machinery, which included a polygraph and some other black boxes that were sheer window dressing. He wouldn't balk at a little torture, but his basically gentle nature led him to use more sophisticated methods. He rarely failed, even with the hard-core. I would walk a thousand miles of chalk line before I would voluntarily submit to interrogation by the Kingfish.

"What do you think this man was doing here?" the Senator asked.

"They would naturally want to keep an eye on you, sir," said Stone. "Possibly nothing more than a watching brief. But this changes things quite a bit. The colonel is going to be very interested to hear that his man has disappeared. We're going to have to give some thought to protecting you."

"I've been protecting myself for more years than I like to think about, son," the Senator answered. "You just get on with your work and let me worry about that. I have some people I can call on. Now, what are you going to do with your prisoner—turn him over to the police?"

"Not quite yet, sir. We want to chat him up a bit, first—but the less you know about that, the better," Stone replied.

"All right. Since I have never seen the man, I can't know anything about him, now, can I?" The Senator sat back in his chair with a satisfied air and looked around at his troops. "Anyone have anything to add to all this?" he asked. "It seems we are making some progress, each in his own way. It's not true at all, what they say about never getting good help anymore."

Each of us looked at him, and then at the others, but no one seemed to have anything to add. We all started making the little moves and shuffles that end conferences, and I started thinking about a bed for my body. We were all milling around, looking for coats and hats, saying the small things that don't mean anything but indicate an awareness of group membership, when the Senator pulled me aside with a hand on my shoulder.

"I'm a little worried about you, John T. With both the police and, I suppose, the colonel's troops looking for you—I mean, if the colonel really is involved—you could be in some danger. And as a target you aren't exactly small. I don't want to get you killed, even in a good cause, Boy." I laughed and shrugged my shoulders under his fatherly hand.

"It comes with the territory, Senator. And don't worry about me. If this was any easier, they'd have women and children doing it. Come to think of it, we do have some women doing it, and they're not dragging their feet, either. But I will be careful. Rancho Useless doesn't have an heir, yet." That stimulated another idea, and I turned to ask Sara if we could have a chat, but she was already on her way out with Sam. I was going to have to get off the mark faster if I wanted any idle conversation with that girl. I shook the Senator's hand and then followed King to the back of the house.

I helped King with the man he had stashed under the porch. We carried him through the shrubbery to the driveway in front of the house, tossed him into the trunk of the Chevy and closed the lid on him. I hoped he would continue to breathe until we could get him out again.

"Your airplane still standing by, John T.?" asked King. "We better take this dude out to that cabin of yours."

"Yes, it is, King. But what if the police have it staked out?"

"Not to worry, old boy," Stone reassured me. "I'm sure we'll think of something." I was sure he would, too, so I told them to get on their way. They would just have time to get airborne before dawn and have clear sunlight for the setdown. The weather would be perfect for flying, as the norther had blown past on its way to the Gulf.

"You're going back to the apartment? What if the colonel has it staked out again? You could have a bit of bother yourself," said Stone.

"Not to worry, old boy," I mimicked. "I'll think of something, I'm sure." He smiled, told me he had sent the girls home with Sam and Sara, and drove off. I got in the Ford and headed home.

I parked the Ford in a parallel alley a couple of blocks from the apartment. I had looked at it earlier, so I had no trouble melting into the shadows along the fence as I started to work my way along to the rear of the apartment complex. I settled down to work, keying my senses to the alertness necessary, and began a stalking approach. It took me half an hour to find all three of them. The first two were easy, but I might never have found the third in time if he had been older and more experienced.

The Second Coming Apartments had been built in the form of two hollow squares, side by side and facing the street, and surrounded by single-family dwellings. An alley ran down the side of each square to the parking lot, which was the width of both buildings combined. The alley which ran by my rear corner apartment continued on to the next street. The alleys and parking lot were screened from surrounding houses by a six-foot redwood board fence masked by thick shrubbery. The side of each square building was open at the side nearest the street, and at each side at the rear.

The first watcher was exactly where I expected him to be, in a car on the street where he could watch both front and alley entrances to my apartment. The second, again predictably, was in the shrubbery along the fence behind the parking lot. The third could have been in any one of half a dozen places from where he could watch my front door. After I spotted the second man, I eased into the driveway between the two buildings under cover of the foundation shrubbery. I had reached the opening that led into the courtyard of my building and was getting ready to cross the sidewalk to the other side when the rear door of the apartment right beside me opened. I heard a man cough and spit, then open a car door. A small-car engine turned over once and fired, and a blue Volkswagen pulled around the corner into the driveway and stopped right in front of the rear entrance. I froze—and considering the temperature that morning, it wasn't difficult.

The man got out of the VW, leaving the engine running, and came back past me to the front door of his apartment. He was young, with long hair and a droopy moustache that framed his mouth. He was dressed in ski pants and a parka with the hood hanging down his back. He looked like an off-duty troll. After a minute, he came back carrying two pairs of skis and poles and started lashing them to the rack on top of the bug. I heard the apartment door open again, and a pretty young girl with blond braids and a happy face came by me carrying a couple of backpacks and a thermos bag. She had a right to be a lot happier than I was. It was Saturday morning of what promised to be a bright, clear day, with the first snow of the season waiting on the mountains. She was young and healthy and had her man, with the prospect of a perfect weekend in which to enjoy him. She put the packs down and offered him a swig of coffee from a thermos bottle, then a dozen or so kisses from laughing lips. He went along with both swig and kisses, but I could tell he wasn't much interested in the kisses. Who can be that early in the morning except a woman? They each made two more trips back to the apartment, loading the VW with enough supplies and equipment to last a VC platoon a week, and then drove off for the virgin mountain snow. I was wishing I could have stepped out of the bushes and begged to go with them when I heard the hiss-splash-tinkle of a man pissing against a brick wall.

I had found the third watcher, and I was lucky—he had a small bladder. I had him spotted now, a deeper shadow in the shrubbery across the entrance from where I stood. I had been ready to dart across that open spot, and I would have landed right in his arms. I waited for him to finish his business, but he didn't seem to be in any hurry to put it away and zip his fly. Then his breathing got deep enough for me to hear it. I decided he hadn't been able to get his mind off that delicious girl we had both been watching, so I rushed him.

He still had his dick in his hand when I hit him—solar plexus and throat, and a chop to the back of the neck as he half-turned and started to fall. I had the momentum of my rush behind the first blow, and he didn't make a sound as he went soft all over. I hoped I hadn't killed him. Die in the saddle, yes—but not alone, and on a stick horse. I checked his pulse and breathing and decided he hadn't left us yet. He might live, if he didn't die of embarrassment when his pals found him unconscious with his joint hanging out. If he did survive, he would be a better person for it.

I searched him quickly and found a .38 S&W in the side pocket of his hip-length black leather jacket, with a handful of loose cartridges in the other pocket. An inside pocket yielded a transistorized walkie-talkie of the kind you find under Christmas trees, so they had rudimentary communication between outposts. I picked up the black beret from where it had fallen. It fit my own big head, so I stripped him of the leather jacket, too. A man can always use another beret and leather jacket. It also fit, which was a surprise. He was a big man, but I felt fat when I hit him. Young, stupid, fat and inexperienced. If this was the caliber of El

Patron's storm troopers, I didn't have much to worry about.

I heard a low squawk from the walkie-talkie then, so I put it to my ear. Number One was talking to Number Two, checking the post, and I had suddenly run out of time. Fortunately it didn't take long to pull one of Stone's tricks on the front door of the young couple's apartment. I was inside with my nose at the high bathroom window when Number One finally got around to making a personal check on his sleeping beauty.

After he got his sudden surprise, disgust, and fear under control, he left his man where he had fallen and ran up the driveway toward the street. He would probably call in more troops and proceed to kick down the door of my apartment. Troops that thick-headed will try anything. Well, they could pitch a tent in my place if they wanted to. I was perfectly happy where I was. The young lovers were on their way to a happier time, and I had their pad to myself for at least a day. So I bolted all the doors, checked the windows, drank half a carton of milk from the refrigerator, and got into bed. It was still rumpled, but it felt just fine.

Chapter . 11

I DON'T SLEEP soundly when I'm working, and I don't like strange beds, but I still felt a lot better when I woke up at noon. I took a long look out of each of the windows and didn't see anything, so I figured it was safe to go ahead with shower, shave and breakfast. It was just after one o'clock when I got on the telephone. I called one newspaperman I knew well enough to horse-trade with, and promised him an inside look at the story of the year in exchange for an inside look at his morgue. I called all my cohorts to warn them that the apartment was of no further use, then lay down on the couch for another siesta. I had been medium dumb to trap myself in this apartment for the whole day, but I needed the rest, and there was nowhere else to go. It had seemed like a good idea at the time.

Just as it started to get dark, a noisy party erupted a couple of doors down, and people started coming and going with some regularity all over the compound. It was a simple matter to join one group going by and walk with them to the street. Sam Anderson was waiting a block down where I had asked him to meet me. I got in the car and told him where to take me, and we drove off.

"Anything new, Sam?" I asked.

"They found that girl's body—Muñoz's secretary. They'd knocked her in the head and left her in the bushes by a stock pond outside of town. The police would like to talk to you about it. A Sergeant Sanchez was at my office asking questions this morning."

"We had better get this show on the road, then. It's only a matter of time until they drop on me, and I want something more than my bare face to show them."

"What are you looking for at the newspaper office?"

"I have a long list of names involved in this, Sam, and I have no idea what any of them look like. I'm hoping the paper will have some photos and some background information that will be useful. And I'm looking for a face."

"I wondered when we would be getting around to that. The man who set up the 'Calhoun' accounts had to resemble the Senator. But what if he isn't one of the people on your list?"

"Then I won't find him, will I? They could have brought in someone from out of town, even, someone we will never connect with the job. But I doubt it. That was too important to leave to someone else, and I also have a hunch the whole thing grew out of the resemblance in the first place. It doesn't have to be that close, you know. The same general build and features, with a false moustache and glasses and a little makeup, would make it work."

"I'm still not used to the idea," Sam mused. "It's a new brand of politics to me. There was no mention of it in Poli Sci Four Hundred back at Harvard."

"Then you weren't paying attention, Sam. This brand of politics was old when Christ was a corporal. It's one of the brands we have for export. It's the only kind that won't weigh you down too much when you parachute into another country at night. Pull up right here. We have to wait for a signal." After about ten minutes, a slender man in a gray suit came to the front entrance of the shabby three-story brick building that housed the paper. He motioned with his hand, and Sam eased the car down to the entrance and I got out.

Jim Tabor was my age and I had known him since high school. We weren't all that friendly then or now, but he smelled a story when I called him and was willing to go along. I would have been surprised if he hadn't smelled news in something that stank as high as this deal did. He held the door open for me, and I walked into the empty business office. A watchman's desk with a telephone stood by the door, but there was no guard to be seen.

"Where's the watchdog, Jim?" I asked.

"I sent him upstairs to the press room. He's used to it. Come on, the morgue's on the third floor."

When we got to the big file room I gave Jim a list of names. I expected to start rummaging in dusty files, but he motioned to a microfilm reader and went into a small room behind the file clerk's desk. He came back ten minutes later with a small handful of film cartridges. All I had to do was slip the cartridge into the reader and punch a button. The information was projected on a screen against the wall. Jim showed me how to work it, then sat down in a chair beside the machine.

"Are you going to give me anything now, John T.?" he asked.

"You know what I'm doing, don't you, Jim?"

"Well, you haven't been very quiet about it. From the names you gave me, it looks as if you've found a Chicano tie-in, which figures, of course. So what the hell is going on?"

I told him enough to keep him quiet, and promised more details later. He asked a couple of questions and then went off somewhere, leaving me to my homework.

The filed information on Gutierrez substantiated what Stone had said, except that there was only a suggestion that a lot of people had been pissed off at him in Korea. There were several pictures of him—a solid, erect man of medium height with cropped black hair and a military moustache. He didn't have more than a hint of the flat Indian face, a slight tilt to the eyes and wide nostrils. One photo showed him in the uniform of a West Point cadet. He had gone there on a congressional appointment in a day when that was rare for any Spanish-speaking kid, so I figured that must have been a tough election year. I wasn't interested in which congressman had needed some Chicano clout that year.

Teofilo Gonzales, congressman for the nineteenth district, which started at Guadalupe Street and went south for a couple of counties, was pretty much the same story. Good record in school, a couple of small scholarships, and then nothing while he attended law school. There was quite a bit of gobbledygook from the time he entered politics, and I wasn't surprised at any of his political opinions.

I went through the entire list of lawyers, politicians, and middle-class businessmen without a glimpse of anything that looked helpful. I didn't find anyone who looked enough like Latham to carry off an impersonation. None of them was tall enough, for one thing, and many were at least a quarter Indian. After going through the complete file, I ran back through the faces. I was sure I had never met any of them, yet several, including Gutierrez, looked familiar. I put it back on the low burner and went to look for Jim Tabor.

"Okay, Jim, I have everything I can get from your files. How do I get out of here?" I asked, when I found him in his little cubbyhole office.

"You don't until you give me a lot more than you have, John T. Just consider yourself a prisoner in a Chinese rumor factory. Now give!" He was smiling but he wasn't joking. I had whetted his appetite; now he wanted steak and trimmings. I wondered how much I could trust him, and decided not much. But then it didn't matter; I didn't have any secrets I wanted to keep anyway. "I'll even offer further inducements," he said, opening a small credenza behind his desk and pulling out a half-filled bottle of scotch—a medium-priced brand that at least had the dignity of having been bottled in Scotland.

"You said the magic word, Jim," I said, and grinned at him. "If you have some Canada Dry, I'll even name names."

"Then we'll have to make a daring midnight raid on the managing editor's pantry. He keeps all the fancy fixin's. Be right back." He was back a moment later with a bottle of club soda, an ice bucket, and two tall glasses. He mixed drinks and we sipped them while I told him everything but the details of Stone's and Kingfish's participation. I didn't want to blow them unless absolutely necessary. They were the only semisecret weapons I had.

"John T., if I broke this story the way you tell it, the whole city would come unglued. The city—hell, the entire Southwest. Are you on dope?"

"Wish I were, Jim. So what are you going to do about it?"

"As soon as I get you out of here, I'm going to wake up the managing editor and either get fired or get assigned full-time to this story. Then I'm going back into the morgue and memorize those files you had me pull. If I'm still sober when I finish that, I'm going to finish getting drunk, because I don't think I'll have much time for frolic when this thing starts to break. Hoo, boy! They'll have to call out the National Guard, the Marines, and maybe even flood the streets and include the Navy. Are you sure you're not smoking hash, John T.?"

"Just get me out of here, Jim. Save your boyish enthusiasm for your editor. But I want another deal. If you stumble on anything, let me know. I still don't understand all I know about these people, and I don't have much time. With both the cops and Gutierrez's black berets looking for me, I stand a good chance of getting lubricated with both barrels." I stood up to leave, but he motioned me back to my seat. I started to speak, but noticed that his attention was on something behind me. Then a quiet voice told me not to turn around. I turned my head anyway, very slowly. Sergeant Vittorio Sanchez stood in the doorway to the small office, pointing a .44 Magnum at my back. His partner was behind him and to one side, with his own cannon giving me the eye.

"Lie down on the floor now, Mr. McLaren, please. Slowly—with your arms stretched out in front of you." He came to my side and leaned down, snapping a cuff on my right wrist. "Put it behind you, Mr. McLaren. Now the other one." Good police technique, perhaps, but he didn't know how vulnerable he was, or would have been if his partner hadn't been covering me. Or maybe he did. Juan Silva had told me a couple of things about the way Sanchez hits to suggest he might know a thing or two. I submitted to search without saying anything. He took the automatic and the young man's revolver and put them in his pocket. He also took my buck knife and the extra ammunition I had in my pocket. He looked into my wallet, then gave it back to me. He stood back then and politely read me my rights, which is well enough. I didn't say anything, but took the time to look at him, and then at his partner, and finally at Jim Tabor.

"Was it you who called them, Jim?" I asked.

"I swear to God I didn't, John T. Perhaps I should have, but we made a deal." He turned to Sanchez and asked if he could go along to the station with us.

"I would rather you didn't, Mr. Tabor. If you insist, I can arrest you for harboring a fugitive, and you can go along that way."

"You wouldn't get away with that for ten minutes, Sanchez. And I am going along, as a reporter for this newspaper. I wouldn't like to see Mr. McLaren stumble on the stairs or anything like that."

"As you wish. Come along, McLaren!" Sanchez's eyes were flat and opaque, and I hoped he never found Jim in a vulnerable position. I could see what Juan had meant about his meanness.

I went along quietly to the jail. No one spoke during the short ride to the station, and I was taken straight to the desk, where the sergeant booked me on two counts of murder one. Then Sanchez personally conducted me through the jailing procedure: fingerprints, photographs, strip and shower. When I was dressed in the nondescript denim jail uniform, he went with me and the jailer to the cell block. When he had me locked in, he stood there looking at me through the bars for a long minute, then turned and left. I sat down on the narrow steel bunk and meditated on my sins.

Having led a blameless life, that didn't take long. The false accusation was another matter entirely, but I wasn't too worried about that, either. If you think about it, the case against me was very thin. Only the pistol, legally registered in my name, and the alleged phone call from the secretary put me on the scene. The secretary was no longer available to testify. The charge that I had killed her also wouldn't hold water for a minute. Within an hour of her call, assuming she had made it, I was with Sam Anderson, and had been with witnesses from that time until nearly dawn except for the half-hour walk in the rain from Hector's gallery. That didn't give me much time to abduct her, stash her somewhere while I made all those witnessed rounds, pick her up again and drive her outside of town to the killing ground.

Muñoz's killer had been in too much of a hurry, operating

on the spur of the moment, to do a tight job on me. The killing had backfired, of course, and had given us too much corroboration of what had been guesses until that time. I very much doubted that I would ever go to trial for the crime. That decided, I concentrated on the rest of the problem.

If our reasoning was valid so far, we were close. Muñoz had been recruited on the fourth level of the citizens' group, which put Teofilo Gonzales on the fifth. Considering the importance of his role in the scenario, that made me think it was the top, with only El Patron above him. Gutierrez had to be the second man at that level, leaving one more to identify if they had carried the three-man-cell idea all the way. There was no reason why they had to do so, but my feeling was that they had. So who was the third man, and who was El Patron? I didn't have the foggiest idea.

The busy community of the cell block wasn't the best place in the world for a thinking man to be. I was in a cell alone, but most of the others were full, and more clients were moving in every minute. It was Saturday night, and that is a busy time for the fuzz. The noise was constant, prisoners talking back and forth, borrowing and lending cigarettes, and the frequent noise of cell doors opening and closing as new prisoners were brought in and others taken out. I was learning why the characters refer to jail as the "slammer."

The cell doors weren't the swinging type with individual keyed locks that we have learned from old movies to expect, but sliding steel frames operated electrically from outside the block. The turnkey was literally that, since his key was a big steel wheel with which he dialed combinations to individual doors. When he wanted a prisoner out, he would call the name and then dial the combination to the door. When the relays connected, the door would slam open with a grinding crash. It was very public and very noisy, and I noticed after a while that I was beginning to anticipate the action and to come alert every time a name was called or a door opened. After an hour or so, my name was called and the door slid open. I went to the block door and waited for it to open. Two uniformed policemen were there to take me to the same conference room where we had visited the Senator.

Jim Cash was there waiting for me, with his briefcase open on the table. When I came in, he stood up and smiled. I shook his hand and thanked him for being so prompt.

"That's my job, John T., assuming you want me to represent you. Do you?"

"You bet, Jim. You're just what I would have ordered if I had taken my phone call. How did you get on to this?"

"Jim Tabor called Sam, and Sam called me. I checked with the desk when I got here, and it looks as if they have you tagged for two big ones. Like to tell me about it?"

"You've heard most of it, Jim. Except for the girl, the rest of it happened the way I told it last night. We weren't thinking too much about her then." I told him my schedule for the day of the murders, and he agreed that there wasn't much of a case because of the time requirements.

"I don't think the grand jury can indict on the evidence, John T. Have you been arraigned yet?"

"No, just processed like a steer through the yard and tossed into a cell."

"Have they questioned you? Have you made a statement of any kind?"

"Not a question, Jim. And that's funny, in a way." I told him about Sanchez, who had shown no emotion, no curiosity. He had just looked at me with that flat, opaque stare, the way you look at a man already dead.

"They have plenty of time for that, John T. They probably know that it won't do much good to interrogate you, anyway, so they can take their time. Well, that's about it, then. I'll see you later."

"What are you doing about getting me out of here?" I asked. "I've got work to do."

"Well, I filed a writ of habeas corpus thirty minutes ago. Now I have to talk a judge into setting a speedy hearing, and hopefully, into letting you out on bail. That will take a couple of days, at least, so you're here for that long. I'll try to make it as comfortable as I can, but you'll just have to put up with it."

"All right, Jim. Do what you can. I'll be here."

"When they do get around to questioning you, don't say anything. You have the right, and nothing to gain by making a statement."

"Mum's the word, as they used to say. Get out of here and get to work on that judge. Judge Bradley might be a good bet. I've known him all my life." We shook hands again, and I reflected that I had done that with Jim more in the last three days than in the previous twenty years. The same two cops took me back to the slammer, which was even noisier than before. I sat down on the cold steel of the bunk and listened to the uproar. After about thirty minutes, a trusty brought a thin mattress, a pillow, and one blanket. I tried to get some sleep.

I didn't have much luck at that. I have already said that I don't sleep well in strange beds, and this one was as strange as any I had ever tried. The closeness of the semidarkened cell, the noise, and the smell were enough to give a mole claustrophobia, and I was used to the high lonesome. I drifted off several times into the same nightmare.

I was at the mountain rendezvous, stripped to the waist, knife in hand. I could feel the texture of the smooth bone handle, feel the cold mountain air on my half-naked body. I strained and shoved, exerting every ounce of strength to force the knife into the soft throat before me. I could feel his hands locked on the wrist of my knife hand, and I could feel his strength leaving him. I saw the empty eyes fill with fear and pain as he cracked and I drove the knife into his throat. I stood there then, the dripping knife in my hand, panting and heaving, feeling myself grow cold with his death as the spectators formed a line and marched past me. Each would pause, look at the body on the ground and then look at me. The big Indian on the Appaloosa was the one exception. He just sat there, motionless, and looked at me.

I was at a formal reception, dressed in the evening clothes of a century past, watching the guests in a long line shaking hands with a dignified gentleman with a large head and a mane of wavy gray hair. As they passed him they would look at me, and I felt the knife in my hand, the cold air on my body, and I looked down at the bleeding corpse on the floor.

I was in a cow camp, standing by the fire with a tin plate in my hand while cowboys filed past the tailgate of the chuck wagon and filled their plates. As each one left the wagon, he walked past me. I felt the knife in my hand again, the cold wind again, and I could not avoid looking down at the corpse at my feet.

I don't know how many times the scene repeated itself as I slept and woke and slept again. It was warm in the cell when dawn came—the temperature never varied—but it still felt cold and depressing, though I was wet with sweat.

The memory of the fight was real, of course, but it had taken place many years ago, on another mountain in another country. I had killed the man quickly and neatly with my parachute knife, and there had been no witnesses. Except myself. It was the first time I had killed a man, and I was never able to submerge the memory, and never able to remember the man I had been in the years before that moment.

I wasn't the only one awake in that cold dawn. There were sounds coming from other cells, where prisoners were pissing in the seatless commodes, grunting and stretching as they flushed the night's accumulation down the drain. I sat huddled on the bunk with the blanket wrapped around my shoulders, wishing I had a cup of coffee or a drink of whiskey. After a while a young black trusty came with a steam cart and gave me a cup of black coffee and a bowl of oatmeal, with a couple of pieces of dry toast. I drank the coffee and shoved the untouched food back under the door. The coffee helped, but not much.

That long Sunday passed into memory as the slowest day of my life to date. I was taken out of the cell only once, when Sanchez came to interrogate me. He was accompanied by two other detectives who didn't introduce themselves, and the questioning was perfunctory. I told them that, on the advice of my attorney, I had nothing to say. After a few questions which I didn't answer, they took me back to my cell. Sam and the others knew where I was, but they had plenty to do without holding my hand, so I didn't expect any visitors.

The day was long but it passed. I spent the time going over the events of the last few days, trying to find the handle I was sure was there. I didn't find anything but a headache. Just before lights out at nine o'clock I bribed a trusty to get me some aspirin. I took four of them and tried to go to sleep. Again I didn't have much luck until after midnight, and the nightmares came again. I woke up twice, soaked in perspiration, and stood looking out the little window until my nerves quieted enough to try sleeping again. The second time I said to hell with it and stayed awake. The hours until dawn were even longer than the day. I kept going over and over the few facts I had, turning them this way and that until they began to fit. The wall I was building went up slowly, and it wasn't much more than waist high when the shouting started. I went to the little window and tried to see the street, but the angle was too steep. I could hear loud, confused voices in the street, and I listened, trying to figure out what it was. I decided it must be the people picketing the jail. It sounded as if there were more of them than I had been led to believe, and they were a lot noisier. The general shouting died down after a while, and a single voice started a chant. It was soon taken up by many voices, but I couldn't make out what they were saying. I heard my name, then, and the big wheel turned the combination to my door and it ground open.

Two cops picked me up at the block door and told me I had visitors. They took me a different way this time, leading me past Latham Cameron's special cell, which was away from the common drunks and noisy brawlers. I slowed down as we passed.

Cameron was sitting in a leather-covered armchair in one corner of the room, which was considerably larger than my own. There was a floor lamp by the chair, and a small table stacked with books. Another man, with his back to the corridor, was sitting on the single bed which had replaced the regulation steel bunk. I had to crane my neck past the guard to see who he was.

It was Hector de la Cruz, busily sketching the Senator as he read in the big chair. I learned later that Hector had been given permission to sketch the trial, which is customary since they banned cameras from courtrooms. He was getting his background studies done ahead of time. Well, the murder trial of a United States Senator would form an interesting chapter in Hector's pictorial history. I wasn't surprised that he was there. That boy could go anywhere, at least in this state.

We went to the same conference room again. Sam, Jim, and Sara were there, and Stanford Stone was standing by the window, looking down at the street. They were still shouting and chanting down there. I said hello to everybody and went to the window. I wanted to get a firsthand look at a sprouting riot.

The street in front of the jail was full of people, some

formed in marching, chanting groups, others just milling around aimlessly. They carried signs that suggested they would know what to do with the murderer Cameron if the police would be so kind as to deliver him into the street, and then I got a small shock. A couple of the signs said that they also knew what to do with the murderer McLaren. Well, as I had told the Senator, it comes with the territory.

"Can we get this over with, John T.?" Sam Anderson asked with an irritated rasp to his voice. He was mad as hell, and I didn't blame him. I was just another complication in his life at the moment. I nodded and sat down at the table. Stone stayed by the window, but he gave me a small smile and a wink as I sat down. I didn't wait for Sam or Jim to start the prayer meeting. Stone had something, and so did I. I had a lot.

"Okay, Sam, Jim. And Sara. How do we stand at your end? Any developments since I saw you all night before last?"

"Let's talk about you first, John T.," said Cash, but I waved him down.

"Never mind me. That can wait. What else is new?"

"Well, I believed Beulah Johnson when she said this crowd thing was going to get hairy. I requested a change of venue, and requested that Latham be moved to the state prison to await trial. I don't expect them to try to lynch him, but anything can happen. So he's scheduled to move this morning. Coley Brannon has assigned a couple of detectives to escort him, and they'll leave in a few minutes."

"Anything else?" I asked, before somebody tried to take the ball away from me. All these people liked to run meetings, and I wanted to run this one myself.

"That's all," said Sam, "except for the mess you're in. Why couldn't you wait a couple of days before you got yourself arrested? One case at a time is too much, and now we have two." I could see then that Sam was not as irritated as he had sounded. He was just blowing off a little steam. I started to drop my bomb, but Sara Connelly spoke.

"I have something, John T.," she said with a diffident little smile. "It probably isn't important, but I have a line on the man who impersonated the Senator." Sara was no slouch as a gunner, herself. Everybody turned to look at her, and Stone's smile was a wonderful thing. Smug, that's what he was. I told Sara to go ahead with her little bomb.

"I went over the check records and statements for the Calhoun bank accounts. There were three checks that didn't fit the pattern. They were for small amounts, written to local merchants. One was to a filling station, and the man who took it has been gone for months. Another was given to the carpenter who changed the locks on the apartment doors, and he too is gone from the city. But the third was written to a big chain supermarket, presumably for groceries. This store makes a practice of photographing check cashers, so I have a photograph of 'Lawrence Calhoun.' "

It was a joy to see the expressions on the faces at the table. I reflected that as soon as I recovered from the nervous breakdown I had earned on this job, I was going to do something about marrying her. I had the perfect place in mind for a honeymoon.

"What?" said Sam and Jim simultaneously.

"Do you know who it is, Sara?" I asked. She shook her head.

"I think I know who it's going to be," I said. "And I rather think that 'Calhoun' is El Patron himself. Anybody care to make any bets?" Stone signaled even odds with his fingers, and I took him for a hundred. I asked Sara for pencil and paper and wrote a name on the page he gave me from his pocket notebook. Sara put the five-by-seven photo face-down on the table beside the slip. "I also know where he is at this moment," I said. "Anybody want a hundred on that?'' Jim Cash had recovered from his surprise and got into the spirit of the moment. He took the hundred on location. Sam, of course, was only interested in the business at hand.

"Let me see that photo," he demanded quietly. Sara turned it face up.

"I don't know this man," Sam said. "Do any of you know him?"

The photograph was a head-and-shoulders shot, with the check and a driver's license superimposed across the bottom. The signature was that of "Lawrence Calhoun," as was the driver's license, but the face was that of Hector de la Cruz y Velásquez, who was sitting just thirty feet or so from us in Cameron's cell. It was seeing the two of them there together that had tripped the handle and spilled the jackpot into my hands. Two tall, slender, aristocratic men with lean faces and high-bridged noses. Two men who dressed like diplomats and bore themselves like statesmen, with the imperious manner that comes naturally from generations of authority and perfect self-confidence.

My nightmares in my cell had had a point, obscured by my own real anguish and fear of the ghosts that filled my past. The faces I kept seeing in the lines of men who witnessed my agony were the faces I had studied in newspaper files. The scenes were all from Hector's gallery, and the faces were in his pictures. Teofilo Gonzales, Gutierrez, even Muñoz, and the big Indian who watched me kill the mountain man. Vittorio Sanchez, the homicide detective who was always around when something happened we didn't particularly fancy.

"Are you sure you know this man?" asked Sam, pointing at the photograph."

"I have known him all my life," I answered. "We are distant cousins, and his ranch isn't too many miles from mine."

"That's Hector, all right," confirmed Cash. "Even with the moustache and glasses, I'd recognize him in a minute. The check and the driver's license are all we need in the way of evidence, of course." He turned to Sara, then, and gave her a deep bow from the waist. "Fine work, Sara. It cost me a hell of a large defense fee, but I might manage to survive that." He turned up my slip of paper, where I had written Hector's name, and made the same bow to me. Stone silently counted out a hundred dollars and passed it to me, then went back to his vantage point by the window.

"Now let's see about getting Señor Patron de la Cruz arrested and Latham out of this jail. I'm on my way to see the DA," said Jim.

"Aren't you interested in knowing where Hector is right now?" I asked with a grin. "I need your hundred dollars, Jim." Cash nodded and nearly had a hemorrhage when I told him that Hector and Latham were at the moment occupying the same cell.

"I have to admire his balls, then," he said when I explained what he was doing there. I added that everything about Hector was admirable, if not strictly honorable. Jim rushed to the door and told one of the cops to get Chief Brannon on the double. When the guard hesitated, Jim told him to get his ass in gear if he didn't want to be working Guadalupe Street for the rest of his life. He got in gear, and Jim sat down again. Sam was up and pacing, and I could hear the click-click of his tongue against his teeth.

I told them about my research, and the pictures in Hector's gallery, and we discussed the names and the chances of tying them into the murder.

"This still doesn't get you off the hook, John T. The photo doesn't tie Hector to Muñoz's murder, and it could be some time before we get it all sorted out. We now have to find another killer, or at least some evidence," said Jim. Stone turned from the window and started to speak, then did a double take back to the window.

"What the hell . . . !" he exclaimed. "There's a sniper on that roof!" He was looking across the street at the building opposite the police station. It was one story higher than the building we were in and had a low parapet around the edge of the roof. I jumped up just in time to see a rifleman silhouetted on the parapet as he squeezed off a shot. His shoulder jerked with the recoil, and I heard the flat report of the rifle. He stayed there looking down the rifle barrel into the street for a moment and then ducked behind the parapet. Stone headed for the door and I followed him. I had forgotten all about being a prisoner until the second of my guards put one hand out to stop me at the door. He had the other hand on the butt of his pistol. I stopped, but Stone kept going. I went back in and sat down at the table.

We sat there speculating on the sniper and his target, and worrying bits and pieces of the case for twenty minutes, until the guard Jim had sent for the chief came back.

"There's been a shooting down in the street," he said. "Chief Brannon says he don't have time to talk to you now."

"Was anybody hit?" Sam asked. "We saw the sniper. He's on the roof across the street."

"Yeah, one guy got shot. Some artist that was here drawin' the Senator. He ain't dead, though. They're loadin' him into an ambulance now."

"Artist? Do you mean Hector de la Cruz? Is that the man who was shot?" I asked.

"Yeah, I think that's his name. I heard somebody call him that. Now, you—it's time to take you back to your cell, if you're all through talkin'. Chief said you could take your time."

"Jim, I don't see us gaining anything by talking. You just get busy and get me out of here. I don't like my cell any more than Latham does." He promised to do just that, and we shook hands all around. I held Sara's hand for a long minute and tried to get a little mileage out of looking into her eyes, but she was too preoccupied to pay much attention. Then I went back to my cell.

It was another long day, and I was a lot more impatient than I had been when they first arrested me. All hell was breaking loose out there, and I didn't know what was going on. I thought about it for a while, and gradually my nerves came off the edge. Then there was nothing else to do, so I went to sleep. I was used to the smell, now, and the constant noise was just background to what was going on in my head. Also, what with one thing or another, including two nights of bad dreams, I needed it. I slept soundly for three hours, and when I woke, Stone was at my cell door. A guard was with him, so when my door opened I waited for them to come in. Instead, Stone grinned at me and told me to get my lazy ass out of there; the vacation was over.

"It took you long enough, podnuh," I said. "Now tell me what's going on."

"It'll wait until you get a cup of coffee," he said, and led me out of the cell block to the jailer's office area. He waited while I signed the forms and reclaimed my property, including my knife and two pistols. Then we went to the coffee shop across the street from the station. I was hungry, so I ordered breakfast to go with the coffee.

"Where shall I begin, then?" Stone asked. "Gutierrez, of course. The man we took to your mountain retreat sang nicely, and he knew more than we expected. He told us a lot of things about the colonel. He was financing his end of the venture with a bit of judicious bank robbery, and slowly moving to control some lucrative rackets, including drugs, prostitution, and gambling. A familiar pattern, of course. More to the point, in your interest, he told us the name of the driver who took Gutierrez to see Muñoz. He also saw Muñoz's secretary in the car with Gutierrez after she was said to have been abducted by 'the murderer McLaren.' Not conclusive, of course, but put with all the other things we had to present to the District Attorney this morning, enough to create a reasonable doubt in his mind. So, he was happy to authorize Cameron's release, and then, after some more discussion, your own. That's how we got you out of the slammer, old felon.''

''So Cameron's out? That's good; but what about Hector? Was it him the sniper shot? And where is he?''

''It was—and I can only surmise that the sniper thought he was shooting at Cameron, who was scheduled to move to the state prison this morning, and was to be taken out the side entrance Hector used. We will never know, of course, because the sniper was killed by police before he could be questioned. He was one of Gutierrez's black berets, of course. De la Cruz was taken to the hospital in a police ambulance. Detectives have been detailed to arrest him at the hospital and to keep him under guard there.''

''Not Detective Sergeant Vittorio Sanchez, I hope?'' I asked, with that feeling you get when you know the answer is going to be all bad. It was.

''Yes, I believe it was Sanchez. Indian sort of fellow? He was the man who organized the search for the sniper and killed him somewhere in the building before his patrolmen had completed surrounding the building.''

''I don't know how to tell you this, Mr. Stone, sir, but in just about nine months we might give birth. We have just screwed ourselves. I think Sanchez is in it up to his scalp lock. I never got around to telling you about that this morning.''

''Would you say that again, John T.? Slowly, carefully, using basic English?''

''Sergeant Sanchez is a bad-ass. The chances are good that it was he who actually set up Malena Vasquez and finally killed her. He and Hector and the colonel are buddies, and they are even now probably on their way to distant climes. We have fucked up!'' Even as I said it, getting a small perverse pleasure out of perturbing the imperturbable Stone, the shit was hitting a big fan-jet at the airport.

Sanchez had acted quickly after learning that the gaff was blown. We learned later that he had gone immediately to the hospital and taken Hector out. Hector was wounded, but not too seriously, and was able to walk out under his own power. They had met Gutierrez at Hector's apartment, where Hector hastily packed an airline bag and armed himself. They then headed for the airport. They had bought tickets for Buenos Aires and were getting set to board the fan-jet which would take them to Los Angeles for the connection to South America.

One of the sky marshals assigned to the flight had been more alert than usual and had sensed something off key in the fugitive trio. He had given the signal to his partner, who had alerted the airport police, and they were getting ready to search the line of passengers waiting to board. But Sergeant Sanchez had his own antennae finely tuned for any hint of interference. He didn't give them time to get set, but spoke a word to Hector and Gutierrez and they moved as a unit. They went through the airport police like hogs through a melon patch. Sanchez had been on the sky marshals like a slashing wind, working his leather-covered slapstick in perfect rhythm.

The three of them had made it to a runway where a shuttle helicopter was landing. They forced the two passengers and the pilot out and took the chopper. They were last seen on a southeast heading, miles into the desert. Coley Brannon had just heard about it when we got to his office. It just wasn't Coley's day, but then, that's Mondays for you.

Chapter . 12

HIS SECRETARY TRIED to road-block us, but we went in anyway without giving her time to warn him. He was on the phone when we walked into his office, so Stone and I found chairs and sat down. Brannon had his ear glued to the receiver and was grunting acknowledgments from time to time. Then he dialed an intercom number and started barking instructions. He hung up after scheduling a meeting in his office in fifteen minutes. There was small joy on his face when he turned to us.

"Hello, John T. I'm glad you came in so I can apologize for the little bit of trouble we gave you. I hope it didn't make you too unhappy."

"Never mind that, Coley. We forgot to tell you something this morning—that is, I forgot to tell my people, and they didn't make the connection. Your detective Sanchez is involved in the deal."

"Now you tell me Sanchez is involved in the deal. Sanchez just took de la Cruz out of the hospital and tried to board a jet with him and Gutierrez. Some sky marshals and airport police got in the way, so they hijacked a helicopter and took off into the boondocks. I was just getting my people organized when you came in.'' He turned back to his desk and started to shuffle papers, so I gathered we weren't as welcome as his pension would be.

"Can you fill me in a little, Coley? And we would like to be somewhere near your communications so we can move when you get a line on them.''

"I'd like to oblige you, John T., I sure would. That would be a small recompense for jailing you—but I can't. This is police business, and you would be in our way. Let us handle it, John T.''

I couldn't think of a better time to pull my deputy sheriff's rank on Coley and suggest that Sheriff Tom Bradley, who is Judge Bradley's oldest boy, would appreciate his cooperation. Coley's disgust was a monument to the dead and maimed in the long feud between county and city police forces everywhere. But he went along, and we stayed for the meeting that quickly outlined a fairly efficient air and ground search, with roadblocks and other esoteric police methods planned as needed. Lieutenant Allen was the staff officer in charge of the search, and he filled us in on the details.

"We checked with the company that operates the shuttle, Mr. McLaren. That unit had made several round trips before they hijacked it, so it has maybe a third of a tank of gas left. That means they have to put down somewhere soon, and that won't be too far from here.'' He made a couple of computations on his pad, then used a string compass to draw a circle on a map, with the city in the center.

"They have to get gas somewhere within this circle, or abandon the chopper. So we've alerted police in all the included towns, and they will be covering the possible locations where they can get fuel. That will include Tres Hermanas, here; Los Palos, here; Callan Pass, here; Brickman Wells, and several other smaller places. They will all be covered, and there's no way they can get out of the circle without being spotted.''

"Bullshit, Lieutenant. There are also fifteen or twenty big ranches within that circle, half of which have planes or helicopters, plenty of gas, and other supplies they might feel they need. Including my own, which is very near Hector's and is as familiar to him as his own bathroom. I have a helicopter pad and nearly a full tank of aviation gas, and nobody there to stop them if they're careful. So what are you doing to cover the ranches?"

"I know about those ranches, Mr. McLaren. I was born on one of them, and I have communications calling the ranches to warn them now. If they land at one of them, we'll hear about it."

"Well, we'll just have a seat over here and let you get on with your work, then. Let us know if we can help." There was an empty desk with a couple of chairs in a corner of the room, so Stone and I occupied it. I sat down and leaned back, thinking about the next step. Whatever it was to be, it would include transportation, so I called the airport and told them to get my plane on the line. I also told the cab company to station two taxis with meters running in front of the station until I told them to secure. Then I sat back to wait. We didn't have to wait long. Lieutenant Allen hung up his desk phone about twenty minutes later and came over to the desk.

"You called the shot, Mr. McLaren. The helicopter just left your ranch with full tanks. They also raided your house and took food, clothing, and weapons. They took a couple of shots at one of your men, but nobody was hurt." I was on my feet and headed for the door before he was half-finished with the report, with Stone stepping on my heels. I handed a cabdriver twenty dollars and told him to hustle. He hustled fairly well, and we were lifting off from the airport in less than forty minutes. From there it was just a short hop to Rancho Useless. I used the time to check Stone out in the 310, and I let him land it when we arrived. He touched down as if he had been shooting landings all day and brought the plane around into the wind on the hard stand. Juan Silva, still walking on eggs but with a rifle in his hand, met us halfway to the house. He told us about El Patron's visit on the way to the house.

"I was in the bunkhouse restin' when they landed, boss. I got up when I hear the chopper and look out the door. I figured it was okay when I saw Mr. de la Cruz with Sanchez. I was just hopin' Sanchez hadn't come to give me any more trouble. They went up to the house, and they're in there maybe twenty minutes. Then I see them come back out again and they're carrying a bunch of stuff. Sanchez had the Weatherby with the fourteen-X scope and he was wearin' one of your coats. That looked sort of funny to me, so I started out to get a closer look and maybe ask them what's comin' down. That's when the other guy—he was still with the chopper, gassin' it up—took a shot at me. I went inside and got my rifle and took a couple shots at them as they took off. I don't know if I hit anything or not." I clapped him lightly on the shoulder and told him to go on back to the bunkhouse. Stone and I continued on to the ranchhouse. Juana Sanchez met me at the door.

"Did Juan tell you what happened, Mr. McLaren?" I nodded, and she went on with her version. They had come to the door, and Hector had explained very politely that they needed a few things. He led the way to the gun room and they helped themselves to my favorite game rifle, the Weatherby; a couple of pistols, ammunition, and a .30-caliber M1 carbine. I was glad they didn't know about the concealed gun cabinet that held the modern military weapons. I have enough of them to arm a platoon, with a good supply of ammunition. Never mind how I got them. They had taken sporting rifles, and that might be a handicap to them. They also went through my closets and took some heavy coats and gloves. I imagine it had been sort of cold in the chopper in their business suits. They had Juana pack them some cold cooked food, and then Hector gave her a thousand dollars to pay for it all. The perfect Spanish gentleman, was Hector. His pet Apache told her to stay inside or he would kill her. The perfect bronco Apache, was Sanchez. Juana snarled like a cat as she told of it. I'm glad they didn't give her a chance. She would have gone for them with a gun herself, and she would have been killed. I told her to fix us a drink and some lunch and to serve them in the gun room.

"What now, m'lord?" Stone asked.

"Now we go to work and earn our money. They're on their way out of the country, and they're already out of Brannon's jurisdiction. They have committed a felony in my jurisdiction, so I am authorized to go after them, no matter where they go."

"You mean to go after them, then? Wherever, and for as long as it takes?"

"Wherever," I agreed. "The job isn't finished until they're in the sack."

"Where do we start, then? We aren't really equipped for an all-out search, and they could be anywhere at the moment. That seems to be a large empty space out there. Surely you're not thinking of getting on your horse and riding off in all directions?"

"Of course not. But the police will be somewhere behind them, with some vague idea of where they're going. We just let the cops bird-dog for us. Simple as that."

Juana came with the lunch then, and we ate cold grouse, washed it down with scotch, and talked about the old days.

"By the way," I asked, "weren't you and King on your way to South America somewhere? Uruguay?"

"Yes, but I'm not really all that interested. After all, it is government work and I'm rather fed up with that. I think I'll send them 'Mr. Stone regrets' and go along with you, for a while at least. I'm sure King will agree."

"Where is King? I haven't seen him since you took off with that dude we picked up at the Senator's."

"He's around with his chick somewhere, I suppose. He came to the jail with me this morning. Beulah was trying to talk the blacks into shucking the demonstration, so he stopped to lend a hand. The blacks were gone when I went down after the shooting, and so were they."

"Well, let him enjoy himself for a while. It will be some time before we know where we're going, anyway." I was starting to pour myself another drink from the decanter when Juan Silva and Pony Blue came into the room. They were doing their damndest to appear nonchalant, but I could see the excitement in their eyes and in the small bouncing steps Blue was taking in his tiny boots.

"Boss, you have any need for a old helicopter somebody left up by the waterfall?" he asked with elaborate calm.

"I can always use a helicopter, Blue. What shape's it in?" It's a nice game to see who blows open first. Blue didn't.

"It ain't busted much, boss. Couple bullet holes in it."

"See any sign of people, Blue? Three men, perhaps, wearing my clothes and carrying my guns?"

"Well, they was some tracks, looked like maybe three men in city shoes, goin' into the brush up by the waterfall." I almost blew my cool then, but I resisted the temptation to hug and kiss a dirty old cowboy and a smirking halfbreed. I gave them a bonus instead and told them they didn't have to come back to work until they were broke. Considering the size of the bonus, I might never see them again—until they ran out of open country, that is. City pavements would soon drive them back to Rancho Useless.

"Well, chappie," drawled Stone, "the gods must love you. They are delivering the ungodly into your hands, and on your bloody doorstep. Shall we go and gather in the sheaves?"

"In time, Mr. Stone, in time. That's a rather large doorstep out there—a few thousand square miles. A bit larger than Vietnam, and just as hairy in its own way. Let's think about it first, gather some equipment, and see if the Kingfish would like to join us. Then we can look at a few topographical maps and see if we can guess where they might be heading."

This was our real element, the kind of operation we had been trained to carry out with a minimum of fuss. Search and destroy, in the open country, with no innocent bystanders and no interference. The police didn't know about the helicopter going down, and since it was on my property, I just naturally figured I had sole jurisdiction. There was one legal base I did want to touch, however, before we went ahead with my plan. I got on the phone and called Sheriff Tom Bradley, my nominal boss as a deputy sheriff of Velasquez County. Yes, of course it was named after our ancestor. After all, he had owned all of it once.

"Sheriff's office," answered a voice I recognized as Deputy Cal Brady's.

"Cal, this is John T. Where's Sheriff Tom?"

"Well, he's on his way to your place, John T. We got a teletype from the city about those hijackers hittin' your place, and he left here about twenty minutes ago. He was gonna stop and get gassed up and have the car checked, but he oughta be on his way by now."

"Can you patch me into him?"

"You bet, John T. Hold on." There were some clicks and squawks, and a couple of minutes' delay, then Tom Bradley came on the line.

"What's goin' on, John T.? I was just on my way out to see you," Tom drawled. Almost all of his Harvard accent was gone by now, but then it had never been more than skin deep anyway.

"Where are you now, Tom?"

"Just pulled out of the gas station when Brady called."

"Good, Tom. We can save some steps if you'll cut over to the judge's and get a couple of bench warrants to bring with you. We just might get a chance to serve 'em."

"No shit? You got 'em treed somewhere? Okay, give me their names and I'm on my way." I gave him the three names and listed the charges as armed robbery and assault with a deadly weapon, listing myself as plaintiff. As far as I knew, they hadn't been charged with anything in town, and I wanted to keep this as legal as possible in my own backyard.

Stone got on the telephone and started looking for King. I told him we would probably need a chopper of our own, and to have King bring one out. In the meantime, I sent Blue and a couple of the Indians back up to the downed helicopter to guide us in to where the tracks started. I had no intention of following them from scratch, but the direction they took would tell me something about where they wanted to go.

I spread the maps out on the big table in the gun room and started briefing Stone on the territory. He hadn't seen Rancho Useless before, so I filled him in with details of the geological anomalies that made my valley a paradise in this weary land.

The U.S. Geological Survey maps showed a landscape as rumpled as an unmade bed, while the USAF charts, which use even outhouses as landmarks, showed how empty it is. After my ranchhouse, which is clearly marked on the chart, there wasn't even an outhouse for seventy tortured miles.

I showed Stone the path up from the valley floor, past the waterfall where the stream fell into the valley, where Pony Blue had seen the tracks of three men in city shoes. I showed him the pass between the mountains, which was the only way they could go unless they doubled back into the valley. The pass led north and ended at the jumbled badlands of the canyon face of the fault-block barrier range. Where the pass bisected that canyon, they could go right or left. The right fork led them farther into desert badlands, sloping down to the slashed and arid plateau. The left fork would take them, after twenty or so miles of rugged walking, to a weathered cowtown nailed to a secondary state highway. That was the nearest food, water, and transportation. Hector and Sanchez would know that.

We took a quick run up to the waterfall in the Cessna, after I had given Blue sufficient time to get there in a pickup. I pointed out details of the landscape to Stone, reminding him of what he had seen on the map. We spotted the downed helicopter on the first pass. Blue gave a long sweep of his arm toward the trail up past the falls, and we circled as he and one of the Indians walked up the steep path. They got to the top and studied the ground, and then the Indian trotted off up the trail toward the pass. We followed in low circles until he had gone half a mile, then dipped the wings at him and headed back down the valley.

Sheriff Tom Bradley was just topping the rise from the desert floor into the valley as we returned, so we buzzed him once and landed. Stone started a serious check of the plane for the flight we planned for the morning. He took nothing for granted, which is always a good habit. I went over to the ranchyard entrance and waited for Tom Bradley.

Tom plays his Western sheriff role to the hilt. He is tall and lean, and his starched, tailored khakis, wide-brimmed Stetson, boots and tooled cartridge belt complete the picture of the local cowboy-turned-lawman. In the last few years he has cultivated a wide handle-bar moustache, and it wouldn't surprise me if he took to chewing tobacco. The getup fools a lot of people who never suspect the Harvard Law and FBI Academy background. He is a dedicated lawman and a stickler for the right way of doing things. He even insisted that I go to the police academy for the course before he would consent to deputize me. It was a good deal for both of us, of course. I kept a goodly slice of his county clean, and he stayed off my back. But it was still on his terms. Now I had a bill of goods to sell him, because this was the first major crime in my bailiwick in fifteen years, and I wanted dibs on it.

"Tom, what are you going to do when the badman comes to town and insists that you draw on him?" I asked as he stepped out of his jeep and stalked toward me on the high-heeled boots.

"Why, I'm going to shoot him, John T. At least that's what I did to the last two who tried it. So what's going on?" he asked seriously.

"Come on up to the house and have a toddy and I'll tell you about it. I think we still have some Wild Turkey around the place." He nodded judicious assent to that sensible proposal, and we walked up to the house. Stone was still fooling around with the plane, so we went up to the gun room for a briefing. When I had taken him through the whole story, he leaned back lazily and stretched.

"Well, I'm pretty sure you have a plan, John T., so why don't you tell me about it and see if I'll let you do it?"

"Only one thing to do, Tom—cut 'em off at the pass."

"Ahuh. Go on." I pulled out the maps again, and we went over my plan. I told him about Stone and King, and the helicopter King was bringing with him.

"It's sort of hare-brained, John T., but I guess it can be done that way. It'll save the county a lot of money if it can. Well, bring your boys in so I can deputize them, and we'll get on with it."

"We can do that after supper, Tom. I figure we should take off about four in the morning, which will put us over the jump point just at dawn. They won't get to the party until eleven or so, so that gives me plenty of time."

I turned the phone over to him, and went down to the village to get my Indians organized. I collected Stone on the way and introduced him to his squad. I just hoped that twenty-four hours of association with him wouldn't corrupt them too much. I don't know what I would do with a bunch of Apaches who wore silk scarves tucked into their shirt fronts and spoke like Michael Caine.

King made it just before dinner. We ate a leisurely meal and then started getting equipment together. Tom Bradley had set up his people to cork the jug at the western end of the canyon, and he was free to help. We had the plane and helicopter loaded and ready on the line before nine. After another drink or two and some casual conversation about nothing much, we all turned in for a few hours' sleep.

Takeoff in the morning was uneventful. We didn't want to fly over our quarry, so Stone flew the long way, north over the mountain peaks and then east. When it came decision time, I wanted them as fat, dumb and happy as it is possible for three hunted animals to be. I jumped at the end of the long pass, miles ahead of them where the pass intersected the canyon along the face of the barrier range.

It was a-good landing, by which I mean I didn't break anything. Bones and equipment were all intact, and I was less than a thousand yards from my planned ambush. Stone made one pass over me at minimum safe altitude and I waved him on. He started winging back to the ranch, where he would plug the backtrail with a squad of my Indians. I grinned at the thought that they were trapped between us. Yes, each of us had only a hundred square miles of broken country to cover to bottle in one experienced hunter, one ex-colonel of Rangers, and a bronco Apache. Whom the gods would destroy, they first make silly. But there was a better than even chance it would work.

I had landed near the middle of a diamond-shaped flat at the intersection of the pass and the cross canyon that paralleled the barrier range. The flat was sand and gravel, washed into a tiny alluvial plain not more than a thousand yards wide in any direction. It was the only flat, open space in fifty miles, and it made the canyon intersection into a duck-soup shooting gallery. The fugitives would have to come into the open and cross it to take the left fork of the canyon, which led to the only food, water, and transportation in a thousand square miles. The alternatives were to double back to Rancho Useless, or to take the right fork into desert badlands, or to climb straight over the mountain. None of the three was much of a choice, though all were possible.

I had plenty of time, so I used it to scout the way they would come and to choose my ambush cover. Before scouting the road, I took my equipment packs off and stashed them by a granite outcrop. The radio was wrapped in two sheepskin pouches Juana Sanchez had put together the night before. I strapped the pouches to my feet, fleece side out, before moving into the area where my targets would be. The soft heavy fleece would help mask the tracks I was sure to make in the loose sand and gravel, blurring the outline and making them difficult to see.

After a long, close look at the target area from a duck's-eye view, I picked three firing points among the rocks in the left armpit of the T. Those were chosen to give me not only clear fields of fire, but also cover from answering fire and concealed passage from one to the other. After making the circuit from one to the other and back to the initial point, I settled down to wait.

I still had plenty of time. They had better than fifteen miles to come, and I doubted that they would be doing better than one mile per hour. They were wearing city shoes on rough and rudimentary trails, and one of them was wounded. I didn't expect them until noon or shortly before. I turned on the transceiver set and reported to Stone.

"Blue Dog One to Useless," I said, because codes are useful on radios, even if they do sound a bit silly.

"Go ahead, Blue Dog One."

"Store's open; no customers," I replied.

"Ten-four, Blue Dog One." The great temptation when you have a radio is to talk your head off—which has resulted in some of the brothers getting same blown off. I waited some more.

They came just before eleven-thirty, slowly and cautiously, in good marching order. Sanchez led at left front flank, Hector walked the center, and Gutierrez followed at right rear. They were at intervals of about fifteen yards, and the flankers were as alert as hunting wolves. Hector wasn't in such good shape. The cold night and the long walk must have aggravated his wound, and it would be giving him hell. It wouldn't have been so serious if he had stayed in the warm hospital. I looked at them over the sights of my piece, and when the first man crossed the chosen line, I put a shot at Hector's feet.

Sanchez, slightly ahead and to the left of Hector, moved faster than I have ever seen an ambushed man react. It seemed that, while my bullet was still in the air, he was off his feet, down and rolling into the shelter of a limestone boulder at the side of the flat. As he rolled, his own rifle was coming to his shoulder, and he was throwing steel at me before Hector got around to raising his eyes from the path in front of him. His shots were poorly aimed and wide, of course, but they did what he wanted them to do. I got my head down and moved to the side before I took another look. Hector was under cover by then, and so was Gutierrez, who had reacted only slightly more slowly than Sanchez.

Both Sanchez and Gutierrez were shooting at me by then, so I moved back and up into my second firing position. I waited there a moment, then put a shot as close to

Gutierrez as I could. I didn't aim to hit him, but I put the bullet close enough to make him uncomfortable. I wanted them alive, or as close to life as possible, and that was the entire reason for setting up the ambush the way I had. I could have killed at least two of them with the first shots, but I had what seemed like a better plan.

I wanted to keep them from taking the left fork, where they had a chance of reaching the little town if they weren't killed at Tom Bradley's roadblock. I wanted to herd them into the right fork, where it would be possible to wear them down to the point of surrender. Stone was behind them to plug the gap in back. King, in the helicopter, and armed as I was, would have set up a second ambush about five miles down the right fork of the canyon. If I could turn them, get them moving in that direction, I could chase them right into his arms. Then they might decide to give up. Then again they might not. In the meantime, I was trying to nip them just enough to turn them.

They didn't herd worth a damn. Sanchez knew what was, or rather what wasn't, in that direction. He also knew he wouldn't make any money where he was, so naturally he came right at me.

I had expected that, of course, and I even knew how he would come, up a shallow trench to the side of the mountain, to a ledge where he would be above and behind me. It was one of the roads I had scouted earlier, and I knew just where it led and how long it would take him to get there. My third firing pit had been chosen with a view to making that ledge as uncomfortable as the flat. It was too bad Sanchez didn't follow my plan.

He came up the trench, all right, but he started sooner than I had expected and moved much faster. He had found the ledge and gone beyond it by the time I started for my third fire pit.

The folded strata of the mountain were standing almost

on end at that point, and erosion had peeled the skin off, leaving a series of steps like the tops of rows of books leaning against each other. I had to climb a leaning slab of limestone to get to the next step up, from which I could command the ledge. I scrambled up and tumbled over in a rolling slide, coming to a stop on my knee with my rifle at high port. Sanchez was already there, struggling up the last few feet through a layer of loose rock. It was poor footing, and he was trying to move too fast, and that saved me. He slipped and staggered as he was trying to bring his rifle to bear on me. The burst from my weapon, which I had switched to full automatic after leaving the last position, took him high in the chest before he could recover his balance. It nearly sawed him in half. He fell backward and slid a few feet in the loose rocks. One hand twitched, seemed to try to grasp one of the flat limestone chips, and then relaxed.

The flat crack of the Weatherby told me where Gutierrez was. True to his training, he was looking for some high ground of his own. But he was older and slower than Sanchez, and a lot more cautious, so he had backed up the canyon a bit and was climbing the hogback a couple of hundred yards from the point where I had first fired on them. He was halfway up, sheltered behind another great leaning slab of limestone, and I couldn't see any way of keeping him from making it to the top. Well, I had known from the start they would go either of two ways. They had both chosen to go for me. I started moving then to improve my own real estate position.

The uplifted layer of limestone at my end of the ridge had split into two equal halves, leaning side by side against a thinner layer of sandstone. The limestone had weathered faster than the sandstone, rounding the tops of the triangular slabs and widening the gap between them until they resembled two gigantic breasts with exaggerated cleavage.

Gutierrez was moving up the steep slope to the top of the left breast, while I was near the top of the right one. I moved back behind the top of the slab under cover and reviewed the situation.

The sandstone layer formed a bridge between the two weathered slabs and was the only highway between the two. It had weathered to a sharp and bony ridge as jagged as the edge of a broken windowpane, and in places was only a few feet wide. That narrow spine was no expressway, but it led where I wanted to go.

I saw Gutierrez only once after the shot that told me where he was going. I switched to single fire and squeezed off a round, but he was already under cover. I gave a thought or two to Hector then. I hadn't heard him fire once, and I couldn't see him anywhere near the ambush spot. I didn't think he was in any shape to climb the ridge, so I put him aside for the moment.

I couldn't afford to wait too long to go after Gutierrez. Once he got to the top, it was an easy slide down the other side of the hogback, and I would have a hard time coming up with him in the broken country down the left fork of the canyon. I took another sweep to see if I could spot Hector, then started inching along the spine on my belly. It took me almost thirty minutes to make my way to the high point in the middle, from where I could see the entire length of the ridge.

Gutierrez had taken too long to reach the same decision I had. I reached the high point at least ten minutes before he did, and I watched him make his long, slow, cautious approach. He was crawling in approved fashion, flat on his belly, with his weapon cradled in his arms, using every inch of the available cover. It wasn't enough, of course. I could have popped him at any time during the last eight minutes of his progress. I waited until he reached the point where he could stand up and rush the high point, and then stood up myself. It was the first time we had met, and the long, silent minute we remained frozen, looking at each other, was the only formal introduction we ever got.

My weapon was aimed at his head, and he was helpless on his belly, but I could see that he was still thinking of trying one. I didn't want to kill him, but if he tried to shoot it out with me, there was only one probable outcome. As is usually the case in real life, it was the nature of the weapons we held that made his decision for him. Gutierrez was carrying a long-barreled sporting rifle, the perfect weapon for long-range shooting at helpless deer but clumsy and inefficient at close quarters. A bolt-action weapon, it gives you one shot with a long second and a half before you can ram another home. It isn't the best gun in the world for hip-shooting, either. I was holding a rifle designed for the work. Short and light, it is equally at home with automatic or single fire at long or short ranges. Push a little button and it becomes a machine gun with a respectable output of little lead slugs. I had pushed that button with my thumb before I got up, and he was looking at sure death.

He decided to live. The tension went out of him all at once, and the Weatherby slid to one side as he let his arms lie loosely, palms down, on the rough sandstone. I told him to get up, and the rifle slid noisily down the side of the ridge as he raised himself to his knees.

"Come on up here," I said. "Carefully." He walked up the incline to the high point and stood looking at me.

"You must be John T. McLaren," he said finally. I nodded and told him to turn around and put his hands behind his back. I snapped a pair of handcuffs on him and nudged him back down the ridge to where I had stashed my pack. He smiled slightly when I offered him a canteen of water, and he drank thirstily while I held it to his lips. So did I, taking long, slow sips, trying to wash the brassy taste out of my throat. Fear dries you up, preserving the body's fluids in anticipation of coming need in life's bloody business. I opened the pack and took out my syringe case and a bottle.

"What's that?" he asked when I made him kneel and rolled up his shirt sleeve to give him the injection.

"Chloral hydrate," I told him. "It'll put you to sleep in a hurry and keep you out of my hair for a while. You'll feel like hell when you wake up." He went out quickly, and I rolled him onto his side and left him there. I didn't remove the handcuffs. I used the radio to report.

"Useless, this Blue Dog One. Do you read me?"

"We read you, Blue Dog One. How's it going?"

"Two down and one to go. Sanchez is dead, Gutierrez in custody. Secure Blue Dog Two, then pick them up. You'll find them both at the ambush point. I am in pursuit."

"Roger, Blue Dog One. Need assistance?"

"I don't think so. If I do, I'll let you know. Hector is left, and I think he might double back. Be on the lookout. Ten-four."

I packed up my gear and started a slow and cautious stalk down the trench Sanchez had used, walking carefully in the loose chips that had betrayed him. Hector, as I recalled, had gone to the other side of the canyon in a stumbling, staggering run. I studied the spot where he had disappeared, then every cranny of the broken wall. There was no sound, no movement. Finally I jumped up and crossed in a crouching zigzag run and fell flat on the other side. No shot, no sound. After a close look and listen all around, I got up. There were Hector's tracks in the sand and gravel, leading into a narrow corridor between the canyon wall and the granite outcrop. I followed slowly and cautiously. The tracks went up the canyon the way they had come, back toward Rancho Useless. I followed until the canyon widened out a bit. I could see for several hundred yards. The tracks went right down the middle for as far as I could see them, but Hector was not in sight. I studied the canyon for a bit. There was no shelter for him within the area I could see, but he must have continued on the back trail.

His steps, from the evidence of the tracks, were more and more uncertain as he staggered up the rough trail. He had made no effort to conceal them, and he was walking straight down the middle like a tourist. After a time I started jogging, stopping from time to time to study the tracks and the terrain ahead. He was in bad shape, beginning to fall now and then, and once he crawled for a few feet before getting up again. I caught up with him about two miles from the ambush. I had been hearing him for half a mile.

I could hear his voice rising and falling around a turn in the canyon wall as I came up to him, slowly and cautiously. As I came close enough to understand the words, I could hear him saying in his pure Castilian—"for mine is the kingdom . . ." over and over.

He was still in the big middle of the canyon floor, on his knees in the rough gravel, sitting back on his heels with head bowed forward.

"For mine is the kingdom . . ." he said again. He wasn't praying. He did not say "Thine is the kingdom." He was cursing, the accent always on the harshly rising "*mio*." The carbine lay in the dirt by his side. He made no move to touch it as I came up to him, my weapon on full auto and aimed at his head. He didn't even look at me, but looked straight ahead at nothing, his pain-filled feverish eyes wide and staring. He was in a wild delirium, but with the final goal of his plan held tightly in the fingers of his mind.

I threw the carbine out of his reach and searched him for other weapons. He had none, so I gave him water from my canteen. Then I lifted him to his feet and walked him into the shadow of a rock and helped him to lie down. I turned him on his stomach and got the coats off him, but I had to cut his shirt off the wound, soaking it with water from my canteen. His shoulder and back were swollen into a misshapen hunch, with bloody pus seeping from the exit crater. The sniper must have used a soft-nosed bullet to tear such a hole in him. The area around the wound was red and angry. I packed it with sulfa from the first-aid kit and gave him a massive dose of penicillin. Then I injected Demerol for his pain. After a time he quietly went to sleep, still lying on his stomach, with his head pillowed on the fleece sacks from the transceiver. I rang up Stone and told him how to find us. He acknowledged and promised to get to us as soon as possible.

It was midafternoon then, and I didn't expect them before dark, so I started making preparations. It wasn't very cold, but I made a fire near Hector anyway, and wrapped him in my own pile-lined coat. A chill now could kill him. There wasn't much in the way of wood on the canyon floor, so I had to range pretty far up the slope to find enough dead juniper to keep a fire going. I checked Hector each time I made a trip, but he was still sleeping peacefully in the drug dreams I had shot into him. I had enough wood for a fire on each side of him and for a signal fire in the middle of the canyon by five o'clock. The sun was gone by then, hiding quickly behind the sheltering mountain, and it got suddenly colder. I sat down with my back to the big rock, between it and the fire, and searched my pockets for what was left of my food. I found a couple of chocolate bars with nuts and slowly munched them. Hector stirred a couple of times and then was quiet. The warm fire made me drowsy, so I decided to make coffee. I made a rack of stones to hold the canteen cup, and was searching for powdered coffee in my pockets when I remembered it was in my coat. I went to Hector and started to ease my hand under him into the pocket to get the coffee. That's when he got my pistol, and I stood convicted of carelessness for the second and final time in that one day.

He had been lying there, awake and rational, for several

minutes when I came to get the coffee. I had knelt by his side and leaned over him. The butt of the .44 was just too tempting to his hand. He snatched it and rolled onto his back in a single movement, just out of reach of my hand. I saw him wince and stifle a groan as the sudden twisting movement sent agony through his body, but the pistol did not waver from the deadline to my nose. I rocked back on my heels and looked at him in the flickering firelight.

"Hello, John T.," he said, with a hint of a smile hovering around his lips.

"Hello, cousin," I answered.

"What now, John T.?" he asked, looking at me over the long barrel of the pistol.

"I don't know, Hector. What do you think?"

"Vittorio? Ramon? You're here, so they're dead, eh." It wasn't a question.

"Sanchez is dead. I took Gutierrez alive."

"I'm almost dead, John T. I would have been dead in another mile, I think."

"No, you'll make it, Hector. Your wound is infected, but I think the stuff I put on it will stop the blood poisoning. We'll get you to a hospital and they'll take care of you." He couldn't get away, of course, even if he killed me. I expected the helicopter with Stone and King and the doctor any minute now. He had had his run. I told him that.

"Sure, I know that, John T. I had had it when Gutierrez's idiot sniper shot me instead of Cameron."

"What was it all about, Hector? What did you hope to gain?" I knew what I hoped to gain by keeping him talking, of course. The longer we talked, the longer I would live.

"You probably understand it better than I do, John T. I wanted to run things, of course. As my family did for a hundred years before the gringos stole the world. They owned half of this end of the state, John T., by authority of the hand of Felipe el Rey. Including your little valley. My great-great-grandfather who gave that valley to your crude ancestor was the first to relinquish a single inch of our land. I am the first in five generations to move to get it back.''

He was one of the sports, all right—one of the throwbacks who come along now and then, in whom the old black violent conquistador blood has not run thin. He was ready to take this land that had been his, using all the weapons available to him. Cortez, that wily old murderer, would have admired his talent for treachery and intrigue, which was always the most useful weapon for the Spaniards who brought the cross of steel to the New World.

Hector's little plot was not a question of morals, of course. Every foot of this old earth is held by right of ancient conquest and present force of arms. Hector's claim was as good as any if he could have made it stick. So were those of Sanchez and Gutierrez. Each had owned the land in his turn. But I own it now, I and the others of my generation who hold this land. It will be ours only so long as we are capable of fighting for it.

''Who killed Malena Vasquez, Hector?'' I asked, changing the subject.

''Sanchez, of course. Gutierrez killed Muñoz and his secretary, if that is of any interest to you.'' I heard the helicopter then, the waffling, drumming sound of the rotary wings loud in the confined space of the canyon. Hector looked at me out of glittering eyes, sunk deep now in the pain-racked face. He smiled, drawing sunken cheeks into a death's-head grin. He gestured slightly with the pistol.

''Get back against the wall, John T.'' I had been set to jump him, but that one thin thread of life I had in my teeth was too strong. I held on to it. I duck-walked backward until my hips touched the rock and waited.

''Take care of my son, John T.,'' he said.

''Your son?'' I asked, in complete surprise.

"Yes, my son. I married, long ago in Spain, and there was a son. I left them there when I returned to this country. Never mind why. But he is my heir—to what is left. Please see that he gets it, and help him hold it." The pleading note was strong in his voice.

"Sure, Hector," I answered, "but . . ."

"Good-bye, cousin," he said, lying there on his back with the pistol leveled at my head. Then his face seemed to relax, and he turned the piece to his own head and pulled the trigger.

"Adios, *hermano*," I said through clenched teeth as a long racking shudder shook my body down to the heels. I stood up in the sudden chill and looked down at him. What was left of the head was a grotesque corruption, white and pink and red in the firelight. I retched suddenly and almost vomited on the corpse. I turned and leaned against the canyon wall and emptied my churning stomach. When there was nothing left but dry spasms, I stood straight and wiped my mouth on my sleeve. I wished I had the coffee I had planned to put in the canteen cup, which was now boiling merrily by the fire. I kicked the cup into the fire and stood there while the chopper landed.

Stone and the Kingfish walked slowly out of the darkness when they saw me standing in the firelight. They looked at the body on the ground and then at me. King went back and brought the doctor up. Doc Maldonado, who took care of my people on Rancho Useless, took one look at the body, at the shattered head. He didn't speak, and he didn't take a closer look at Hector's corpse. He had seen enough cadavers, I suppose. Haven't we all?

I helped carry the stretcher to the helicopter, but I was all thumbs when it came to strapping it to the frame. King completed that, then clapped me on the shoulder. I got into the passenger seat in back and the others loaded in, King in the seat beside me. As Stone jockeyed the machine straight up between the canyon walls, he handed me a flask of whiskey. I took a deep pull and handed it to King. He took a sip to keep me company and passed it back. I took another drink and leaned back into the seat. Nobody spoke during the ride back to the ranch.

They kept coming past me, my new recruits to my private death march. Sanchez and Hector, already dead; Gutierrez soon to die; all marching through the big door. Death has a thousand doors, and each man somehow chooses the one for his own exit. I was just a doorman.

Chapter . 13

WHEN WE ARRIVED, the ranch was lit up like Saturday night in town. All the hands were clustered near the helicopter pad when we sat down, and at Doc Maldonado's direction, a half dozen of them quickly unstrapped the body and took it into the freezer plant. I asked King to see to the money belt I had seen strapped around Hector's waist, and then went on up to the house. Tom Bradley, Jim Tabor, and Juana Sanchez were waiting on the long gallery. I nodded to them and led them inside. Juana went off to see about drinks and food, and I led the way into the library.

"You were right, Tom," I said, when everybody had found and claimed a chair. "It was a hare-brained plan."

"But it worked, John T.," Tom said gently.

"If you call a truckload of bodies a success, I guess it did," I answered. "At any rate, it's over."

"All but the shouting, John T.," said Tabor, and I looked at him. I guessed I did owe him the story, not only to complete our deal, but for going along when Sanchez arrested me. I will never know whether or not the detective had the *ley fuga* on his mind or not, but it wouldn't be the first time an inconvenient prisoner hadn't made it to the station.

"That's your department, Jim. If you can stick around until tomorrow, I'll see that you get some facts to shout about. Right now I'm beat."

"That's not all the shouting there will be," said Tom. "I've had calls from everybody from the Governor's office on down. The FBI, IRS, District Attorney—you name it, and it will probably be here tomorrow."

Juana and one of the maids came in with a bar cart loaded with drinks and little sandwiches. I told her we would have a small army for dinner, and she smiled. Teach your granny, the smile told me, and I stopped worrying about my guests.

King joined us after a time, and we sat and drank and talked all the way around the subject on everybody's mind. Finally I got loose enough to give them the details of the ambush and Hector's suicide.

"One thing, Jim," I said when I had completed the story. "As far as your story is concerned, Hector died of the wound from the sniper's bullet. He has a young son in Spain, and it won't do anybody any good to know he shot himself." He agreed, and we went on talking. I was tired, but I didn't want to sleep. I didn't want to drink, either, but what I really wanted to do was equally out of the question.

I wanted to head for the high lonesome with a survival pack. I wanted to get far above the sight and sound and smell of men, wash myself in icy streams, sleep on stones and doze by medicine fires through the watches of the night. I wanted to see wolves at play, follow lions patrolling the escarpment, and find out if the bears had gone to sleep. I wanted to howl and rave and beat the earth to dust, far from the crumbling towers.

But the feudal system doesn't allow for self-indulgent romantic escapes. After dinner I excused myself and went into executive session with Juana Sanchez.

A ponderous machine had been set in motion. It was

called the Law, and Government, and sometimes, playfully, it referred to itself as Society. The machine would roll over the scene of the recent crime, crushing the fallen stones to powder, sifting pebbles, mixing mortar, and finally patching together a hovel they would call justice. The process would be a king-size drag. I could expect innumerable interviews, conferences, phone calls, depositions and statements to be required of me. I could expect the FBI, the IRS, the DA, and every other set of busybody initials in the land, until I would no doubt welcome any sort of revolution that would promise to end it. The details would be boring enough, so I won't follow them any further.

I told Juana what to expect, and told her to put Connie Salazar, one of the brighter girls from the ranch who had worked her way through secretarial school, onto the job of keeping the appointments and phone calls and records straight. She had been doing a part-time bit as my secretary, so I decided to make it a full-time job before she got ants in her pants and went off to the city.

The days that followed were as advertised, so I stuck close to the ranch. I worked out in my private *dojo* in the mornings, with Stone and King. I met and talked and answered questions for anybody who came along, signed statements for them, and made myself generally helpful to the big machine. I also met with Peter and turned the money over to him, with instructions for distributing about half of it to some people who had been hurt, principally the families of Muñoz and his secretary. The remainder, with the balance from Senator Carlsbad and Latham Cameron's reward, which I had claimed, would help prop up the ranch for another six months or so.

Things had begun to taper off a bit after a week, and I was pleasantly surprised when Connie came down to the *dojo* one morning and told me that Senator Cameron and his two assistants were on the way out to the ranch. I was at the pad when their helicopter landed, and I helped Sara Connelly out of the machine with the first real pleasure I had experienced for days.

"I hope you brought a trunk full of everything you're going to need for a long visit," I told her. "I'll shoot you that elk I promised, and maybe it will even run to a fiesta if I can get the village interested in a little celebration."

"You're on, John T. Now that everything has calmed down, I would like to see how a feudal lord lives when he's at home." I gave her hand a squeeze and then shook with Sam and Latham Cameron.

"You look well, Senator. Glad to see you out of the pokey."

"Thanks to you and your friends, John T." He looked years younger than he had in the cell, and he almost bounced on the short walk to the house. As much as his innate dignity would permit, of course. Sam was his usual self, calm and phlegmatic. He made himself useful, directing a couple of the hands in unloading the bird. They had brought a respectable amount of luggage, so I could expect them to stay for a day or so. Connie met us at the door with the news that another chopper was on its way with Peter, Julia Conrad, and Beulah Johnson. I told her to find Stone and King and let them do the honors for that one. I turned them all over to Juana, then, and started thinking about the best way to get Sara off into the boondocks for some serious conversation. I needn't have bothered. Ten minutes after her luggage had been delivered to her room, she appeared in riding clothes and demanded a horseback tour of Rancho Useless.

"That should take about a week, m'love," I said. "If we don't stop to count anything, that is. As for horses—well, I bought a couple of Irish hunters at an auction over in Texas last year, and they need a lot of exercise. Give me ten minutes to change."

We didn't have much opportunity to talk for the first half hour of the ride. The hunters were feeling their oats in the bluebird weather which had returned after the first storm, so we let them run. She rode well, relaxed and cheerful but in complete control of the big horse. The animals settled down after a time, and we rode side by side at a walk. Then I discovered I was as tongue-tied as a movie cowboy. I knew what I wanted to say and do, but I shuffled from foot to foot, stuck on top dead center. I pointed out landmarks and big black steers and deer tracks, and she made appropriate responses. Finally I gave it up as a bad job and relaxed for the first time since she had stepped out of the helicopter. That's when she took a firm stance and knocked me into the first-row seats.

"About that proposal of marriage, John T.," she said. "I'm ready to talk about it. That is, if the seat is still open."

"I'm glad you mentioned that," I said. "Shall we go back to the house and call the preacher?"

"I said I was ready to talk about it, John T. I guess I should be flattered, but you're too eager, Boy!"

"Maybe I am. Okay, let's talk."

"I've thought a lot about you in the last two weeks. If I hadn't been so busy, starting up the Senator's campaign and then cranking it down, I suppose I would have been like a schoolgirl going steady. But the work kept my head level, and I was able to look at things more or less objectively. What it boils down to is that I have no objection to marrying you, but I also have some plans of my own."

"Say on," I said.

"I want to run for Congress in the next election. I have it on good authority that Gonzales will retire from politics, if he doesn't go to jail, and his seat will be open. The election is a year from now, which will give me time to get set up for a campaign. Sam and I are going to trade jobs. He will go to Washington, and I will run Latham's office here until it's time to throw my hat in. I have a good chance to win, so where does that leave us?''

We rode in silence for a moment, and than I answered.

''That leaves us about five miles from the house,'' I said. ''If we start back now, we'll just about make it in time for lunch.''

''Slamming the door, John T.?'' she asked, with the hint of a smile playing around her lips.

''I truly don't know, Sara. Maybe I just need time to think about that. It wasn't part of my plan, old girl. I had something entirely different in mind. Not that I object to lady congressmen, or to your having a career of your own. But there's a little matter of children, which is very important to me, for reasons you know about.''

''Yes, there is that. And it would be difficult to do much campaigning with my tummy out to here,'' she said, laughing as she indicated a point midway between her horse's ears. ''But it might get me a lot of women's votes.''

Neither of us had a lot to say after that. We got back to the house a few minutes before lunch was served, and I used them to have a couple of drinks in my room while I changed. The big table was full when I came back down. Latham and Sam, of course, Stone and King, Peter Heilman, Julia and Beulah. Latham had had a couple of drinks before he sat down, and was more expansive than I had ever seen him.

''I wouldn't recommend it as a steady thing, John T., but I suspect this affair will guarantee me a dozen more years in the Senate. I've had a hundred calls, from some of the most radical liberals in the state, telling me how this has made them start thinking about the realities of politics. It has scared a lot of them into taking a long look at their own hole cards. As I said, I wouldn't want to do it again, but it has been a good thing, politically speaking.''

''I told John T. about my own plans, Senator,'' Sara said

then. "And for the rest of you who don't know what I'm talking about, I am going to run for Congress in Gonzales's district next year."

"You made up your mind, did you?" said Sam. "So I guess I will have to start packing for Washington. Congratulations, Sara. I think you have a better than average chance of making it."

"She has an excellent chance," said Latham. "She will have the full support of the party, and a lot going for her besides. Being young and beautiful won't hurt, either." Congratulations were offered from all sides, then, and the lunch threatened to become a party caucus until Honeypot spoke into a short lull in the animated conversation.

"I have a small announcement of my own to make," she said. "I am going with Mr. Stone when he returns to Virginia." You could have cut the silence with a knife until Peter Heilman stood up. He looked at her, then at Stone, and then at me.

"Did you know about this, John T.?" he asked.

"No, I didn't, Peter. But now that I think about it, it doesn't surprise me much," I answered.

"Well, it surprises me. I should have known it would happen sooner or later, but I was hoping it would be much later. Mr. Stone, do you know what you're doing with the best young investment banker in the state?"

"I rather hope I'm going to marry her, old boy," said Stone with a smile. "Sorry if it upsets your organization and all that, but it did seem to be a very good idea. You do agree, don't you, Honeypot?"

"You mean you're going to marry me, too?" Honeypot said with a giggle. "I thought you just wanted someone to keep your checkbook balanced."

I ordered champagne for everybody, and the quiet lunch turned into a sort of celebration. It tapered off after a while, and people separated into groups of one or two or three. I didn't talk to Sara again, and I wasn't surprised when she had her bags brought down and boarded the helicopter with Latham and Sam, on her way back to the crumbling towers. She would do what she could to bolster them in her own way. I wondered if I had made another bad mistake.

Stone and the Kingfish met me at the door when I returned to the house. They were carrying luggage of their own. I called one of the hands to help them with it, and walked with them to the rented helicopter King had brought from town.

"Sorry to see you fellows go," I said. "Why not stay another week? We never did get a chance to go after those deer."

"Another time, John T. We'll be back, now that we know the way. But I have to make a fast trip back to the old homestead to warn the guv'nor to get set for a wedding."

"I hope we worked enough of the fat off you to last till we get back," said King. "You been shapin' up pretty good the last couple of times on the mat. You keep in shape, now. Hear me?"

"I hear you, Kingfish. And *dom arigato* for the workouts. Have a good trip." I stood back, and Stone started the helicopter. They were both waving as the machine hopped straight up and then leveled out for the trip out of my valley. I went back to the house and sorted through some things with Peter and Julia, then saw them off with Beulah in their own machine. Then I was alone for the first time in two weeks. Not just by myself. Alone. I yelled for Juan Silva and told him to get me a couple of horses ready. Two hours later I was headed up the slope, packhorse trailing, headed for the high lonesome. I left no messages for anybody.

TWO ~~ONE~~ **WEEK BOOK**
TO BE RETURNED ON OR BEFORE

Jul 13 '76	Sep 17 '76	Dec 16 '76	Mar 18 '77	May 1 '78
Jul 20 '76	Sep 25 '76	Dec 27 '76	Mar 28 '77	Apr 11 '78
Jul 27 '76	'76	Dec 30 '76	Apr 18 '77	4 '88
Aug 6 '76	Oct 13 '76	Jan 10 '77	Jun 1 '77	
Aug 13 '76	Oct 20 '76	Jan 15 '77	Jun 9 '77	
Aug 23 '76	Nov 10 '76	Feb 1 '77	Jun 16	
Sep 1 '7	Nov 29 '76	Feb 14 '77	Jul 5 '77	
Sep 10 '76	Dec 9 '76	Mar 1 '77	Oct '77	

For every day beyond this there sh 5¢

Daily Overdue
Fines on this book:
5¢ first week
10¢ second week
15¢ third week